Adriaan van Dis

MY FATHER'S WAR

TRANSLATED BY
Ina Rilke

VINTAGE

Published by Vintage 2005

2 4 6 8 10 9 7 5 3 1

Copyright © Adriaan van Dis & J. M. Meulenhoff bv,
Amsterdam, 1994
Translation copyright © Ina Rilke, 2004

First published in Great Britain in 2004 by
William Heinemann

First published in Dutch in 1994
under the title *Indische duinen* by
J.M. Meulenhoff bv

Vintage
Random House, 20 Vauxhall Bridge Road,
London SW1V 2SA

Random House Australia (Pty) Limited
20 Alfred Street, Milsons Point, Sydney
New South Wales 2061, Australia

Random House New Zealand Limited
18 Poland Road, Glenfield,
Auckland 10, New Zealand

Random House (Pty) Limited
Endulini, 5A Jubilee Road, Parktown 2193,
South Africa

The Random House Group Limited Reg. No. 954009
www.randomhouse.co.uk/vintage

A CIP catalogue record for this book
is available from the British Library

ISBN 0 09 944354 6

Printed and bound in Great Britain by
Cox & Wyman Limited, Reading, Berkshire

Contents

Preface

The girls wanted to see the coast. They heard excited voices in the passage and the loudspeaker blaring out over the decks: Holland in sight. The steam whistle blew, feet thumped on the stairs, gulls screeched. The girls clambered down from their bunks and dragged the big cabin trunk over to the porthole. The little one was allowed to have the first look, her two sisters hoisted her up. Pressing her nose against the pane she said: 'It's just waves.' The glass steamed up.

In the corner of the cabin by the door, the mother was having her morning wash at the basin, splashing water on the floorboards. She took her towel from the hook and looked in the mirror with a sigh. She felt exhausted as soon as she got out of bed these days, just as well the hot water had steamed up the mirror, for it spared her the sight of those deep lines in her face as she towelled herself dry. It was stuffy in the cabin. She crossed to the porthole and twisted the bolt to open the window. Cold salt air rushed into the room, the girls shivered and quickly pulled their jumpers on over their pyjamas. A gull flew past, lazier than the gulls that had been following their ship, so this one had to be a land-gull. 'Now me,' the middle girl said, pushing her mother out of the way. She poked her head through the porthole and pulled a face. No land in sight.

'Down, you've got to look down,' the eldest said, 'Holland's below sea level.' She got up on the trunk, placed her feet wide apart, thrust out her bottom and curled her hands to make a telescope.

There was a knock at the door and a bald-headed man stepped inside. He was already dressed in his day clothes and held a military jacket over his arm. The youngest girl ran towards him and leaped into his arms. She locked her legs around his waist and let herself fall backwards, arms flung wide: 'Justin, Justin!' she cried. 'I've seen the sea of Holland!'

He lowered the child gently on to the bed and tickled her brown stomach. 'It's called the North Sea,' he said. 'A couple more hours and we'll be in Amsterdam.' He kissed the mother and leaned over to the middle girl. She ducked away.

'Now, Ada,' the mother said, 'you should answer when Justin says hello.'

'Hello,' Ada said gruffly.

She went over to the washbasin and started brushing her teeth.

The bald man shrugged his shoulders and smiled. He moved to the window. 'Come now, Jana, you'll catch cold,' he said, putting his arm around the eldest's hips and drawing her close. 'You're looking in the wrong direction, the coast's on the other side, to starboard.'

The mother noted how the back-light made Jana's legs in her pyjama bottoms look thinner than ever.

The girls got dressed; in the meantime the man drew an orange ribbon from his trouser pocket. 'Today's a special day,' he said. 'It's Princess Juliana's birthday.'

The 30th of April, how did he remember things like that? She herself had stopped keeping track of the days, she had no idea how long they'd been on board ship: even her body was ignoring the calendar. She was nauseous and long overdue. The mother snipped the ribbon into three equal lengths. The stiff fabric rustled between her fingers, but her daughters' hair was too short to hold a bow. Before embarking all the children had had their hair shaved off by a nurse, on account of the outbreak of scabies at Palembang.

The girls couldn't wait to see their new homeland. They dashed into the passage, skipped impatiently at the heels of slow-moving passengers and squeezed themselves up the stairs alongside the handrails. They wore long pants under their skirts and the mother insisted they fasten the toggles of their new duffel coats and put the hoods up over their heads. She was wary of the Dutch spring weather, and the children were still full of diseases. After Port Said there had been one epidemic after another, measles, scarlet fever, whooping cough. Warm clothing was the best prevention. The mother shuffled after them, holding on to both rails for support. She had trouble climbing stairs, her legs kept letting her down. When she pressed a fingertip against her thigh in the morning after washing, the dent would take ages to go away. She took calcium tablets and vitamins, but the oedema persisted. It was odd that she'd been so tough when things were really bad, while here on board ship where she had nothing to do all day she felt too tired even to take a turn in the lounge. The girls brought her supper in bed and Justin kept her company until nightfall. After the eldest had gone to bed he returned to his cabin.

But this time she forced herself to go up on deck with the children, she dearly wanted to point out the first Dutch village to them, and they'd never seen a stone pier before, had they? Nor a lighthouse, for that matter, or a sluice-gate, or black-and-white cows. She shivered from the cold, for she hadn't found herself a winter coat that fitted in the Red Cross supply, which only ran to small sizes. Someone had thrown her a coat as she stood on deck at Ataka, but she had cut it up to make jackets for the three girls. The main deck was teeming with people. Where had they all come from? Entire families of dark-complexioned colonials jostled for a place at the railing. Hardly any of them had shown their faces in the lounges, but now they were all mingling with the Hollanders in their eagerness to glimpse their new homeland. The mother cast a pitying eye over the women wearing the

East Indian sarong and kebaya. Imagine arriving in Holland in such a state, she reflected, they're in for a hard time, no matter how many blankets they've got.

Justin draped his jacket round her shoulders and rubbed her arms to warm them. Leaning against him, she was shocked by the sensation of her hip poking sharply into his side. She felt ashamed, she'd been strong when she first met him in Palembang, even though she was nothing but skin and bone. The will to fight was still in her then, but since they'd left the Mediterranean behind, the grey northern sky had drained the last vestiges of energy from her body. Her eye teeth were loose and she kept finding grey hairs on her pillow – delayed shock, she told herself. How could she have danced night after night under the starry Egyptian sky? The band of musicians that had come on board in Aden stayed until Port Said, where they disembarked to join a ship heading south. She had felt safe in his arms, he had held her firmly as he danced, but would he play a part in her future?

The adults jostled together at the railing. The children's view of the coast was blocked by trouser legs and flapping skirts. Justin lifted the little one up on his shoulders and the mother rose shakily on tiptoe beside him. She was a head taller than he, but like him all she could see was a grey shroud of drizzle. The engines pounded away as the ship veered, the heaving subsided, they could feel the waves coming from behind, people pointed . . . over there! the great sluices! An Ambonese machinist thought he saw a windmill.

'At the first sight of Holland you can make a wish,' the mother said. 'A colouring book,' cried the youngest, drumming her fists on Justin's head. 'It's got to be a silent wish, Saskia, or it won't come true,' the mother said. She took a deep breath and stepped forward. 'These children have never seen their motherland,' she declared in a loud voice, 'now it's their turn, please don't begrudge them a precious memory.' She grabbed Jana and Ada by the hand and, apologising profusely, tunnelled a way through the densely packed crowd. To her surprise she noted that her tone of voice was edged with the harsh Dutchness of her girlhood. Her speech had softened in the Indies, but in sight of her homeland the old intonations came flooding back. Forgetting how sick she felt, she cleared a section of railing with a grand wave of her arm, seized a few stray children by their collars and chivvied the whole lot of them to the front. Justin and Saskia followed meekly behind.

The ship's siren sounded and at that very moment the sun broke through, albeit cautiously. There were the sand dunes, row upon row of them, the clouds tore apart in the light and the sand turned golden yellow. No one spoke, seagulls swooped over the shore and the sun dappled the dunes like a shadow-puppet play in the cold. Husbands and wives exchanged looks and reached for each other's hands. 'What are those?' Saskia asked. 'They're sand dunes,' the mother said, 'Dutch dunes,' and her voice faltered a little. 'Just like cake,' Saskia said. Bystanders laughed and cried at once. A woman cleared her throat and started singing: 'Where the white dune-tops shimmer in the sunshine.' Everyone joined in the old song, but the girls kept their mouths firmly shut, for they adored cake and were making their silent wishes. Justin looked up at the sky so no one would notice he didn't know the words. He was shivering, too, but it was more from the cold than from emotion, he failed to see what the fuss was about – this sun was too feeble to set anything ashimmer.

The ship entered the lock and the water level sank, but the countryside sank even lower. The passengers applauded. A group of men stood about waiting on the quay, then propped a gangway against the ship's side, slung their briefcases on deck and, just before the floodgate opened, leaped on board. The Ambonese machinist saluted and the adults milled around the newcomers. This was a solemn moment: Holland was bidding them welcome. But the men picked up their briefcases without a word. Not even a greeting.

The children took over, cheering and shouting at the tops of their voices: such enormous cows, they'd never seen such monsters, nor so many churches. And all those flags, all in their honour. And the mother gave them instruction: yes, that was a meadow and that low-lying stretch of land over there was called a polder and that shaggy mound with its crooked roof a haystack, a food-store for the cows in winter. She recognised the smell of the land, this was where she was born. You could tell by the look of her, even though she was weak and emaciated, with those hands strong enough to turn a calf. Her father was a well-to-do farmer, 'tough as old boots', as they used to say in her birthplace. She had inherited his build, and like him she had a hearty constitution. She was amazed at how delicate and fragile her girls were, that a farmer's daughter could produce such daintiness, the slender fingers, the small flat noses and the little folds of skin by their almond eyes – her children were quite delightful. She was enchanted by their beauty, they seemed so much browner in the pale Dutch light than in the glare of the tropics, only here did the coppery sheen of their skin, the *kulit langsep* they'd inherited from their father, appear to full advantage. Didn't her daughters take after her in any way? Would they be up to cycling against the driving wind; wouldn't the bitter cold be too much for their little bats' ears to stand? Cod liver oil, that was the first thing she'd buy when they landed. Survival in Holland meant swallowing a lot.

And survive they would, that much was certain, for there was one thing the mother and her daughters had in common: they were adaptable. They would adapt to anything if they had to. They proved as much, too, on this Royal birthday: the pilot had come on board accompanied by his children, who'd chalked a hopscotch game on deck with a hell and heaven of a kind her daughters had never seen in the Indies, and just look how quickly they'd caught on to the strange rules – not half an hour in their new country and they were already beating the Hollanders at their own game. That was the spirit, and they'd got it from her.

And yet she was afraid, for she was at a pretty low ebb. All those uncertainties – no money, no home, and her health failing, too. What was she to do, hope for better times, resign herself to the inevitable? Her stomach turned, for a moment she thought she was going to faint, but Justin's arm held her steady.

The passengers returned to their cabins, having been told to collect their hand luggage and await further instructions in the dining saloon. It wouldn't be long before they stepped ashore amid flags and bunting, nor would it be long before they were caught up in red tape. The Dutchmen who had come on board distributed sheets of paper – they were officials, their welcome consisted of printed forms to be filled in. What was she supposed to put: 'married', or 'previously married'?

The girls descended the stairs backwards. Now that the sea breeze had dropped it was even stuffier in the ship's belly. Justin left them to fetch his duffel bag from his cabin, their mother wanted to lie down. But there was upheaval in the passages, for the officials were inspecting the cabins. When the girls arrived at their door, they saw at once that the lock on the big trunk had been broken. The mother groped for an arm to hold on to and fainted.

It was nothing serious, the ship's doctor said, just a dizzy spell, too much emotion, that was all. A whiff of smelling salts and she'd be on her feet again in no time. Oedema, he could tell, yes, and he palped her slightly distended lower abdomen. He drew a stethoscope from his bag and placed the chrome disc on her belly. He smiled, probed again, and then a grave expression crossed his face. 'Off you go, make yourselves scarce for a bit,' he told the girls. The doctor washed his hands and studied his papers. 'When did you last see your husband?' he asked.

'Back in '42,' the mother said.

'And have you had any news yet?'

'No, the Red Cross was very slow.'

'When you get home you should have a proper medical check-up.'

Home, home, did she have a home to go to? She couldn't bear the thought of returning to her father, for he'd never forgiven her for running off to the Indies when she was so young. He only knew her husband and children from the snapshots she'd sent, he'd never seen them in colour. No, not just yet, she needed more time. She'd go to some reception centre, she'd fend for herself, even if it meant scrubbing floors.

'Well,' said the official in the dining saloon, 'where are you planning on going?'

'I don't know,' the mother said.

'Relatives?'

'I haven't been able to reach them yet.'

'Why ever not? Weren't the postal services working properly in the Indies?'

'I want to lodge a complaint.'

'You can send a telegram from here, free of charge.'

'My tea's been stolen.'

'Let's get the list done first, madam.'

'They broke into my cabin trunk.'

'Lady, you should be grateful to be welcomed here at all,' the official said, without looking up from his papers. 'Any preference?'

She didn't understand what he meant.

'North? South? Town or countryside?'

She turned to seek advice from Justin, who was chuckling with the girls and reciting the names of the Dutch towns along the railway line from north to south: Roodeschool, Groningen, Assen, Hoogeveen, Meppel . . .

'I don't know,' she said.

'I've got a place for you on the coast.'

'To the dunes, to the dunes,' chanted the girls.

'That business with the tea being stolen', the mother said a few weeks later, when they were settled in the house in the dunes, 'upset me more than three and a half years of camp.'

1

Death to the Family

Forty-six years later I was present at my half-sister's deathbed.

Ada died with her eyes open. She could see something that was hidden from our view, and we saw ourselves reflected in her tears – mother, brother, sister, son and husband, specks floating in the pools of her eyes until they vanished down her tear-streaked cheeks. Then the light broke.

Saskia pressed her sister's jaws together and tried to shape her lips into a smile; then she lowered both eyelids in one fluid movement of her hand. You could tell this wasn't the first time she'd closed the eyes of someone who'd just died.

The family had been gathered around Ada's deathbed since early morning. She hadn't slept for days, was reeling in cycles of pain and wakefulness. We didn't want her to be alone when she went. Outside, the weeds swayed behind the curtains, the sun was past its zenith and children's voices rang out in the summer gardens, but however hard I tried to concentrate on other sights and sounds, Ada's raucous breathing ripped everything to shreds. She had a hard time dying.

Her son Aram stood wide-legged at the foot of the bed. He gripped the rail with both hands, his knuckles white, as if he were straining to keep his mother away from death's door. He was still young, just fourteen, but that day he was determined to be a man, brave and in control. Aram cringed away when Saskia put her arm around him, drew back his fist when his grandmother made to give him a pat on the hand. His body was tense with rebellion, the muscles in his neck throbbed, he could no longer hold back his tears, large drops spouted from his eyes and hit the blanket with the force of a boy's first ejaculation. I felt bad to be thinking of such life-giving things as semen at this deathbed, but Aram reminded me too strongly of the time when my father lay dying, and of my own growth from boy to man.

I was eleven when I lost my father. I wasn't there when he died, my mother thought I was too young for hospital visits (as if I had no notion of death at all – and yet I poked dead seals on the beach with a stick and fished tar-covered seagulls out of the surf). I did get a glimpse of my father fighting for his final hours, because I listened carefully to everything my mother and sisters told me. To me listening was seeing with my ears.

My father was an unruly patient, I saw him writhe in pain, kick out his legs, knock his medicines off the bedside table and almost choke to death. The nurses had to secure his oxygen mask to his face with sticking plaster. His goggles, was how my mother referred to the mask, and I pictured an aviator in goggles. Biggles suffocating. 'They've put goggles on him,' she said when she got back from the hospital. 'He says I smell of garlic.' She made each of us smell her in turn, her mouth, her hands . . . but she just smelled of Mother, the white cream in the jar with the blue lid by the washbasin, fresh as ever. 'He could smell his own death,' the GP said later, when he came round to offer his condolences.

According to the night nurse my father's last words were: 'The sea, the sea.' He had torn off the sticking plasters and couldn't breathe. The oxygen mask lay gurgling on his stomach. My mother arrived too late to see him off across the ocean.

In my imagination my father turned into a sea serpent with rolling eyes that could see through walls and blankets, and a couple of years later, when I masturbated for the first time, he swam past the bottom of my bed, hissing with disapproval. My semen smelled of garlic, too.

Aram's tears fell on my hand. We adults sniffled quietly or were dry-eyed. Perhaps it was the beauty of Ada's wasted body that made me think of sex. She was beautiful, all the roundness turned inward now, her jutting bones giving new definition to her shoulders, arms and hands, and the skin of her chin drawn into the hollow beneath her jaw. She was an Indonesian child again, six or seven years old. 'A child of the camps,' my mother said.

Saskia spoke soothing words to her sister, asking whether she was comfortable, whether there was anything she wanted, and although Ada could no longer speak and there was not even a flutter of acknowledgement from her eyes or lips, Saskia translated her wishes out loud: 'Ah, she's thirsty,' and she took a teaspoon of water and carefully trickled it between Ada's teeth. Her gums were receding too, making her teeth look like those of a skeleton. Saskia mopped her clammy forehead with a flannel and fetched an extra blanket, for her sister had imparted to her that she was cold. She did all this lovingly and efficiently, she was the only member of the family capable of changing sheets and washing an invalid while they were bed-ridden. It was as well that she had trained as a nurse when she was young, for Ada didn't want any strangers at her bedside. It's a calling, Saskia said, attending to the dying is a calling. 'Yesterday the doctor wanted to give her a tablet for her heart, just think, a huge pink pill at the back of her throat. Let me do it, I said, she might choke otherwise. I ground the tablet into powder and dissolved it in water. Oh, they're such a clumsy lot, they are.' I felt too guilty to disagree.

Saskia had been nursing Ada for weeks now. She came every day, washed, ironed, tended bedsores, and every evening she gave me a call to say how tired she was and how much had to be done for our sister. I didn't tell her that Ada had been complaining to me, too: 'She's nursing me into my grave. I'm not going to die. I may not be very well now, but that's only temporary, and anyway the bad patches are getting fewer.'

But as the bad patches got fewer they also got longer, until there were no ups left for Ada at all, just downs, a steep downhill slope. She was confined to her bed, her skin lesions refused to heal, she lost kilos of weight, became incontinent, her legs swelled up to such an extent that the fluid collected behind the lungs. Her breasts had shrivelled, but now in dying she gained two fluid-filled pouches on her back. Supplies for the journey ahead. Saskia could see her skin turning livid. We didn't see that, we didn't smell her dying the way Saskia did, but we hadn't received training for these things.

Ada didn't take any painkillers, she was opposed to polluting her body. There was no chemotherapy, no surgery, all that mattered was the quality of life. Only nature could heal her, so she took injections of Iscador, an elixir made from mistletoe. The way mistletoe saps the life from a tree, so this elixir was to sap the cancer from her body. A symbolic cure, in keeping with Rudolf Steiner's anthroposophical principles. Alas, my sister was not a tree.

As her body weakened her mind embarked on a desperate quest for an anchor, or so the titles in the bookcase by her bed seemed to say: *The Question of Life, Mysteries of the Soul, The Path to Knowledge of a Higher Universe* . . . volume upon volume of esoteric wisdom. There was also the dingy calendar from the organic food store, with images of expanding universes, misty creatures with auras and chakras, smudges and swirls in pastel shades. Still, there was something comforting about their familiarity, for our house by the sea had been full of such pictures. Our mother was a firm believer in the ineffable forces at work between heaven and earth. She knew this to be so through her experience in the Indies. There was a hole in the Indonesian universe, and if you lived there long enough and were sensitive by nature, you became insightful. She used to draw a new horoscope for each of her children on their birthdays, she sowed and planted when the moon was full, and on Christmas Eve, she put a whole-grain loaf out on the doorstep so it would absorb the positive rays that pervaded the cosmos at such holy hours. This beneficial exposure made the loaf mould-resistant, and anyone who showed the least sign of ill health was immediately give a slice of irradiated bread to eat. Even Ada was not spared her portion. It was a secret world that belonged to the sand dunes and to the old *guna-guna* magic of the Indies, whose essence still lingered in the cabin trunk.

Saskia refused to give her sister the Iscador injections. When Ada grew too weak to administer them herself, Saskia dumped all the syringes and ampoules in the rubbish bin. The cancer had spread too far, there was no sense in further resistance. As a former nurse she dedicated her talents to life, she said, she wasn't one for torture. She used complicated words, spoke of her Hippocratic oath

and of her respect for death, which got the better of us all
in the end. Her nursing career had, as it happened, been
brief, but that didn't make her any less principled.

All Ada was granted in her dying days was a single
paracetamol at bed-time.

Saskia was in full command at her sister's deathbed. Pulse,
respiration, the slightest irregularity was noted with a
raised finger. With Ada's breathing becoming so shallow
it was clear she was sinking fast, Aram's resolve, too,
weakened, for all his efforts to steer his mother clear of
death. He slunk out of the room and started kicking a
football in the corridor. Maarten, his father, who'd been
sitting with Ada since early morning wedged in between
the bed and a parched *Ficus benjamina*, looked up with a
frown.

Nothing happened for a long while, until Saskia
forbade us to leave the room any more and summoned
Aram to come back. He put the ball down under the bed,
glanced at his distraught father and drew himself up. The
sun poured into the back room by the bucketful,
somewhere in the distance a bunch of kids took a garden
by storm, Ada's throat rattled, and Saskia declared
solemnly: 'She's gone . . .' She felt for her sister's pulse and
glanced at her watch. 'Ada passed away at a quarter past
five.' She shut her sister's eyes and stifled a sob.

Maarten buried his face in his wife's pillow. We started
towards the door. But Ada wasn't gone. She started
shaking, her husband jerked upright and the ficus shed a

few leaves at the jolt. Her chest heaved up and down, squealing and rattling like an old farm cart, but she was breathing. She gazed at us tearfully.

Saskia sprang into action, pressed the eyelids down unceremoniously and blew the tears away. This time she didn't let go, as if the glue needed time to dry. Rigor mortis was a while coming. 'It's post-mortem reflexes, that's all,' Saskia declared, 'perfectly normal.'

'But maybe she isn't dead yet,' I ventured.

'I've seen hundreds of people die. I know,' she said in a hurt tone.

Her word was final. Ada was dead. We kissed her farewell and again she opened her eyes . . . brown diamonds. Half an hour later she drew her last breath. Air from no man's land. Her eyes had turned to dusty charcoal.

We huddled together in the front room and shut the glass-panelled sliding doors. Saskia stayed behind to tidy up the bed. She whipped off the blankets and smoothed the sheet, turning her sister into a white-shrouded manikin. Ada gaped at the ceiling, the smile refused to stay put. Yet she had died with a smile on her face. After all the pain came a moment of peace, during which she must have had wonderful visions which lasted until death.

The anthroposophical doctor turned up (thick woolly socks, sandals and a whiskery beard – some clichés are surprisingly true). He wrote out a death certificate and left quickly. Too quickly for my liking. Had he guessed that I wanted a word with him in private? This man had encouraged Ada to deny that anything was wrong with her, and here he was, filling in forms next to her dead body. I couldn't help calling him a murderer, in a voice that was a little too loud. The family got so nervous that they hustled him out the front door before I knew it.

We sat and waited for the undertaker.

'My sincerest condolences to you all,' intoned Mr A. Korst of Verduym and Son Funeral Management ('Your personal consultant in times of bereavement', it said on his business card). He set his bulging black briefcase down on the floor next to his chair and gave a little bow, which caused his black trousers to rise slightly at the back, exposing a slice of hairless, fish-white leg. There was indeed something fish-like and slimy about his appearance, the bulging eyes, the mouth gasping for air, the black three-piece suit shining and scaly.

'Been in the business forty-two years, madam,' he told my mother, 'not that one ever gets used to it. The grief, I mean. I cannot lessen your grief, madam, but I can lighten your burden of cares.'

We all nodded in assent.

'Milk and sugar?' Saskia inquired.

'That would be very nice, thank you. But I think I had better look in on the dear departed first.' Mr Korst crossed to the back room and stooped over the body.

'He's going to kiss her,' Aram said.

'No, just having a sniff,' Saskia said. We all felt grateful for her nursing background.

★

'Quite delicious, madam,' Mr Korst said, swilling round the remainder of his coffee before downing it in one gulp. 'At home or in the funeral chapel, sir?'

'I think Ada would prefer to be at home,' Maarten said.

'It is entirely your decision,' retorted Mr Korst. 'It's not the same, of course. Plenty of parking space at the funeral parlour, and then there's suitable music and a constant supply of fresh flowers.'

'I'd rather she stayed here,' said Maarten.

'As you wish, sir. We'll see to it that Mother looks her best.'

The coffin. Mr Korst displayed a folder with seven samples of timber to choose from, as if they were discussing a new floor. Maarten looked away, but my mother quickly stabbed her finger at the cheapest wood. 'This one will do,' she said. 'Ada liked birch trees.'

'Austerity, indeed yes, madam, I take it your preference inclines toward the simple and the modern? We respect that.'

The funeral cortège. 'Two limousines? Perhaps an extra one for the convenience of elderly mourners, so they can be driven right up to the entrance. It's quite a long walk from the car park.'

Large auditorium, small auditorium? Coffin exposed or placed in a discreet niche with a soft orange glow? Black or grey border for the envelopes? Coffee and cake or just coffee? Glass of wine? Anything was possible, there were still plenty of choices to be made after death.

The urn. 'An urn is not required? Attendance at the scattering of the ashes? No? In that case, do you wish to receive notice of the date of the ceremony?'

Mr Korst noted everything down. 'Your funeral expenses policy extends to fifty envelopes. So for a hundred that'll be an additional 105 guilders. And an extra limousine, that's another 250. Scattering at sea perhaps? No? So we'll settle for the rose garden, then? Well, that keeps it all nicely within the budget provided by your policy. Plain and simple also has its virtues,' he concluded when the total lit up in red on his Japanese calculator.

'What about the announcement in the newspaper?' he added, while he was writing out the invoice. I handed him three texts that we'd drawn up just before he arrived, as we were sitting together at the kitchen table.

'Do forgive me,' he said, 'but I see you've written "after a *short* illness". We tend to recommend employing the expression "a *brief* illness", given that a temporal qualification is referred to rather than a spatial one.'

'Another cup?' Saskia asked.

'Excellent coffee, madam,' Mr Korst smiled, underlining a word. 'Isn't *at* preferable to *in*, and may I change *ever after* into *for ever after*?'

'I'd rather you didn't.'

'What I mean is, we want to strike a respectful note, which would be more in keeping with the gravity of the occasion.'

I lit a cigarette – my first for months, pinched from Saskia's handbag – and blew a puff of smoke in the direction of the glass-panelled sliding doors, temporarily screening Ada from view.

'I have forty-two years of experience in the trade, you see. Have you spared a thought for the music yet?'

'I want to play my horn,' Aram said.

'Do you really think that would be a good idea, young man?' Mr Korst said. 'You'll be grief-stricken, you know. People have no idea how nervous they'll be on the day. You might play the wrong note. We tend to advise against this kind of tribute, on the basis of experience.'

'You can play at my funeral, if you like,' my mother said.

'We'll play one of your tapes, Aram,' his father said.

'With two intervals of ten seconds each, please, one to give people time to sit down, and the other for them to rise again,' Mr Korst said. Aram stomped out of the room. 'Indeed, emotions can run high at such times,' Mr Korst went on. 'I buried my own mother-in-law not so long ago. Well, that'll be as easy as falling off a log for you, people told me, and I laid her out myself – nothing to it, you'd think, after forty-two years. Well, I stood there and cried, madam, cried with a capital C.' He slapped the letter with his right thumb and forefinger. 'I was amazed at myself.'

'Yes,' Saskia agreed. 'When I was a nurse I witnessed the passing of hundreds of patients. Still, family's different.'

'So it is, madam. You and I know what we are talking about, speaking as dyed-in-the-wool professionals.' Mr Korst shifted his chair towards Saskia. 'What do you say, hadn't we better amend the text to read "for ever after"?'

She threw me a questioning look. 'Perhaps that would be better.'

'Quite so,' said Mr Korst.

Aram's football bounced in the corridor.

Saskia had already received three messages as to when Ada would die. She'd been getting a lot of messages in the past few months. She was in contact with one of the astronauts on the Challenger which had exploded during take-off a few years ago, killing all the crew. Sheila was her name. She was now in orbit round the earth in a cocoon, and had chosen Saskia as her medium. Ada would die on the ninth day of an unspecified month, which my mother thought sounded convincing, seeing as nine stood for Mars. Besides, the number nine had loomed large in the family from death to birth. Nines were fiery and passionate, their lives were characterised by hardship and struggle, but they were unafraid. She knew this for a fact. Both her husbands were born on the 27th (which added together makes nine), like all three of her girls. Just to stay in tune they'd all got married on the 27th, too. She'd also picked names with an A in them for each child, because A (= one) stands for sun, which in turn stands for positive energy, creativity and spiritual enlightenment. At first Saskia thought it would be the 9th of July, but on that day her cleaning woman died instead of her sister. A sad loss, too, but the wrong one.

On the 8th of August she rang round to tell us to

prepare for the worst. 'Will I see you in the morning?' she'd asked her sister while she was putting the ironed laundry away in the wardrobe. 'Yes, why do you ask?' Ada had responded. The next day one of Saskia's neighbours died. She'd never met the man, but his death affected her just the same. One month later she got it nearly right: Ada died on the 6th of September. The month was right at least, and it was understandable to get the six and the nine confused from an upside-down vantage point in the sky.

Sheila also put Saskia in touch with our deceased fathers, hers and mine, our mother's first and second husbands. Not only were they born on the same day of the month, they were both called Justin. To distinguish between them the family referred to them as Just One and Just Two.

Just One had been an 'Indo boy', which was what you were known as if you were dark-skinned and born in the East Indies. And you remained a boy all your life, however grand you looked in photographs, in dark dress uniform with stars and braiding and ribbons, stitched collar, white-plumed helmet and a sword dangling at your side. Justin van Capellen, First Lieutenant in the Royal Dutch Colonial Army, son of a Dutch planter and a native woman.

My father, too, had served in the Colonial Army, although his rank had been lower and his uniform ordinary battledress. If he'd had a sword it would have trailed over the ground, because by the time he died his trousers were already getting too short for me. He was undersized, but he was handsome, even his baldness suited him. His tanned skull gleamed like a peanut, but he wasn't anything like as dark as my mother's first husband. Just Two said he had a 'tropical tan', it was the climate, he thought; at the equator the sun shines right through your clothes. (Was his body as sallow in death as it had been in life?)

His family was still purely European after six generations in the Indies, and Roman Catholic to boot. That mattered to him, I'm afraid – not his faith, for he had lost it in the prison camp by then, but the colour of his skin. He thought of himself as a Dutch chap (the way he pronounced those words sounded like shrimp fritters in boiling oil), and joined the army at sixteen, a chap even at that young age – he never was a boy. He must have impregnated my mother just before sailing for Holland, at Palembang, where hundreds of former internees were awaiting repatriation. They had time on their hands. Which was how Just Two had taken on the role of stepfather to Saskia and Ada, and also to the eldest, Jana, who would emigrate to Canada when she was eighteen. The girls and I didn't look the same and we had different surnames, but in the sand dunes we played together as one family. Words that might erode that family bond were avoided in our house. Step and Half were banished to nasty fairy tales.

Sheila the astronaut also sent Saskia versions of her father, including one in which Just One, in full regalia, made ready to receive his dying daughter. He appeared under a canopy of palm fronds in the greenish dawn, with a string of bearers in his wake. In the car on the way to the funeral parlour she saw her father yet again, this time girding on his sword. 'He's still watching over us,' she remarked to her mother.

'I expect he's been waiting for her,' my mother said matter-of-factly. To her the world was a place of transit, a coming and going of old and new souls.

My father, too, put in an appearance. 'He sends you his regards,' Saskia told me, the first time I encountered her at Ada's sickbed. I hadn't seen her for a couple of years, and I immediately remembered why. She always used to go on about my father, what a warm and special person he was, he was the best, remember all those elaborate *rijsttafels* he would prepare (numbingly spicy), the stories he used to tell over supper (we'd stay awake all night in terror), the kindling they used to gather for the fireplace (she ended up carrying it all), all the books he read (war stories), his imaginative ideas, his high-mindedness (pain is the best discipline, the death penalty for all traitors and, with any luck, for the Socialists, too, for it was they who had sold out on the Indies).

Oh yes, he had a temper, he could be hard, Saskia admitted that, but he was a gentle man at heart (which explains why he squandered my mother's money, dressed like a dandy and never lifted a finger, a spoilt colonial, that's all he was). But she, Saskia, had known he was special early on, she had understood him, they were kindred spirits. Being torn between talent and duty, that was another thing she recognised. He had taught her to draw, and to use a camera, which had been truly enriching. She was laying it on so thick you'd think she had sprouted from his seed, the man she was conjuring up was such a perfect father that I actually felt jealous.

Saskia was adamant. Watching her bustle about the sick room I was struck by the size of the scar on her left thumb. The tendon had been severed, which prevented her from lifting a cup by its handle. She wore the evidence of my father's love on her hand.

Mr Korst finished filling in the forms. ('Ah, the whole family was born in Indonesia I see. The emerald archipelago. Our best clients come from there, such warm-hearted people.') After the final signature two funeral attendants came to the door. The coffin. Chipboard with birch veneer, solid wood not being covered by the insurance. He had phoned the 'mortuary lads' a while back to tell them what was required, adding: 'And, well, bring a hearse-cloth, too, while you're about it.' We sat there and did nothing. In addition to the hearse-cloth the undertakers had brought a cooler, which they dragged to the back room. There was a weekend to get through before the cremation, which meant my sister had to stay in shape for five days. We turned the backs of our chairs to the sliding doors and stared outside, where the hearse was double-parked. Some kids from next door flattened their noses against the frosted glass windows; they were disappointed to find it was still empty. Saskia drew the curtains, which left us staring at folds of cheesecloth, while from behind our backs came the sound of a bed creaking, rubber wheels squelching, a zipper being fastened, Mr Korst cautioning his men: 'Careful, lads, easy does it.'

I was seeing too much with my ears and went through to the kitchen in search of a tablecloth and drawing pins. As I was pinning the makeshift screen to the glass-panelled sliding doors, I glimpsed Mr Korst shaking out the folds of a clean pair of my sister's pyjamas, and having trouble undoing the buttons with his stubby fingers. For all his forty-two years' experience, his hands were shaking.

They had said they'd do Ada proud, and Mr Korst put his head round the door with a few final queries. The wreaths. The mortuary lads had dropped off a catalogue, why didn't we pick something out of there? 'Guaranteed fresh,' he said, holding up colour plates of floral wreaths, crosses and artistic ensembles studded with asters and carnations. 'No chance of petals dropping off before they're placed on the coffin, not like some. Dreadful, that is.' We quite agreed. I couldn't take my eyes off the illustrations. There was even a boat-shaped arrangement, and a musical note in white carnations (Ada sang in a choir), even a portrait in flowers was possible – an exact copy of a photograph, a mere 1,000 guilders that would be. We were duly astonished at the scope of floral tributes they could provide. 'We'll have flowers from the garden,' Saskia said. She'd already bought some florist's foam to stick the flowers in.

The funeral oration, who was to deliver it? All eyes turned to Maarten, sitting in a corner mumbling to no one in particular: 'Ada's gone, Ada's gone . . . unbelievable . . .' For years he'd been suffering from a debilitating disease that attacked his nervous system so he could barely walk, in fact the disease had already spread to his brain. No, he didn't think he was up to it, he said, but maybe I would like to express a word of thanks on behalf of the family? So that was that, and I resolved to give them a piece of my mind.

'You will keep it short, won't you?' asked Mr Korst.

'No, I've got quite a lot to say.'

Mr Korst leafed through the policy. 'You're entitled to twenty-five minutes in the auditorium. If you require more time we'll be obliged to charge extra.'

The mortuary attendants presented themselves. They looked the part: deathly pale with twisted backs from too much lifting. 'What about the mouth then?' the head undertaker inquired. 'It's half open at the minute, very natural, but we can close it if you like . . . It's up to you.'

We didn't know what we preferred. I started hunting for Saskia's cigarettes and our hands touched over her handbag. We gave each other's fingers a little squeeze. When had I last touched her? Not since my father's funeral (which I wasn't allowed to attend – too sensitive) had I kissed her. Reluctantly, for she had wept too copiously that day: my father was mine alone and I had no desire to kiss a traitor. 'With the lips closed people often say, no, no . . . that's not like Mother,' the head undertaker said. As we all held nature in high regard we opted for the slightly parted lips.

A few minutes later Mr Korst invited us to step in and inspect the result of their labours. Ada was laid out in a coffin draped in grey and covered halfway with a sheet of glass, her up-swept black hair looked dull, there was a smudge of colour on cheeks and lips, or was it merely the reflection of her pink pyjamas patterned with blue swallows flitting among forget-me-nots? In her hands she held the framed portrait of her father – Saskia's idea. At her feet lay a white plastic-covered folder: a dance card for her final ball.

Maarten held his camera over the glass and took a flash picture of his wife, whom he hadn't seen looking so lovely for months. From beneath the coffin came a humming sound which gradually grew louder, making the floor reverberate. Ada was shaking (so was I), and the glass panels tinkled in the sliding door. Mr Korst crawled under the coffin to see what was up. The men got down on their knees ('There wouldn't be anything wrong with the cooler, would there?') while the family turned to leave. Then Aram's football rolled out from under the coffin, leaving a trail of slime on the linoleum.

I said I'd be round in the morning to address the envelopes.

★

Maarten didn't possess a diary, his days were too empty for that, he had no address book, nothing, it was Ada who'd kept track of all his appointments. Maarten had no idea who her friends were, or who ought to be invited to the funeral, he was too fazed for any of that. All he wanted was a quiet cremation ceremony, into the furnace a.s.a.p. and with as little fuss as possible. 'Ada, no more Ada,' he kept repeating, like a dull prayer. I couldn't get another word out of him.

We started off with the family, uncles and aunts. Aram knew pretty well where they all lived, but didn't know their surnames. It took a lot of phone calls to draw up a provisional list, hardly good for a single row in the auditorium. Surely this wasn't right for the sister I knew, for my sister Ada who was always writing letters, who never missed a reunion either of people she'd known in the camp or of friends from her schooldays? Surely she had some correspondence tucked away somewhere. 'Try the drawers at the bottom of the bookcase behind the coffin,' Aram suggested.

I couldn't face going into the room just yet, I'd seen Ada die all those deaths there the night before, her shallow rapid breathing still rasped in my ears. So I had another go at Maarten. 'Where does Namunia live? And what about Aunt Nikki?' I asked.

'Namunia . . . who's that?'

'Your Moroccan cleaning lady, according to Aram.'

'Namunia, Namunia . . . never seen her.'

'And Aunt Nikki?'

Maarten shrugged. 'Dunno.' The glass panels started rattling again as the cooler switched itself on.

'She's the one who saved Mum's life in the camp,' Aram explained.

'Haven't heard from her in years, no need to let her know.'

'Are you sure that would be right?'

'Yes, yes.'

'What's the name of the choir she sang in?'

'Something Christian-sounding, I think.'

I abandoned my attempts at cross-examination and plucked up courage to enter the back room. I'd have to go through Ada's things, perhaps I'd find addresses there. I had no choice.

I was met by a gust of hot stale air, as if someone had put a pail of ditch water on the boil. It turned out that Saskia had brought her flowers early on, sunflowers they were, arranged with long wild grasses of course, just the way she wanted. Aram had put the vase by the gas heater, but the heater was still on because Ada had felt cold when she was dying. The stems had gone all mushy and the heads were drooping, what with the cooler competing with the heater. Ada was in an even worse state, with her mouth agape and her eyes half open, even though the ficus had done its best to shed its leaves by way of camouflage. I blew the leaves off the glass and covered her face with my handkerchief.

Rummaging in someone else's personal possessions is enough to send the adrenalin pumping, but doing so next

to the owner's dead body is downright scary. The drawers
were full of private keepsakes: postcards of museums and
foreign holidays, receipts, press-cuttings, souvenirs, snaps
from the Indies – Ada playing on the veranda with a
raccoon dog, Ada standing proudly beside her father
who'd shot a tiger – and Ada half rubbed out, in a drawing
of her with her sisters, all three with bows in their hair.
'Justin', it said underneath, in the same fine hand my
father used for his signature on my school reports. The
paper was creased and ragged at the edges. I also found
piles of envelopes from which the addresses and stamps
had been cut out. I sniffed them, looked inside, read bits
of the contents, love letters from her days as an au pair in
London, photos of old boyfriends. My hands shook. It felt
like sacrilege. I tried to stop myself from reading, after all
it was addresses I was after and it was wrong to snoop.

I started with the bottom drawer, on my knees, with
my head level with the coffin, but the higher the drawer
the better I could see Ada peeping out from under my
handkerchief. I didn't want to look, but her droopy eyes
compelled me and I caught myself whispering urgently to
her: didn't you keep any addresses at all? Surely you've got
something written down somewhere?'

The top drawer angled slightly upwards and jammed. I
banged it with my fists and wrenched until it suddenly
gave way, slipping from my hands and only just missing
the glass lid on the coffin. A fan of green notebooks spilled
out on the linoleum, yellowed and bleached by the sun.
One of them had come apart at the seams, but the loose

sheets had already been pillaged: pictures had been peeled away and pages torn out, scraps of dried-up sticky tape lay on the floor.

I gathered up the sheets quickly, so as not to be too sorely tempted, until my eye was caught by the word Bankinang, the name of the camp where my sisters and mother were interned. This was different, it might be of use to me for my speech, and I started reading at the top of the first page that came to hand.

> *It was boiling hot in the day and cold at night. There were five big sheds, sixty metres long, each with five hundred women and children, two corridors, dormitories left and right, no privacy, four lights, one above each entrance. We had a tiny space. I could just stand up in it, Mama had to stoop. We had two mats for the four of us. Auntie Nikki lived overhead, she was a committee member and she snored. When she peed beside her pot in the night, it rained down on us. The place was full of busybodies, all of whom we had to call Auntie. They stole each other's laundry, I saw it with my own eyes, and they blamed us kids. Liars, the lot of . . .*

The end of the sentence was crossed out. In the margin Ada had written: *Women among women worse than Japanese!*

That's my Ada, I thought, dear old grouch. What could this be, some sort of private memoir? Why the half-finished sentences, the exclamations?

The pages didn't follow one another in any recognisable order, entire passages were crossed out with brown ink (Ecoline it was, a whiff of school), with comments in a clearly more grown-up hand, as if later she'd decided to edit her memory with pen, scissors and sticky tape. In the margin she'd written 'Indies=Indonesia!' several times. 'Japs' had been crossed out and 'Japanese' written above.

Mama says hunger has a bad taste. I now know how to eat the most disgusting things: tighten your throat, hold your nose and swallow. I keep thinking of the two Japanese guards at Fort de Kock who took our piglet and cut its throat and drank the blood with us looking on. It was cruel and revolting. Afterwards, I too ate fried blood and had to squash a sapi eye. Mama couldn't bear to do it herself, but it was good for enough cooking oil to last for ages. Once you've had goat's bladder with glue you can eat anything.

This wasn't getting me anywhere, East Indian cooking was not the stuff of a funeral oration. I'd move my listeners to laughter, or to tears, but the camp? No, I had no desire to say things that the entire family was well aware of already, even though they had all told a bunch of lies.

I sat down on the linoleum beside the grey drape, in the chill of the cooler, which was itself no wider than her wartime mat, and reached for the notebooks. Some of them bulged with pasted pictures and dried flowers: primrose, wild violet, milkweed, briar rose and snapdragon, the flora of my birthplace.

War and school were jumbled together. Page after page of teenage scrawl, decorated with magazine pictures of Rock Hudson and one of Edmundo Ross in front of a red double-decker bus, singing London is the place for me! Even then. I never knew my sister kept a diary and scrapbooks. But these, too, must have been censored later on: the more adult her writing, the more scrupulous her editing. Even the film stars didn't escape her scissors.

One of the notebooks seemed to be more or less intact. It was the oldest one, judging by the childish script, and it was decorated with pictures from the Van Nelle albums. 'From the tropics', it said on the label, with a different colour for each letter, in keeping with the wobbly anthroposophic style.

I was born in Malang. An old woman told us malang means bad luck. When my mother heard that she walked round our house with a candle several times to drive away the evil spirits. There was a kuntilanak in the mango tree, an evil spirit to whom the natives sometimes sacrificed a water buffalo. We never had any bother, though.

A composition written for school, probably. Useless. I turned the pages quickly, glancing at the Van Nelle pictures: women weaving, a Balinese dancer, bulls with pink parasols tied to their horns. The pictures were glued along the top. I lifted up the bottom edge of one and saw that the space underneath was covered with writing. Was it part of the other entries or was it something else? Her handwriting was so tiny and so compressed within the rectangle covered by the pictures that I had to screw up my eyes to decipher it. I felt I ought to get up and ask Ada's permission face to face, but my curiosity got the better of me.

What are memories? Things you remember. I've forgotten such a lot, often I can't remember anything at all. Last week I was ill and shivering with fever, and suddenly I remembered things from the past. We were sent to three different camps on Sumatra, after we were under house arrest in Fort de Kock with five other families. First there was a transit camp, then that awful Boei prison in Padang. There were a thousand men there already when another 2,300 women and children came to join them. We ended up in Bankinang concentration camp miles away from anywhere. It was Aunt Nikki who told me how many people there were. All I know is that it stank of pee. The pounding surf kept us awake all night, some mothers thought it was the guns of allied ships come to liberate us.

I had come upon the most secret of Ada's secret diaries. I lifted up the edges of the other pictures, too, as if I were peeping under her skirt, and read on.

What I'll never forget: me in my yellow dress with little black glass buttons, which I had swapped for a pair of trousers. I can hear the women returning with firewood. I'm in the makeshift hospital in the middle of the camp. A chee-

chak creeps up the side of my mosquito net, staring at me sadly. Am I going to die? The room stinks of pus. They bring in a little girl with burns from falling into hot ashes, her mother has wrapped her in a mosquito net and now the netting is stuck to her skin. I feel sick, my stomach has turned to water. All I get is tea with salt and pepper. One of the Japs comes to see me every day. He's kind, talks to me, but I can't understand him, he only knows a few words of Malay. He takes me on his lap and soothes my cramps. The Australian lady doctor tells him to stop, but I let him do what he wants. He says he'll take me to the men's camp, where they have new medicines which will make me better. The lady doctor and my mother don't want me to go. Then he lifts me on to the back of a lorry, and makes me sit on his knee. My mother is standing by the gate, crying.

The Jap sent me back with two coconuts and a whole cabbage. My mother slapped me and made me promise never to accept anything from him again. But that didn't stop them from eating everything up. The Jap did the same with Els. She didn't tell me this until we were on the ship to Holland. We always got something extra if we sat on his lap.

I don't know how long I was ill. When I ask Mama, she says the Japs were nice to children. I've forgotten the rest.

At this point her own memory had done the editing. To what extent had I myself excised memories from my consciousness? How true was the memory I had of my sister? Had Ada, the clever one, cool and collected Ada who disdained fashion and fads, ever moaned about the camp when we were children? 'I was too young,' she'd say whenever the subject came up. Saskia was different, every little ailment was directly traceable to Bankinang. In wet weather, for instance, her right shoulder would ache from fetching all that water. Ada always stuck her fingers in her ears so as not to hear, but she didn't miss a thing. Whenever Saskia said: 'concentration camp', she corrected her crossly: 'It was an internment camp,' and if anyone had the cheek to compare the Japanese with the Germans she said: 'Being beaten isn't the same as being gassed.'

And my mother wasn't having any moaning either. I can still see her at the sink, singing the old camp songs with the girls and flicking the dish-mop angrily when one of them dared to complain about the Japs: 'You learnt how to chop wood, make fires, cook, slaughter animals, sew, mend, nurse the sick, make bamboo picture frames, paint coconut shells. How many children do you know who can do all those things? Positive thinking, that's what you need. You were taught to read and write better than any child in Holland. Your teacher was a lady professor. You have the camp to thank for that.'

That and other things.

But what about the girl called Els, whom Ada mentioned in her diary and who was her confidante on board ship, who could she be? I knew only one person by that name from the old days: Els Groeneweg, whose father was a notary in The Hague. Her parents and ours were friends, her mother had been in the camp with ours. Her father was in charge of the family paperwork, and helped my mother in her campaign against the Ministry of Overseas Territories. No sooner had a buff official envelope hit the doormat than Notary Groeneweg would be summoned, and he'd appear bringing his own typewriter, with a metal ring around each key. His sentences were as long as the ribbon, it seemed, and he read them out to us in a booming voice: missives to the Minister, the pension fund, and petitions to the Queen. 'Petition' – the word conjured up a vision of grown-ups in the yellow lamp-light, smoke-rings curling up from the notary's cigar, the smack of type hitting paper . . . We sent a steady stream of petitions to Her Majesty. The treatment we had received was unjust, that much I understood, but my parents didn't raise their voices in protest. If we had something to complain about, we'd go through the proper channels.

The Groenewegs were well-to-do and respectable. Els wore a signet ring (and my sisters wore her hand-me-downs), her father drove a gleaming black Rover. Half the village would come running when he drew up at our front door, for fancy cars with walnut dashboards and a multitude of dials were rare where we lived. We were used to the greengrocer's three-wheeled van and the Kraut holidaymakers in their DKWs in summer. When the notary was done he donned his top hat and took all us children for a spin on the sea front.

In later years Els would come and visit us in her own

car, a soft-top blue MG sports car. I'd crouch in the dickey seat at the back and bury my nose in her streaming blond hair (and still I can hear the tinkle of the charms on her silver bracelet when she changed gear. All the old sounds come flooding back. My ears have the best memory of all).

Els was my first secret love. She would certainly have to be notified of the funeral.

The doorbell rang. Maarten called for his walking stick and Aram bolted up the stairs. I slipped the Tropical Notebook under my shirt and stuffed the others back in the drawer. Whoever it was would be gone by the time Maarten got there, so I ran to answer the door and caught the visitors just as they were leaving: the next-door neighbour and his son Pieter, who was Aram's best friend. They had come to pay their respects. I called upstairs for Aram and heard a key turn in a lock.

'Would you like to see her?' inquired Maarten, leaning groggily against the wall in the corridor. Without waiting for a reply he turned and shambled towards the back room. I warned them it might not be a very pleasant sight, the undertaker still had to make some adjustments. But the neighbour dismissed my objections with a wave of the hand: 'There's a first time for everything, and Pieter is old enough.'

I went upstairs to find Aram. The carpet on the landing had been ripped out, the tracks still bristled along the skirting boards, the echo was chilling. I had never been upstairs and opened the first door I came across: the master bedroom. Unread newspapers all over the place, piles of unopened mail and a double bed rumpled on one side. Here, too, the floor was bare, just planks with wisps of dust caught in the grooves. Maarten was right, the inside of this place had not been seen by the Moroccan cleaning woman for several weeks at least.

The unused side of the bed was strewn with shakily scrawled memos: 'Aram too noisy! Aram disobedient! Ring meals-on-wheels! Aram: insurance! Pay for music lessons! Aram must help more! Take shoes off, no horn practice in afternoon! To seaside with Ada: book hotel now! Be kinder to Aram!' The resolutions of a worm-eaten memory.

There was a large print up on the wall, yellow and flaky, almost antique-looking. But when I stepped closer I found it was a blown-up drawing in unsophisticated perspective, a study in austerity: a plank floor, four rolled-up mats, reed partitions, four tins, a pail and a broom. The inscription underneath read: 'Our tempat in Bankinang.' So this was the cubby-hole my mother had shared with her daughters. I peered at it again and recognised the Spartan look of Ada's home.

Aram was not in his room. It smelled of unwashed feet and stale sheets, the floor was littered with books, model kits and exercise books, the last vestiges of a dutiful boyhood. There was a poster of a Roman fort and a picture of King Arthur and the Knights of the Round Table over his desk. He wanted to be a knight himself when he was a kid, he loved his storybooks with tales of chivalry, so long as there weren't too many pictures in them because his parents wouldn't approve. At primary school he'd given talks on the subject in class, wearing a home-made cuirass and a cardboard helmet. It also explained why he'd opted for the French horn.

The wall above his bed was hung with trophies of adolescent high spirits: a stolen traffic sign, posters of Guns n' Roses and heavy-metal groups with lots of skin showing, tattoos and leather. He'd also had a go with a spray can. You could tell that Ada hadn't made it upstairs for weeks. This domain had reverted to her son, to Aram the bookworm, amiable and polite with his pageboy haircut, rubber-soled shoes and baggy clothing. There were even comics scattered on his bed. Only a note pinned over the headboard still recalled his parents' dwindling authority: 'Be nicer to Dad and Mum.'

Where was Aram? Not in Maarten's study, in which I encountered a small desk with drawers crammed with dinky toys (now that I'd succumbed to the urge to snoop I'd lost all sense of propriety), not in the bathroom (towels stiff as boards), not in the toilet (recycled toilet paper). I called his name but there was no reaction, until a creaking sound in the corridor attracted my attention. I tugged at the string hanging from the trapdoor in the ceiling, but the ladder didn't slide out. Aram was holing up in the attic. 'Won't you come downstairs?' I asked.

'No.'

'Pieter's waiting for you.'

'Don't want to see him.'

'Why not?'

'Because,' he said with a catch in his voice.

'Are you afraid you'll cry?'

'Yes.'

Who was it up there? Him or me? Both of us were fighting our shame.

The day after my father died they made me go round and tell everyone. My father wasn't married to my mother, which meant that cards couldn't be sent – those were prim and proper days. Off to the post office for starters. Anything overheard there would be all over the village within a couple of hours. The postmistress, a stout woman with a cardboard bust, detached herself from her counter: 'Poor child,' she said, 'we'd been expecting it, but how are you all going to manage now?' and she pressed my head between her breasts. I told the green-grocer, who smelt of booze early in the morning because he'd lost his daughter to scarlet fever two years before, and he pressed me to his beer belly. Mr Klei, retired sea captain, tipped his hat to me. Everyone I passed in the street offered their condolences, and each time I burst into tears, not because my father had died, but because I couldn't stand being the object of their pity. They didn't give me a chance to be a man, which was all I wanted, and men didn't cry.

'It's all right, Aram, you can stay up there if you want,' I said. 'Pieter can come some other time.'

Pieter was waiting on the sofa downstairs, staring glassily ahead, his mind full of his first dead body.

★

That night death came back to haunt me in my dreams. I heard the twang of something striking the spokes of a bicycle wheel. The newspaper boy? The hour between darkness and daylight is the busiest time for dreams. And I saw my mother, still young and yet already old, the way all mothers are in childhood memories. Pedalling hard, hunched forward against the wind on the bike with the frayed canvas panniers I was so ashamed of. I'm eleven and sitting up in bed, listening to the sounds of the night. In my dream I have another dream. My father is lying in hospital, dying. Gasping for air, like a pilot flying at high altitude. The hospital has called: father's sinking fast.

Taps run, doors squeak, whispers in the corridor. Hush, hush, let's not wake the boy, he's not to know, don't switch the light on. I can hear the crunch of bicycle wheels on the garden path, the twang of panniers striking spokes and off they go, my mother and my sisters. Without me.

A storm is raging, the wind tugs at the shutters and there's a creaking sound in the corridor. I can hear the tap of shoes on the lino: my father's tread. He opens the door of my room. There he is, in his motor-cyclist's coat, his face partly hidden behind rubber goggles, eyes sparkling in the glow of my night-light. Shivering from the cold pouring out from under my father's leather coat, I make room for my father to sit on the bed beside me. While my mother and sisters hold their wake, my father has rushed home to be with me. Given death the slip, we have. My father pushes up his right sleeve, making the leather squeak. He takes off his wristwatch and holds it against my ear. The pale green luminous dials pulse like a heart. Thud, thud. I push his hand away, I don't want his watch. It ticks too loudly. I'm scared of the poisonous light, the steel is cold and the strap cuts into my ear. I duck and twist my head but can't escape his hand. The hand which hits, and which, even when it fondles, cannot be trusted not to give a sudden pinch. His traitor-hand with a heart beating in it. Thud, thud.

The newspaper dropped through the letterbox. I was still hearing thud, thud. It was my alarm clock ticking away under my pillow: I had knocked it off the ledge above my bed without knowing. Just shows how dreams play tricks with sounds.

In the final weeks of her life Ada couldn't abide noise. Aram and Maarten had to pad about in stockinged feet and Aram stopped playing the horn. Distant children's voices, the first autumn leaves fluttering against the window-pane, the wind, any little noise was enough to upset her, even the ticking of a watch hurt her ears. She tapped on her wrist (so thin, so brittle) and motioned me to take it off. 'I'm not wearing a watch,' I whispered. And yet she could hear it. Ada knew I never wore a watch, and she knew the reason why.

The night my father died I was jolted awake by the rattle of bicycles returning home. A moment later I heard the tap of flat shoes in the corridor, then a gust of cold air blew through my room, and my mother loomed ashen in the light of the bedside lamp. She knelt down by my bed: 'For you,' she said, 'now that you're the man of the house.' She held a stainless steel watch against my ear. Thud, thud.

I said I didn't want it.

Mr Korst was greatly astonished: 'Must be over a hundred people already, and there's only seating for sixty.' He couldn't provide extra chairs (not in the budget). We should have booked the big auditorium, that would have been more sensible. 'What are we going to do about the cake?' he asked.

I slipped him a 100-guilder note: 'Forty slices extra.' Mr Korst softened. It even occurred to him, suddenly, that there was a cache of folding chairs behind the curtain. The mourning tom-toms had done their work: there were several rows filled with friends from the camp. My mother complained of an aching wrist from making all those telephone calls, but it had been worth it, just look at all those faces from long ago . . . Why, there was Nikki, and goodness me, wasn't that Els? As I escorted her to the front row Mama waved to people, giving little flutters of recognition with one hand while holding the other to her midriff, like a retired diva acknowledging her old fans.

Half the choir was in attendance, too, thanks to the

neighbours round the back who'd tracked down the conductor. What a crowd. All we were waiting for now was the music. Where was that French horn? We were all set for a spate of sobbing, but there wasn't a sound. Mr Korst stepped to the front and made to introduce me as the speaker. 'Music,' I whispered. He bent over – again there was a flash of pale white leg – and said, with a nod in Maarten's direction: 'The gentleman does not wish it.' 'Take no notice, my sister was very fond of music,' I said. 'Surely you have something appropriate in stock?'

Saskia understood what was going on. No, you couldn't leave anything at all to Maarten nowadays. This was typical. She'd brought a CD along just in case, something with violins, would that do? She didn't have any music with French horns, She handed a brown envelope to Mr Korst, who hurried with it to the back. Aram gave his father a poke with his elbow.

Shoes shuffled nervously on the tiled floor, questioning faces all round. 'We shall have some music first,' I announced over the heads of the crowd. A moment later weeping violins with plenty of tremolo filled the auditorium, like syrup spread on a tooth cavity.

Shame burnt on the back of my neck, *we shall have some music first*, how dare I take over like that, and now these awful violins. Hardly an example of Ada's refined taste, which I intended to mention in my eulogy: 'She opened her home to the beauties of music and literature, banishing all vulgarity, materialism and ugliness.' That was what I'd jotted down the evening before. I wanted to show Ada the way I had known her as a girl, not as the austere woman she grew into, constantly searching for higher meanings. It had taken me quite some effort to be truthful without being unkind, I kept having to soften the sharpness that crept into my tone. In the end I had rejected half of what I'd written, and while the music played I ran my fingertips over the crossed-out lines, tangible proof of having kept my anger at bay.

Could any death be more pointless than hers? Had she let them operate in the early stages, she'd be alive today. She denied her cancer. She also denied Maarten's illness. She'd found a magnetician who came twice a week to pray for him behind his back. And she had no doubt that it worked. It was thanks to the healer that Maarten still got by without a stair-lift or one of those electric wheelchairs, even though it took him half an hour to negotiate fifteen paces, after which he had to lie down on the sofa to recuperate for at least an hour.

But I managed to contain myself, and I'd deliver my little white lies in the sonorous tones befitting the gravity of the occasion. Nor did I eschew the occasional stomach-lurching metaphor: 'In her days as a student of English Ada immersed herself in the Arthurian Legends. Like the Knights of the Round Table questing for the Holy Grail, so Ada pursued the highest in herself and in others.'

I didn't know I had it in me. *Pursued the highest in others* indeed. She didn't open herself to others, she shut them out. In these final years she had seen little or nothing of her old friends, she could no longer bear their money-grubbing and their endless complaints about mortgages. Her manners in company grew increasingly stiff, she was harshly critical of others but especially of herself. In her house a peal of laughter sounded like an imprecation. Just the one biscuit with your tea before the tin was whisked away. Penny-pinching became a sport, she'd wear the same shapeless dress (no bra) for fourteen summers in a row, a bottle of wine not more than once a year, and punch jazzed up with a clove-studded orange. Merry Christmas.

She invented more and more rules for herself as she got older. Early to bed and up with the sun. Mopping, polishing, all of it done manually, shopping for organic vegetables and scrutinising the labels on tins and jars with a magnifying glass to track down toxins and preservatives. She was a health freak, we thought, just as she was devoted to her hand-loom and to 'honest' materials. Ada was all in favour of a new purity, she took to eating increasingly unappetising meals such as barley gruel with beans for instance – food being for nutrition, not pleasure. She yearned for simplicity and purity of spirit. In time her home became almost as bare as their *tempat* in the camp.

Ada had a horror of possessions. She refused to tie herself down to a house or to personal property. There could be a war again tomorrow, you had to be ready to flee at a moment's notice. That was how she felt; after reading her diary it all fell into place.

She compared her illness with being ill in the camp. 'I've been at death's door before, I pulled through then

and I'll pull through now,' she assured me the last time but
one that I went to see her. The light filtering through the
cheesecloth curtains reminded her of the mosquito net in
the camp hospital, and she placed a photograph of her
father on her beside table. The less future she had the
more she withdrew into her remembered past. She and
her younger sister talked about the camp, which they had
never done before, and she had wept, which in Saskia's
opinion was an achievement: imagine Ada crying! She
regarded her sister's tears as a gift, the best possible reward
for her efforts to be a good nurse.

In the end Ada didn't really want any visitors at all. The
present had ceased to exist for her, in her mind she was a
little girl again, locked in the empty waiting of their days
in the camp, lying perfectly still and hoping for salvation.

When she finally gave in and let me come and see her,
I tried to raise more pleasant memories. We leafed
through her old art books and talked about the wonderful
exhibitions there used to be, about the wonderful books
she insisted I should read as a boy. And then I wouldn't be
able to resist a little barb, because for all her girlhood
enthusiasm for modernity, nowadays she shrank from the
new: pop music, Hollywood, nudity, they were equally
offensive. The only films she approved of were shot in
black and white by some surrealist film director, they'd
last two hours and would have earned high praise from
some mealy-mouthed critic. Whenever she recommended
such a film to me I'd rattle on about the merits of *Airport*
parts one, two and three all in one. I made myself out to

be more plebeian in my tastes than I was, and defended the mass vernacular with the same argument with which she defended high art and culture. Just to shock her I told her lies. If only I'd known that she'd drooled over a picture of Rock Hudson when she was a teenager.

Why had I felt all that animosity towards her? Here she was, lying in her coffin, and here was I, resenting her. She didn't deserve that. I ought to have been grateful for the guidance she had given me when I was a boy. It was she who gave me my first book of poems: *Poets of Our Time*; it was she who took me to the ballet: *The Green Table* by Kurt Jooss (the first time I saw men with bulges in their tights leaping about on stage); and it was with her I saw my first play: Tennessee Williams's *Cat on a Hot Tin Roof*. I must have been twelve, or fourteen. I didn't understand much of what was going on, it was just that the leading actor, in the role of heartless cotton planter, was exactly like my father, and I imagined I was his son Brick, a sensitive lad, but with the guts to lash out at his old man.

Ada was on my side in my battle with my father. She dared to laugh at him, she mocked his disciplinarian ways. That was our bond, and it would last for ever. She'd written about him in her Tropical Notebook:

'Mummy's new man-friend served under *our father in Java.'* Under – she had seen fit to underline the word three times.

When he comes into my room he always turns my father's photo the other way. I don't say anything, I just turn it the right way again. He thinks he's still living in an army barracks, everything has to go like clockwork. If I'm home one minute late after school I get punished. When he's really mad he slaps us in the face with the flat of his hand, like he's an army major. His favourite punishment is locking us up in the bathroom. Sometimes I spend half my Sundays in there, writing. He tore up my exercise book the other day. I don't show him enough respect, he says. Next time I'll have my flute with me. The calmer I am the crosser he gets.

I had copied this passage out but had decided against using it. No need to rub it in on such a solemn occasion.

The violins having been smothered, I stepped forward and posted myself at the lectern. As I unfolded my speech I glanced up and my eye was caught by a camera with the little red light on, high up on the brick wall at the back. A watchful eye? Was Korst the disc jockey spying on me? The actor within me praised Ada's sensitivity and her maternal side: 'Maarten needed her care and attention, as did Aram's education, and despite her own ill health she kept in close contact with her sister Jana in Canada, to whom, I'm afraid, we shall also be bidding farewell in the not too distant future. Ada, ever helpful, ever modest.'

A frisson of alarm passed through the auditorium. Had Jana fallen ill as well? Hardly anyone knew this yet, and we didn't want to think about it at the time, but when I talked to her on the phone after Ada died she intimated that she had only a few more weeks to live. Cancer. My mother wouldn't hear of it and deluged her eldest daughter with advice about diets, irradiated bread and the latest homeopathic magic. Jana was very compliant, but she had already made up her mind. She had ovarian cancer, and would be undergoing treatment until the birth of her first grandchild. That would be in about two months. She would cradle a little bundle of pulsating life in her arms, and then she would be ready to die.

I felt justified in being straightforward for a change, there was too much covering up and hush-hushness in the family as it was. 'It is unfair that a boy should lose his mother at such a young age. It is unfair that my mother should have to lose two beloved daughters, the children she fought so hard to keep alive during the war. And yet they are to be lost to her, broken and wasted by ill health. Nature is unfair.'

Nature, not God; no reincarnation; man as a chemical process, that was all there was to it.

The cake was delicious and Mr Korst talked with his mouth full. He handed me the register of mourners, the ribbons and the silver frame in which Ada had kept her father's photograph. 'Incineration of foreign metals is not permitted,' he explained. Sounded reasonable. He also had a videotape of the ceremony for me, as a token of company gratitude and also as a keepsake. 'You do not wish it, sir? But it comes with the package, a gift from us to you.' He left briefly and returned with Saskia's CD, which belonged to a collection entitled *Musical Meditations*, fantasies for strings which, so the text on the cover claimed, 'evoke the stillness and sorrow of dying water lilies'.

I was last in the line of family members accepting expressions of condolence. I shook countless hands and had moist kisses planted on my cheeks by old ladies who said they were Auntie So-and-so, though I'd never seen them before.

I recognised Els Groeneweg at once. Blond, high-hipped, hazel eyes, little laugh lines, while the old East-Indian twang was still recognisable in her voice. I couldn't hold back my tears, fell in love with her all over again. Besides, she looked a lot like my girlfriend: fair-haired, same smile, same eyes, same figure, how extraordinary that I should have subconsciously sought out my first love. 'How sad about Jana,' she said. 'She was my best friend, you know. I always wanted her to marry Joost, my elder brother. But he died last year.'

'So if you'd had your way, Jana would be a widow now,' I said.

'A merry widow,' she said with a smile, and I smothered her laugh lines with imaginary kisses. 'Pity it didn't work out between those two. They liked each other a lot. I've still got stacks of her letters. Perhaps you'd like to look at them some time. For Jana leaving Holland was an escape, truly it was, but she wasn't very lucky over there either. Poor girl, life hasn't been easy for her.'

Escape? What was that about? Jana had been my father's poet. Holland, to her and to so many other young repatriates from the Indies, felt cramped. She wanted to emigrate to Australia, but they wouldn't have her: too dark. In the end she went to Canada. I always thought my mother had encouraged her, a woman has to go out and seize opportunity, get out of this chilly backwater, and hadn't she herself left home for the Indies at an early age? Every other summer she flew halfway across the world to visit her daughter, and returned each time with tightly permed hair and a nylon trouser-suit with flowers on it. That alone was enough to put me off wanting to visit my sister.

So what had she been escaping from? Els wouldn't pursue the subject. We exchanged phone numbers and promised to be in touch.

I had never met Auntie Nikki. She was over ninety years old, could barely walk, and had hired a taxi to drive her halfway across the country. She hobbled from arm to arm until she fastened on to me, drawing me to the nearest chair. 'I've come for Letje's sake,' she said. 'Something told me I had to come.'

I had never heard anyone call my mother by her pet name, she was usually Lea to her friends. 'That's very kind of you,' I said.

'You know your mother and I were in the camp together?'

'Yes.'

'Your mother once told me you thought it very odd of her to keep attending our *kumpulan* – the camp reunions, you know. She said you couldn't imagine what on earth she got out of it. But your mother drew strength from our reunions. Letje always put a brave face on things, but she had her low moments, too. I used to cheer her up, give her the odd poke now and then, like poking up an old furnace.' She took my wrist and sprayed spittle as she spoke. 'Without her old friends she'd have been far worse off, she always sets off home again with recharged batteries. You know, morale in the Bankinang camp was very high, and that strength always come back during our reunions. One time she came very close to giving up, she stopped caring, didn't eat, just lay there on her pallet writing, preparing to let go. Yes, she had oedema, and fluid on the lungs. Jana had to take over. Letje, I said, think of your girls, you can't let go, you're needed right here. And now your poor mother'll have to be strong again, there's another ten years of life in her yet. And Aram is going to need her.' We both turned our heads and saw Aram further down the line being mobbed by mourners. 'No need to worry about Ada, she's in good hands. But you must go and see Jana, she doesn't have much time left, and she misses you. She is grieving for her sister, she needs you.'

'Mum and Saskia are planning to go next month.'

'Now!' she said imperiously. 'I foresee a departure in the next week. You must go with them, you have never been to visit. Go on,' she tugged at my wrist as if the plane were already waiting. 'Jana was your second mother, she took such good care of you when you were born, when your mother was too weak.'

She could tell I had no desire to go to Canada. What

for, anyway? Since Jana had emigrated I had only seen her twice, briefly, and neither meeting had been particularly memorable. She had spoken of rubbing snow all over your body in winter. Nice mother. Autumn would have arrived by the time my mother went, and it would already be snowing in New Brunswick.

'You're going, whether you like it or not. I've seen it all in a vision. There's a lot Jana can tell you about your father.' Auntie Nikki clasped both my wrists and fixed me with her gaze. 'You've got his eyes,' she said.

I struggled to extricate myself, but she was adamant. I blinked to avoid her stare. 'Your father had his good sides, too. You think you hate him, but if all you did was hate him you'd not be the person you are now. You loved him, too, and he loved you. He expected such a lot of you, his only son. He must have taken hundreds of photographs of you. But he wasn't well, I know. I remember how much you looked up to him when you were little, how you admired him and longed for his affection.' Auntie Nikki smiled at my expression of surprise. 'Yes indeed, you may have forgotten, but in the first years after the war I used to visit you sometimes, to give Letje some moral support, but when I moved away and my legs went bad all I ever saw of you was the snapshots she brought with her to the reunions.'

I didn't remember her, yet she must have been pretty impressive in those days, a large woman with piercing brown eyes.

'You must allow yourself to think of his good qualities,

they're inside you, too. Hating everything about him means hating yourself.' She spoke sternly and with great assurance, and although my entire body cringed, I was struck by the equanimity of her attitude.

She beckoned Aram, who hung back at first. But after repeated signals he came towards us, looking slightly relieved. 'Well, my boy,' she said, 'you can consider yourself fortunate to have had such a mother.' From the corner of my eye I could see Maarten slumped on a chair, shaking each hand that was extended to him, and looking completely dazed. What sort of a father could he be to Aram in the coming years? No one took much notice of him these days, although he had his lucid moments. He had been largely excluded from the discussions about his son's future.

Auntie Nikki laid her hand on Aram's pageboy haircut. 'I felt a hand on my head in the auditorium earlier, as well,' Aram said. 'It was weird. I sensed someone sitting down beside me and putting his hand on my hair. A man in uniform. Creepy.'

'Right, you're a sensitive lad,' Auntie Nikki said. She seized him proudly by the arm and they made off towards the cake.

Poor Aram, I thought, a good head on his shoulders, doing all right at school, and here he is already in thrall to extrasensory perception. I lit a cigarette and moved towards the corridor.

I was waylaid by my mother: 'Ah, there you are, at last, come here, look! all these relatives wanting to meet you.'

'I can't take any more family,' I said, 'I've had enough.'

'But you haven't met the Van Capellens, and they've come all the way from Groningen.' She was referring to her first husband's relatives, with whom she had lost touch after the war. In the sixties they had turned up in Holland, having opted for Dutch citizenship in preference to Indonesian. They were warmly welcomed as long-lost uncles and aunts by my sisters.

'Spare me,' I said.

My mother stood squarely in my path, elbows sticking out, clutching her handbag. 'Just was there, too, you know.'

'Just who?'

'Just van Capellen, Ada's father.' All I could do was heave a deep sigh. 'He was standing behind the coffin, in his uniform. Holding Ada in his arms. He came all the way to fetch her.' This was the highest trump card. She fought back tears.

'Well, that's nice for her,' I said, and slipped away. I thought I'd take a stroll in the rose garden – wouldn't want to miss the chance of trampling some ashes, now, would I?

At the end of the corridor Mr Korst was already standing at attention for the next funeral. Noting how downcast I looked, he gave me a fatherly hand-shake in passing: 'Ah, well, sir, death is a fact of life, comes to us all, all it takes is living long enough.'

2

Affidavit of Denial

As far as I was concerned the whole family could drop dead. Attempts at consolation were warded off, everyone withdrew into their own carapace of grief. Maarten eyed me glassily when I addressed him, hadn't the faintest idea what all these people were doing in his house after the cremation. While we were busy making coffee he slid a prepared meal into the oven for Ada and couldn't see why he should have ordered one portion less from the meals-on-wheels service. He was sticking to the schedule taped to the kitchen door.

Aram was tense and moody. He shrugged off the smallest kind word, took his food upstairs with him and locked himself away with some heavy metal.

My mother in particular went off into her own separate shadow-world. It was painful to see a perfectly sensible woman falling for all that airy-fairy ballyhoo. Ada was well and truly dead of course and reduced to a heap of ashes, but in my mother's consciousness she was still with us. Her spirit wasn't ready to go, she said, there was so much that needed sorting out: insurance, a guardian for Aram, nursing for Maarten. Ada had avoided any discussion of the future. Maarten had never dared broach the subject, she hadn't either, so now it was up to her to keep an eye on us from the other side until matters were settled.

When I was young my mother's foibles used to make me laugh. And they hardly affected us children, she was too down-to-earth to let that happen. Yes, we'd draw Tarot cards at the weekend or throw coins for the I Ching, and she'd interpret them. We'd giggle over her vague predictions and fail to notice whether they came true or not. Cosmic vibrations were all very well, but it wouldn't do to get carried away. She only half-believed in it, pored over her horoscope to see what the stars had to say about her but if she didn't like what they said she dismissed it all just as easily. The stars pointed things out, they didn't make them happen. Nor did we make sarcastic comments, to us it was just a cheery family game; sarcasm hurt her and she'd had more than her share of hurt already. If you'd had as hard a time as her, you had a right to some astrological relief.

But magic and reality were getting seriously mixed up these days, not least due to her having fallen into the clutches of two old ladies with spiritualist leanings, who lived in the same nursing home. 'Wonderful ladies,' she opined, 'terrific contacts, too.' One of them had been a handicapped child in a previous life, and a highwayman in another. 'She murdered dozens of people, so she's got an awful lot to make up for, she's got to do good in this life, which is why she wants to help me. She's incredibly supportive.' The other old lady found herself in a bus with a Hindu gentleman whom she'd met in a previous incarnation. 'So now he takes tea with her once a week. A very interesting fellow, he has the gift of materialising. He's one of the chosen, imagine coming across the likes of him on a bus.'

'Ada must go in peace,' my mother said. 'Let's help her all we can, there's nothing worse than a restless soul.' That very afternoon, after the cremation, she told me to go over the certificates and the other paperwork. 'Ada will show the way to go forward,' she said. I had to repress the urge to suggest she summon the assistance of her errant husbands. The Royal Colonial Army, at your command.

Grief had washed away the last remnants of my mother's common sense, fantasy was her life-line now. Since Saskia had mentioned to her, as they consumed their funeral cake, that she'd given Ada two sleeping tablets the night she died – unbeknown to the doctor and crushed to a powder which she'd mixed with custard so she could trickle it between her teeth – she was persuaded that her daughter had died of an overdose.

'It was those pills, wasn't it, Saskia?' she repeated at least five times in the limousine on the way home from the funeral.

'They just gave her the strength to die,' Saskia said.

'The pain was preventing her from sleeping, she was too tired to die.'

'Yes, but it was that pill, those pills, that finished her off.'

'Cancer, it was cancer,' I snapped from the back seat. My words struck her on the nape of the neck, causing her brand-new purple hat to lurch forward.

My mother spun round, shocked: 'You! Why so sharp? Why can't you just keep quiet for a change?'

Right, she could have it her way. I'd show her how good I was at keeping quiet. As soon as I got home I unplugged the phone and didn't get in touch for a week.

The only thing that bothered me was the thought of Aram in that miserable house. I wanted to get him out of there, spoil him, buy new clothes for him, throw his smelly socks in the bin for the poor of Eastern Europe, give him treats. It might be a good idea for him to come and live with me. I tried to envisage a life of being home on time, four o'clock tea and overseeing homework. It was a crazy idea, I couldn't very well take him out of his current school and simply tell his father: 'Your wife's dead, I'll have the boy, we'll put you in a nice home.' I changed my will – everything was to go to Aram – and measured up the attic to see if I could improvise an extra bedroom there. And as I made room for my nephew in my head I pictured him tramping down the bare corridors of his school, rubbing the sleep from his eyes, hair sticking out, no one to check his appearance before he left the house. Would he be feeling miserable, or proud? Death always got you extra attention when I was at school: classmates whispering behind your back, a little wave from that girl who'd ignored you before. And what better excuse for truanting and poor marks? Still, I worried about him. His whole demeanour, his clumsy behaviour, everything reminded me of the boy I was when I lost my father.

I recalled being in the playground surrounded by boys, with me telling them about my father's heroic death. Yes, he'd been struck down by a very complicated disease. There'd been a piece in the local paper about him, not that he was mentioned by name, but rather as a medical case. He was the first patient in our part of the country to undergo a commissurotomy. A what? Yeah, it was Latin. Some professor made a slit in his heart valve, and stuck his finger in the hole. A knife in the heart! I pulled up my shirt and pointed to where the chief surgeon had cut the skin and sawed the bone in a three-quarter circle. I was aping my father, who'd bare his chest at the most unexpected moments to show off his scar. At last he had a wound worthy of display, better than the badly puckered scar tissue on his back. This was a wound to be proud of, almost a mark of distinction, more important than his army medals. They snatched the press-clipping from me: wow, you had to be put on ice before a heart operation or you'd bleed to death, unconscious for eight hours straight and the heart never missed a beat! My father was a medical miracle.

But the valve got unstuck, they had nurses watching

over him day and night, bandaging didn't help either. My father turned blue again and this time there was nothing the chief surgeon could do for him.

I was the hero of the playground. A pierced heart! Even the tough boys were impressed. My father didn't have a job, he was always round the house, there hadn't been much reason to brag. Now he was dead I could show off at last.

The trouble was that I was lying. He'd had the operation over a year ago, and his heart had been fine afterwards. What got him was a cold, a common Dutch cold. My father died of Asian flu.

My boyhood crept into my consciousness with everything I did. How I used to watch my father as he shaved (I've got his chin) and think: so that's what it'll be like for me, too – sharp blades, hot water, shaving brushes and grimaces. But by the time I sprouted a beard I found I'd forgotten how to angle the razor. That was the first time I missed my father, it was about six years after he died. There was no man in the house to teach me manly things. To this day I'm not sure which way you twist a light bulb to unscrew it, and instruction leaflets for electrical appliances drive me to despair. Who would be there for Aram? He could hardly turn to that pathetic father of his, all he had on offer was bewilderment and forgetfulness.

I didn't realise that I was not grieving for Ada, but for my father. I thought I had him under control, that I'd smothered him under a blanket of cynicism, but here he was rising from the grave to wind me up. For years I'd been led by hate, everything I did or didn't do was connected to my aversion to my father. He was an army man, so I promptly varnished my nails to escape conscription. He lived by the clock, I lived without, even made a point of being late. Vigour, muscles, sweat, however poor his own health, he always read the sports pages from beginning to end, whereas for me the mere sight of a football boot was enough to make me puke. My hate was a source of energy.

I had no desire to see things from a different perspective, I simply refused to think about him, but as the years passed I couldn't help noticing that I took after my father in more ways than I cared to admit, and if I hadn't seen this for myself the family was always keen to remind me. Like him I was no good with money, I was hot-tempered and self-indulgent, and I also possessed his charm, his talent for conversation, and his tendency to exaggerate. These characteristics repelled me, but how to shed them? As I was shaving one day I saw that my face, too, was looking more and more like his. Gradually it dawned on me that I didn't really know my father very well at all. Since Ada's death I had felt the twinges of comprehension. I was infuriated by this, there was no way I was going to change my opinion of the man who had humiliated me for the first eleven years of my life.

I shut myself up in my apartment and lay on my back mulling over the past, thinking away and wasting a lot of time. My father kept edging into my mind, talking about the old days. I didn't succeed in driving him away with drink, in the end I drowned out his voice with a flood of self-pity.

A week later I was foolish enough to reconnect the telephone. I was ready to face the world again. Saskia was quick to pick that up. The phone rang: 'Look, what I really wanted to say was, I just want you to know, get it off my chest, but don't tell a soul, especially not Mama . . .' She paused dramatically, her voice was hoarse from crying and I knew she was gripping the receiver as if her life depended on it. 'Yes,' I said coldly, 'I'm listening.'

'I've applied to Forty-Five.'

'Forty-Five what?'

'The Nineteen Forty-Five War Victims Foundation. They've taken me on. I'm in therapy, three times a week, one-on-one. I just sit there and cry, all I do is cry.' She broke down into long, racking sobs. I said nothing, just waited patiently at the other end of the line. I kept this up too long, apparently, because Saskia slammed down the phone.

I rang her back. 'Ye-e-es,' she responded in agony. I said: 'Go on, you can tell me.' She started sobbing again, but soon thought better of it and composed herself. 'We do talk as well,' she said with an apologetic chuckle, 'there's so much to say, you have no idea. I wish Ada could have shared this experience. Did you know that the majority of camp children die younger than the rest of the population? It's been scientifically proved. We spent all our lives doing our best to adjust to our surroundings, but deep down the war never ended for us.' She said these words slowly, clearly she had said them before.

'Do you find it helpful?' I asked. It was hard to follow what she was saying, all the therapeutic jargon was getting to me. 'Working through trauma . . . healing old hurts . . . laying bare long-suppressed memories, finding the self, East Indian identity . . . so many years after the end of the war and still awaiting liberation.'

Barely two when she went into the camp, yet her most vivid memories dated from then.

Those Forty-Five Foundation guys must have been having a field day, I thought. Post-traumatic problems? Go on, speak out, shed the past, we are experienced listeners. What with the real victims getting too old to remember, there's room for more clients in our appointment books. We mustn't stand idle, unemployment runs high in the therapy industry. We are here to help you, and by the same token you are helping us. Makes good business sense.

'No one would listen to us for all those years,' Saskia said.

'Come come, what about all those eager-beaver social workers?'

'Remember when the Molluccans hijacked that train? Well, I was stopped and searched three times at the station in a single week, and once they made me lie flat on the ground. We're outsiders, they'll go on reminding us for ever that we're different. We just don't belong.'

I kept silent.

'Why don't you say something?' Saskia asked.

'What can I say? I think you're getting mixed up.'

Saskia dissolved into tears. 'We've kept our mouths shut far too long,' she said.

'It's a good thing you're getting help,' I said. I could hear her lighting a cigarette, and I followed suit. We felt a little less tense.

'I've got so many questions I want to ask Mama, but as soon as I mention the camp she starts complaining about her health. She says I exaggerate.'

'Does she?'

'There are still so many blind spots . . .'

'Blind spots.'

'We've a right to know what happened . . .'

'Yes.'

'She won't talk about it. She's forgotten, she says . . .'

Say yes, repeat the last word the other person has said and they'll natter on regardless, a shrink's trick, nothing to it. In the meantime your thoughts can have a wander. Saskia's reproaches had a familiar ring. My mother refused to listen to her, she was as bad as the rest. No one had shown the slightest interest in what they had been through when they had first arrived in Holland, either. Utter the smallest complaint about life in the prison camp and the subject would immediately switch to the listener's own little problems. She'd had to swallow a lot. People sneering: 'things weren't half as bad in the colonies as they were in Holland. How awful for you to have to cope without servants – still, all that sunshine, and bananas on every tree, eh? Compare that to the winter we almost starved, when we had to eat tulip bulbs to survive.' In this way my mother's hardship was diminished, and she was too weary to protest.

It was over a year after the war that she received official notice of her husband's decease, then she spent years battling with the Ministry to collect his back pay and pension. 'An Indo boy who remained loyal to the Dutch during the war, a bit far-fetched, don't you think? It's common knowledge that practically all educated Indos collaborated with the Japanese, and with the Indonesian nationalists, too.'

'But he had Dutch citizenship,' mother said, 'he fought for Queen and Country, he joined the resistance.'

'Resistance against the Japanese? Dear lady, there was no such thing. Dutch nationals were interned, they had no means of resistance.'

They made her wait five years for her pension. Notary Groeneweg went to considerable lengths to find witnesses who could attest that her husband had fought on the right side. Indeed, he was suddenly deemed a war hero after all, rehabilitation followed in the newspaper and in the end Justin van Capellen was posthumously awarded Holland's highest military honour.

'Too late,' my mother fumed. 'Too late by a long chalk. First I was supposed to be ashamed of my husband and now I'm supposed to buy his honour.' The offer was that the decoration pertaining to the Militaire Willemsorde would be dispatched upon receipt of 36 guilders and 20 cents. 'Why don't you just wear it yourself?' she had written to the minister.

My mother clammed up after that. The 15th of August, the date of the Japanese capitulation, was marked with a cross on the calendar in the lavatory. The second spring after the war my father bought his first Dutch flag: he lowered it to half-mast on the 4th of May to commemorate the nation's dead, and flew it high for victory on the 5th. Those were the only days he put out the flag, never on the 30th of April, which besides being the Queen's birthday was also the date of his arrival in his new homeland. We didn't fly the flag for Holland, but we wanted to show we knew all about the war.

Our mother was not the complaining sort. 'Positive thinking,' she said, and avoided all mention of the camp. When I asked her she said: 'Well, yes, we were hungry, I suppose, but we also had lots of laughs. *Sudah*, never mind.'

And now the daughter was making off with the mother's pain.

'All right, all right,' I said, and Saskia burst into tears.

Between sobs I was given to understand that besides being in therapy she was attending gatherings with a bunch of people who'd been through the same experiences as her. They reminisced together and felt collectively misunderstood. Most of them had been interned in some Japanese camp with their mothers, but some of them were born after the war. 'Our parents keep mum, that goes for all of us children.'

'Children?'

'We were children then,' Saskia said. 'You should come to one of our meetings some time. Do you good.'

'I'm fine.'

'Don't you remember what it was like with your father, when we were living by the seaside, how the war went on from morning till night?'

My ears pricked up at that. That's none of your business, I thought, my father belongs to me. 'Is it because of Ada that you're so involved with all this camp stuff nowadays?' I asked.

'No, I've been weepy for ages. I cry over the silliest things. At the supermarket, for example, I go past the baby foods and paper nappies and I burst into tears, all those smiling little faces on the labels, I don't know what it is. We were never allowed to be children, perhaps that's why.'

The last few weeks had been awful, she'd barely stopped crying. Her husband blamed it on the menopause. 'I keep dreaming I'm a little girl again, all alone, with a barbed-wire fence all around. I wake up every night screaming, drenched in sweat. I can't concentrate during the day, and without my Seresta tablets I don't sleep a wink at night. Doesn't that sound familiar at all? Don't you ever feel that way?'

'I didn't live through the war.'

She sighed, and I sighed. Bad chemistry, we'd wound each other up ever since we were kids.

'A couple of months ago Ada took me to an exhibition

about the Indonesian resistance during the war,' she went on, with renewed energy. 'There was a display about Papa van Capellen's group. They had a picture of him in the prison camp along with three others, so skinny, I didn't recognise him, naked to the waist, a living skeleton. There was another picture of the same group, which they probably distributed as a warning to the rebels. This time they were kneeling, in uniform . . . and they'd been executed. Papa van Capellen's head was on the ground in front of him. I could see his eyes, they were looking right into the camera, upside down, two black dots in pools of white, wide with surprise. His collar was still on the neck, and you could see the muscles, trails of white in the gaping throat. There was a trickle of blood down the front of his jacket.'

She fell silent at the other end of the line, and in a flash I saw the cabin trunk with the framed photo on top, her father in full regalia, with stitched collar and plumed helmet.

'How revolting, I never knew that.'

'Nor did we, Mama never told us. The executioner was standing right next to them, grinning. A dirty sodding Jap, with blood dripping from his sword.'

'But why dredge it all up?'

'I just had to see it with my own eyes. I have a right to know who my father was. Mama told us he'd been shot, and anyway, that's what it said in the War Graves Memorial book, too. We don't know the first thing about him. Another thing I found out at the exhibition was that he'd been a guerrilla fighter for two years, they blew up radio stations, sabotaged points and made trains run off the rails. Fantastic. And d'you know what the caption said, in Japanese characters? "Traitors receive their due." The nerve. My father was a hero.'

A fool more like, I thought. He'd picked the wrong cause, he'd sided with the Europeans who'd stolen the land of his people and who persecuted the nationalists. History hadn't proved him right, either. To console her I said: 'A father to be proud of.'

'We didn't even get a chance to be proud. Mama refused to talk about him.'

That was it. I'd run out of nice things to say about her father.

'I think it's awful that we see so little of each other, soon we'll be the only ones left. And you're the only brother I have.' It was Ada who had brought us together, she felt, and we ought to stay in touch more, for our sister's sake. Her therapist thought so, too. 'He says you and me ought to talk, work through the grieving process together. The counselling is supposed to help me get back to being an autonomously functioning person.'

I began to feel genuinely sorry for Saskia, despite the snivelling and the actressy delivery.

'Can't we make an appointment to meet some time,' she said, 'there's something I want to tell you about your father. A voice from the past.'

Oh God, not Sheila the astronaut again. The receiver felt sticky in the palm of my hand. 'Why don't you come here,' I said in the warmest tones I could muster, 'let you see how I live?'

'No,' she said firmly, 'I don't want to see how you live. You've never invited us to your house before.'

'Then why don't I take you for a drive along the coast, past our old house? We could go for a walk on the beach.'

'No, I don't ever want to go there again. I want to keep everything in my head just the way it was, I don't want to see how it's changed.'

'It's the same as it always was, as bleak and boring as ever.'

'The wood across from our house isn't there any more, someone told me. I'd like to go for a walk in a wood.'

We agreed on the wood behind the sand dunes, we'd go there the next day. Have a good chat and stop at the pancake place. I like to have a destination in mind when I walk.

Weren't Saskia's troubles actually rather more pedestrian in nature? Her failed career as an artist, her floundering marriage? She'd gone on about getting a divorce for years, and kept resolving to take up her painting again, like when she was young and used to hawk her watercolours on the sea front. Half the village had praised her talent, and there was nothing left that art classes could teach her. Saskia was the artist of the family, and all she ever wanted was to leave school and go to art college.

My father had never been in favour of her artistic aspirations. Nursing, that was a sensible profession for a girl. You had to have a profession you could fall back on, preferably with a pension, it was one of life's first necessities. He spoke from experience. Saskia rebelled, she drew pictures in all her exercise books, wore tight sweaters, took in the legs of her jeans and back-combed her hair to look like Brigitte Bardot. By then my father was already too ill to let her behaviour get to him, and so it got to me instead. She played truant from school and Mother secretly slipped her money to pay for lessons with a professional artist. She hid her canvases at the neighbours' and removed every tell-tale spot of paint from her fingers before sitting down to supper. She sat the entrance exam for art college without my father knowing. Hardly had he died when she gathered together her paintbrushes and left home. Which to me was the second good riddance within the space of a few months. She found herself an attic to rent, started painting in a big way and designed ban-the-bomb posters (which our mother tore up because the Hiroshima bomb had saved her life). Saskia blossomed in her rebellion, she even had a solo exhibition. But she didn't sell a single painting, and from one day to the next she went into nursing. Disillusioned. She married, had a daughter and moved to a bungalow in the leafy semi-suburbs. Her husband was a jerk with plenty of money and a peculiar taste in furniture. He favoured rustic antiques, and their first coffee table was a converted wagon wheel. Easel and paintbrushes were put away in the attic. A few years into her marriage and she already wanted to leave him, but she hadn't dared. It was wrong to deny a child its father, at least that was what my mother said, because Saskia and I weren't on speaking terms in those days. Too scared of being on her own, too dependent on his money and the luxuries he showered on her, she had tried to lead the life of the local gentry – some gardening, the occasional bridge party, and fund-raising for charity. Each summer she ran away to her mother to cry her heart out, and after a week of herbal teas, the I Ching and a séance with the old ladies, her husband would come to fetch her and she'd be her old resigned self again. This had been going on for years. Did it have anything to do with the war?

The wind dispersed the briny air and we spotted our old home from afar, looming up from its bleak surroundings, a wide red roof against a backdrop of dunes. Saskia didn't want me to drive past, but I had no choice, there was no other road to the wood. When I pointed to the roof, saying: 'See how green the copper on the belfry has gone?' she looked the other way, towards the patch of wasteland where a beetle-borne disease had killed off all the pine trees years ago. It was the very wasteland she'd said she didn't want to see.

There were sand drifts in the front garden, without a fence the wind had had free rein. Before the war it had been a holiday home for German children, hence the bell up on the roof. After the war the building had been requisitioned to provide accommodation for four families of repatriated colonials (all of them brown, except for my mother and myself, a deficiency that was rubbed in each summer: seven shades of pink, then all that peeling. One freckled nose in a sea of coppery faces).

It looks better kept than in the old days,' I commented, 'the paintwork's looking good.' I couldn't resist pulling up in front of the house. The greater the chaos around me, the more I dive into it.

Saskia turned her head warily, her cheeks wet. She couldn't see properly through her tears. 'Do you come here often?'

'This is the only decent beach as far as I'm concerned. I like it here, the greeny-brown marram on the far side of the dunes, the tufts of lyme grass, blue thistles, yellow primrose, the pallor of the white poplars, the black of the pines. When I have trouble sleeping I think of all those different colours, and at the dentist I try focusing on this kind of scenery.'

'But you always said you were miserable here?'

'Not in the dunes. Knee-deep in the powdery sand, a stick in my hand, roaming the dunes. No one to spoil the horizon around here.'

'What about us then?'

'You lot refused to see anything, you were blind. Look, I was beaten to a pulp once, right there in that corner.' To get a better view I rubbed my sleeve against the side window, which had steamed up.

'We loved your dad. It was us who picked him for Mama.'

'What do you mean? Our fathers knew each other in the Royal Colonial Army. Mine was supposed to be helping Mother find yours, but he went looking in the wrong places and I was the result. No point pretending it was any different. Had his way with the wife of his superior and there she was, up the spout. That's all.'

Saskia flicked a piece of imaginary fluff from her Hermès scarf, eyes brimming again. There I was, being hateful again despite my good intentions. 'We first got to know him early in 1946, when we were waiting to be shipped to Holland. We were staying in some big house in the European quarter of Palembang. It was full to bursting, ten families, just women and children, everything you touched was sticky. No one was allowed to leave the grounds, we cooked in the garden, grew our own *ubi* and played behind the *atap*.'

'*Atap*?'

'The fence. The older children cut little holes in it to watch what was going on in the street. We spent all our time there, peeping out, fascinated by the men because we'd never seen a man in civvies, and if we squealed too loudly when they came past the grown-ups pushed us out of the way to look for themselves. Mama was desperate, worried about the family in Holland, and penniless. She'd sold everything, down to her last ring. The army wouldn't do anything for her until they had news about our father. The Red Cross people wouldn't help either. There were all sorts of conflicting rumours, someone had seen him in northern Sumatra, someone else said they'd heard of him in Borneo, where he'd boarded a ship bound for Java. Anything was possible. Several men from his regiment had fetched up as POWs in East Java, but they all turned out to be white Hollanders. We were led to believe that Papa van Capellen had probably not been interned, at least if the Japs had stuck to the rule that Eurasians didn't have to go behind the *kawat*. Anyone with at least one quarter native blood counted as non-European.'

'You seem very well-informed all of a sudden.'

Saskia looked hurt. 'I hear a lot of stories in therapy.'

'And all those Malay words. I'm impressed.'

'I'm doing a course, it's part of my identity. I have decided to go down that path.'

She reached for her handbag on the back seat and took out a posh notebook bound in expensive leather with a gold-plated ballpoint secured in a ring, your typical little gift for the woman who has everything, and she wrote the words in Malay for my instruction: *ubi* = sweet potato, *atap* = fence, *kawat* = barbed wire. Lesson one for beginners, as if I were a half-wit. She ran her manicured fingernails over the words. There was something indecent about it all: memories of poverty spelled out by a rich woman, a woman who hadn't peeled a potato in years, and her jewellery was obscene, too: emeralds set in gold, shades of the tropics, green on brown. If push came to shove that ring would keep her going for several months.

'At the beginning of the war we had much darker colouring than we have now,' Saskia said, 'but that didn't stop them from sending us to a camp. We lived with the Dutch army, and were put under house arrest straight away. I envied the natives, they could go where they liked. I didn't want to belong with the Hollanders, I belonged with the brown people and still they put me behind the fence. I couldn't understand why.'

No wonder, I thought, you were barely out of nappies at the time. But I was determined not to be nasty so I shut up.

'Funny, come to think of it, perhaps it was then that I first became aware of the colour of my skin,' she said, stabbing her finger at her chest. I'd never heard her referring to her roots with such obvious pride. 'Twenty-five per cent. At Sunday School in the camp we used to sing: "Here we gather at heaven's gate", and I'd picture a whole lot of brown children skipping about in a free heaven. I dreamed of wriggling past the legs and skirts of the women gathering firewood, and making a dash for it, so as to be with the native smugglers on the other side of the fence. It wasn't until much later that I realised it wasn't any safer out there at all.'

It was stuffy in the car, and Saskia's perfume was getting on my nerves. I wound down the window, but she begged me to shut it at once. Her mind was in the Indies, she said, and she didn't want to be distracted by the cold sea air.

'When war broke out Papa van Capellen was away on a secret mission to Borneo. There had been no news from him since. Mama said not to worry, he was bound to be in hiding somewhere. But where? And why hadn't he got in touch with his regiment now the war had ended? No one went looking for him, and anyway the postal services weren't working properly. It was the start of the Bersiap period, with all the purges. A lot of Indonesian nationalists were hostile to the Dutch. Sumatra was unsafe, there was fighting all over, women and children had to be repatriated as soon as possible. If there were any news about our father, we'd hear it in Holland.

'Some colonial official told Mama that Papa van Capellen and some of the other Indo soldiers had joined the resistance. Mama couldn't bear all the gossip, what with some of the Hollanders saying he was a traitor. How could she ever prove this was untrue? Mama was completely in the dark, she didn't have a single official document.

'We didn't have any clothes or household linen left to barter for other things. The English gave us some Jap uniforms, horrible, but what could we do? Mama cut them up to make little mud-yellow dresses for us. She herself wore army pants which ballooned round her bottom, she tied them with a white webbing belt stained with rust around the eyelets. I can see it clearly. But we didn't have shoes, there weren't any children's shoes in the Red Cross parcel, so we wore wooden sandals with leather straps.

'The neighbourhood where we were put under house arrest was guarded by the Japs. They were supposed to keep the rebel fanatics away, so our former enemies became our protectors. Thank goodness they stopped making us bow to them, but I was even more scared then than I'd been in the camp. You heard shots in the night, and you could smell houses burning in other parts of town. After a while the British took over from the Japs. There was a group of men billeted down the road, in an old mission station or something. They used to play football in the front yard, and they were very noisy, especially at night, playing music until the early hours. All the mothers disapproved, but when we were in bed they'd sit in the garden and hum along to the music.

'Us girls were told to keep well away from them at all times. The women we saw visiting that house were wicked. Later on, when things weren't so strict, we ventured past the mission one day, keeping our eyes peeled for wicked women. But all we saw was a bunch of old men, some of them lying on stretchers under the corrugated iron roof of the veranda, others hobbling about on crutches. They looked like tramps, haggard, dressed in rags, nothing like the wonderful husbands our mothers talked about in the evenings, the men they had danced the rumba with before the war. Stooping, with hollow bellies, they looked like death warmed up.

'But there was one man who stuck out. He wore snow-white pressed trousers and brand-new black shoes. He looked like a dancer, we thought, we could hear the metal caps clicking under his soles. I'd never seen such shiny shoes in my life, all we knew was canvas shoes with a hole cut out for the big toe, wooden sandals and boots. The dancer waved and said something to Jana, something friendly, there were none of those nudge-nudge wink-wink remarks that the Allied soldiers were notorious for.

He would be seen idling on the square at the end of the avenue, chatting over the fence with the natives. We were full of admiration for his shoes, and he let me stand on them in my bare feet while he took a few dance steps. He gave us goodies which he wangled out of the locals. I couldn't remember my father at all, but I just loved being so close to a man. Several children in our house were being reunited with their fathers, there were truck-loads of fathers, and I thought I'd pick one out for us. That he turned out to be called Justin made it all the easier. Oh yes, all three of us were totally smitten by him. That was your dad.'

Saskia gave me a meaningful look. What did she expect me to do? Throw myself into her arms and weep with gratitude for her having picked the man who would father me?

'When we told him our surname, he said he'd met our dad when they were recruits. We ran to tell Mama, but she was too tired to go and talk to him. Every time we saw Justin we'd ask him questions. He'd been a champion boxer, and was incredibly good at drawing. We even posed for him and gave the picture to Mama. It got lost of course, thrown out like everything else from the old days. We wanted her to come with us to say thank you, but she was ashamed of her baggy Jap trousers. Jana made a big fuss over him, she was the go-between, she even called him Just to his face. He wasn't really that much older than her. She actually went to the nuns to beg for a dress, and when she got a flat refusal she stole a sheet from their clothes line, she confessed to me later. Mama made it into a tunic.

'They met on the little clearing. That was Jana's idea. Mama on the bench, your dad by the fence, and two hawkers behind the barbed wire. We held up our hands and one gift after another came our way: condensed milk, a length of material, a tin of cocoa, all of it heaped in Mama's lap. He presented her with a flower, too, and a letter, and she accepted it all graciously, although she declined his offer to go dancing. That wouldn't be seemly, she thought. She was waiting for her husband, she didn't know yet that she was a widow, and anyway he seemed far too young.'

'You've got a very good memory,' I said, 'the tunic, the black shoes, the rust stains on a belt . . .'

'It's the little things that stay with you.'

'You were little yourself.'

'I was five, nearly six.'

'And already politically aware.' I didn't think she was telling the truth. I changed gear brusquely and swung into the lane through the wood, a few hundred metres behind our old home. There was a parking lot at the end of the lane, but I didn't stop. In combative mood, I tore up a side-track. The sand whipped up against the side window, the engine howled. I remembered how I used to help Germans who'd got their cars stuck, and now I'd done it myself. We glared at each other. We'd had enough talk for now, I thought, it was time we had our walk.

'It was Ada who told me all these things,' Saskia said

contritely, 'but you know how it is, some things become even more vivid in the telling. And they're part of me all the same.'

In a sudden move to avoid any more snide remarks from me she took an envelope from her bag and laid it on my knee. 'The voice from the past,' she said, 'there, it's a letter for you.'

My old surname was written on the front – my father's surname. It had been mine, too, when he was alive, and I kept it during secondary school, but at university I took my mother's surname. I didn't care to be reminded of my father, and since he'd never been married to my mother, the switch was easy. I thought it would help me banish him from my life. Besides, my mother's family was of much older stock. Not only am I a bastard, I'm a snob.

'It's been opened,' I said.

'It was sent to Ada's address along with the other letters of condolence. Maarten was very puzzled.'

'Who is it from?'

'Go on, read it. Read it aloud. With an Indo accent, you're really good at that.'

Dear sir,
It is with some difficulty that I address you as sir, because I held you on my knee when you were small, but I assume you have grown up in the meantime and I hope for your sake that you merit the above form of address. First of all I wish to extend my sympathy on the passing away of your

half-sister. I remember Ada far more clearly than I remember you. Ada was a strong-willed girl. You must have loved her. The bond between half-brother and half-sister can be very close, as I well know from experience.

It must have been a shock for your mother, please convey my sympathy to her, too. My reason for writing to you is the following: why did you not sign your sister's death announcement with your own surname? Why use your mother's maiden name? Wartime circumstances prevented your father from marrying your mother, he never shrank from recognising you as his legal offspring. He was exceedingly proud when you were born. I remember this well, for I am your father's half-sister.

You deny your ancestry. I have heard, through your mother's circle of friends, that you often disparage your father. I can understand that you may not wish to maintain contact with your father's relatives, but I cannot let your allegations of mixed race in the family pass.

Your father was a highly regarded man and a brave soldier. His family is of long standing, with ancestors who were members of the famous Leiden Drapers' Guild. The family had been in the East Indies since 1827, and was entirely Aryan.

Your grandmother Didier, my mother, was French and of noble descent. There is not a drop of Indo blood in our veins. I wanted you to know that.

Yours Sincerely,

Mrs E. Taulor-van Bennekom

P.S. Do not hesitate to contact me.

'Who is this creep?' I asked.

'I think it must be your Aunt Edmee.'

'Edmee? Never heard of her.'

'She used to live in Cyprus. She was married to a British army officer: Uncle Jeremy, a reserved, pipe-smoking chap with a moustache. They came to visit us once. She was smartly dressed. How could you not remember? I'll never forget her because she wore a hat with a veil over her eyes, very chic.'

'And one hundred per cent Aryan.'

'You were four, or five. Strange, that is – well, not everyone has memories of that age. Perhaps you've suppressed them,' she said, with a bitter laugh.

We left the car stuck in the sand. My temper had subsided, but so had my energy to dislodge the wheels.

As we walked along Saskia asked me to put my arm around her. I did as I was told, although I'd sooner have kept her at a distance. She was over-dressed for a walk, too made up, altogether too lavishly turned out. The pleated skirt over her bottom made me think of a lampshade with a loaf of bread underneath. I soon hustled her down a narrow sandy path which was too narrow for us to be able to walk side by side.

Autumn was creeping into the marram grass, green shimmered with yellow in the breeze, the dry summer had dyed the bushes red and the buckthorn drooped under the weight of orange berries. Signs of a severe winter to come, Saskia remarked. We wondered how cold it was in Canada and whether Jana would die in the winter or in the Indian summer. For her sake I wished for mild weather when she died, Saskia hoped she would live to see the snow.

We have never contrived to agree about anything. As kids we were constantly arguing, to her I was a spoiled brat growing up in the lap of luxury, she couldn't stand me turning up my nose at a plateful of food. For my part I felt excluded. She wouldn't let me share their past on the other side of the world. I was jealous of her war, she was jealous of my peace.

But it went deeper than that, so I learned at the teashop where we stopped for a rest on the way. The sea mist had got under our coats, and we ordered hot chocolate and a pancake each (deep-fried, I didn't finish mine, she ate all of hers. 'I can't bear to throw away food,' Saskia said. 'But I can, I throw food away every day. It's my offering to the lap of luxury').

We had taken a table by the hearth, where the first fire of the season was burning brightly. I asked her if she thought she and her sisters had made the right choice when they picked my father.

'How do you mean? He was good to us,' Saskia said.

'He humiliated you.'

'Sometimes, when I did something wrong.'

'Thirty seconds late for supper, sixty seconds late coming home from school.'

'He lived by the clock.'

'He struck like a clock, too.'

'Not me.'

'All right, he just threatened you and you sucked up to him to avoid his temper. You massaged his neck with tiger balm, you pressed his trousers. You begged for his love.'

'You were jealous.'

'Yes, I was,' I said, my mouth full, 'he was *my* father, however mean he was. You played us off against each other. You were all sweetness when he lashed out at me, and then I felt left in the lurch, or you made fun of him behind his back and then I'd be ashamed. Looking down on him meant looking down on me. And my father enjoyed messing us about like that, he liked to make us squirm.'

'But he was scared of us, too. He'd wince when we reached out to him. We loved him and he couldn't stand it.' Saskia gave me a despairing look. Shoulders hunched, hands outstretched, she was pleading to be understood. We both knew we'd been competing for his affection, which was why we resented each other so bitterly. I ran my thumb over her left thumb, over the scar that my father had inflicted on her. Waved her fork a bit too vigorously and wham, a swipe with the carving knife. An accident, lost his temper, that was all, how was he to know the knife-grinder had just been. I wasn't a witness to the incident at table, I was still in my cradle.

At last we found something to agree on: we had been rivals for our mother's attention. Always patching things up, was our mother, but blind and deaf to our claims to her sympathy. She refused to be drawn into domestic tiffs, kept aloof, soothed quarrels, always ready to acquiesce, always finding excuses.

'She was the most scared of him,' I said.

'She didn't dare take sides,' Saskia said.

'Yes she did, when it mattered. She let Jana emigrate behind his back, and she helped you get extra painting lessons.'

'He was at death's door by then, and it wasn't even her own decision, she'd been to a medium for advice.' Her face relaxed at the memory: 'I'll never forget – she'd been to a séance and I was already in bed when she whispered the magic words in my ear: You must go to art college. Must – that was the message she had received.'

'Why didn't you finish the course?'

'I never dared tell them at home,' she said. 'I was in my second year when I got the chance to show my work at a friend's gallery. I was very keen. Sepia was my colour, I was still into abstract art, monochromes on a white ground. I wasn't expressing a particular idea, it was just the way I felt at the time, that was my colour.

'My friend the gallery owner had put one of my pictures on the invitation card. Soon afterwards she got a call from a friend of hers, who'd shown the picture to a Japanese acquaintance. He was a recent arrival in the country and interested in buying some Western art to decorate his living room. My friend rang me at once, did I want her to invite the Japanese man to the opening. I said fine. Make some money out of my old enemies. It was all very exciting. And he did come to the opening, but when I saw him craning his neck to inspect my paintings, I was panic-stricken. It suddenly hit me what my work was about: terror, detention, wire fences, locked gates. I ran away and never wanted to see those pictures again. For years afterwards I didn't have the courage to paint, and later on, when I took it up again little by little, I preferred doing landscapes, nothing too close to the heart.'

'So you became a nurse.'

'Clean and white.'

'And what my father would have wished.'

'Yes and no. When I helped Mama move to her retirement home I found an envelope at the back of the linen cupboard. It was empty, but there was something written on the outside: Saskia must go to art school. What's this, I asked mama. She thought she might as well tell me now, and explained what a shock she'd had the evening she attended the séance. A message had been transmitted in writing, and the medium's hand had been guided by a supernatural force to write in my father's hand.

'I know you don't believe in any of this, but I also have the feeling it was my father making me paint that way. He wanted me to release my fears in paint. It's a pity I didn't listen to him. I wanted to please two fathers, yours and mine.'

On the way back we took the wider paths, arms around

each other. I pulled an orange shovel from a fire-post and cleared a passage behind by the rear wheels, *Jawohl jetzt geht's* – as I used to assure the Germans in the old days. That did the trick, and together we pushed the car free from the sand. Two pairs of hands on the boot, pink and brown, me in communion with my difficult sister.

'Any news from the hereafter?' I asked my mother on the phone when I got back.

'No, nothing special.'

'They're not giving up on you, are they?'

'We haven't been able to establish contact.'

'What about that Hindu connection of your friend's? Didn't you say he was one of the chosen few, can't you get him to hook you up?'

'He turned out to be a fraud, made off with her table silver. No, it's just that Ada's too tired.'

'Tired? Do you suppose she took her mortal remains with her?'

'Of course not, it's her spirit that's tired. Don't forget, she had a very hard time of it, and then there were all those sleeping pills.'

'By the way, who's Edmee?'

'Which Edmee?'

'I've got a letter here from someone who says she's my father's half-sister.'

'Gosh, don't you remember? The youngest of the lot. Edmee was a daughter of Grandma Didier's second marriage, to a lawyer, if I'm not mistaken. Name of Van

Bennekom, ran a shady practice in Batavia, very crafty he was. My word, little Edmee, so she's turned up again.'

Neither the letter nor Edmee's accusations seemed to surprise my mother in the least. 'No matter how much feuding there is in a family, you always find each other again in the end,' she said. 'It's a mystical bond, a filament of mycelium connecting you to your base.'

Dump the lot of them, set yourself free from all these crazies, rinse your memory with bleach and forget you ever had a family, I thought to myself, but I really wanted to be a good son so I said: 'How nice to have another aunt suddenly.'

'Don't you go bringing her here. I have no desire to see her again.'

'When did you last talk to her?'

'Oh, ages ago, at your father's funeral.'

'So how come she knew what I think of my father?'

'Don't be silly, since you've never had a good word to say about your father and you never missed an opportunity to vent your feelings, it's common knowledge. All my camp friends are aware of it, and you know how people gossip at these reunions. Anyway, everyone knows your father's family and ours don't get on.'

'Everyone except me, that is.'

'They said the girls looked Ambonese. Nonsense. Justin van Capellen's mother came from Menado.'

'What are you on about?'

'Ambonese families are very close, you see, they're clingy. The Hollanders looked down on them because they went on living with forty people under one roof once they came here. Well, you know what your father's brothers and sisters were like, proud of their white skin, all hoity-toity. After he died they wouldn't have anything to do with us any more.'

Well I never. The pot calling the kettle black. Charming family, and there was me all this time in the dark.

'Your father's side of the family were ashamed of us,' she went on brightly. 'You were illegitimate, of course, which is a mortal sin for Roman Catholics. That's why they didn't consider you one of them.'

I wasn't sure how much of all this was true. My mother had a tendency to rewrite the family history every time some new detail rose to the surface, and things were certainly stirring in the pool of her memory. The older and feebler she grew, the more she prevaricated and contradicted herself. A good liar needs a good memory.

My father came from a large Catholic family, so he said, and we took him at his word. There were six children, not counting Edmee. He was the eldest and just ten years old when he lost his father. Suicide was hinted at, but as usual I'd never been told the whole story. I made a mental note to ask my mother about this. Besides my father, a brother and two sisters of his were repatriated after the war, the others stayed behind with their mother and stepfather in what would become the Republic of Indonesia. It wasn't until the fifties, when things got too dodgy for them there, that they left. After a time in New Guinea they emigrated to Australia.

As my father was sent away from home at a young age, he wasn't one for keeping in touch. So it was no surprise to me, after he died, that we stopped hearing from his side of the family. Family – it was like the tide, rising and falling. I wasn't bothered, but later on, it must have been when I started shaving, I became curious after all. Where had they all got to, and what could they tell me about my father? 'Emigrated,' was my mother's response, 'followed the leader, the whole clan's in Australia.' It sounded plausible and I left it at that.

When my father died the Indies died in our house, too. My mother didn't want to be reminded, not only because of the camp, but also and especially because of the strained relations between the families. In her first marriage she had experienced how complicated it was marrying into a brown family: she had never felt completely accepted. However hard she, a girl fresh from Holland, tried to learn Malay and to adapt to local customs, her husband's family never stopped seeing her as a threat and treated her accordingly. She'd had enough. The Indies lay behind her.

So it was goodbye to my exotic uncles and aunts with their pale gold rings and rolling *r*'s and stresses on the wrong syllables. The ceremonial dagger, the decorative batik cloth and the tall stories went back into the cabin trunk. No more steamed rice for supper from now on, just soggy Dutch spuds.

My father had always done the cooking in our house.

He hadn't been able to contribute much to the family's household equipment, but the wok and the steam-cooker were his, brought by him personally from the Indies, as he never tired of reminding us when tempers flared. Sunday was *rijsttafel* day, and each little dish sounded like a spice island: *bami, lombok, sajur, serunding, atjar, ketimun*. The kitchen was his archipelago. He wasn't up to taking a proper job – 'my valve leaks, you know' – and sometimes he was so short of breath that he lay on the day-bed all afternoon. But he always cooked, however poorly he felt. With his apron on he could at least play the chef.

He maintained a complicated web of contacts with East Indian grocers, who provided him with *bumbu* and the *pisang* leaves he needed to wrap his sticky rice in. All my mother was allowed to do was make vegetable fritters with left-overs and breadcrumbs. After his death we found out why: she was a terrible cook. It wasn't until I was a student living on my own that I discovered that a boiled egg needn't be blue in the centre.

My mother wanted things to be straightforward. She simply erased my father, and from then on I was hers alone, hers and her family's: tough farmers, Waldens by name, sixteenth century. But when people made remarks about the colour of my sisters' skin I belonged with the Indos again.

That's how matters stood, and they stayed that way until about a year ago, when my mother's tower of lies was shaken to its foundations. She was troubled by a lump and had to go to hospital. On the eve of her operation, fearing she might die, she gave me a long thin envelope fastened with a seal. 'This is yours by rights,' she said weakly, 'but you're not to open it until after I'm gone. Promise?' I promised, but my fingernail was already scratching at the seal. 'No, look at me now, you must give me your word.'

I shut the door behind me and tore the envelope open. Inside was an official document, with an orange seal and rubber-stamped by Notary Groeneweg, who had himself died several years ago. Had our benefactor had something to settle with me as well? I could hear the tinkle of silver charms and the tick of dashboard-clocks. An inheritance of a million, maybe?

'Statement' was typed at the top of the document, with underneath, in handwriting: 'Transcript of affidavit. Drawn up at The Hague, August tenth, nineteen hundred and fifty-seven.' That was one month before my father died. A message from the graveside.

The attestation was that 'on January thirteenth, nineteen hundred and forty-two, a marriage was contracted between myself and Mrs Sophia Munting, presumably resident of Indonesia, whereabouts unknown; I have been separated from my aforesaid spouse since being summoned for active war service on second March, nineteen hundred and forty-two, after which date I never saw her again; on twenty-seventh November of the same year, during my absence, my aforesaid spouse gave birth to twins, whose paternity I do not acknowledge. However, disestablish-

ment of paternity could not be validated due to Mrs
Munting's failure to sign a deed of acquiescence; . . . I
have no knowledge of further children born to Mrs
Munting . . .' And so forth and so on.

Such convoluted prose, I wished he'd get to the point.
Pausing halfway down the corridor from the surgery
ward, I took another, closer, look at the document, and
spotted a surprise attachment. On the back was pasted a
hand-written note with 'Affidavit of Denial, nineteenth
August, nineteen hundred and fifty-one' written in the
margin, presumably by the notary, because the writing
was in the same ink and hand as the signature beside the
stamp.

In this statement my father reiterated his denial of
paternity. Despite the efforts of a lawyer in Batavia on his
behalf he failed to obtain confirmation from Sophia
Munting. A dozen missives had been dispatched but Mrs
Munting had failed to respond. Same gist, except that in
this version the twins had names: Roeliana and Roediono.

Sounded like a Colonial Army circus act.

I already knew, even when my father was alive, that
he'd been married in the Indies before the war, and also
that his wife couldn't be traced afterwards, which was why
he couldn't marry my mother. And I'd also heard the
rumour about the children, but they had supposedly been
born years after he left. The family version of events,
nothing new there.

So why had she never told me about the envelope? Did
she suspect that the twins were his after all? I stared at it

yet again: called up for war service in March '42 . . .
Roeliana and Roediono were born in November of the
same year. That was nine months later. My mother can't
have missed that. This was weird.

I was sorely tempted to go right back and confront my
mother. What did it matter that I'd broken my promise to
her, she wasn't exactly trustworthy either. But aside from
my anger I felt small and humiliated: she was still
manipulating me. It was absurd – there she was having her
stomach cut open while I found myself lumbered with my
father's children. Twins, no less. What were they, boys,
girls, a boy and a girl? The brother I had longed for when
I was a kid? A boy with whom to share my dreams under
the blankets, who'd hoist me up to climb a tree and rescue
me if I got too close to the quicksand? That evening,
belatedly, I was to have my brother.

Perhaps my father had acted in good faith, he may even
have had proof of his claim – who knows what Sophia
Munting got up to in the turmoil of the early days of the
war? But why was my mother so secretive about it, and
why had she kept this document from me for so long? If I
hadn't opened the envelope, I'd still be none the wiser
today.

My mother was a great one for reserve, she would leave
awkward truths to mature for a bit, the way we hung the
game we bought from the local poacher. This time she
had left them too long. I had to hold my nose and make
for the exit.

While I was in the lift stuffing the papers into the

envelope, I noticed a pencilled scrawl on the outside: 'For my son, so he will understand.' My father's handwriting. That took away the last doubt.

I ran across the hospital parking lot, brimming with energy to drive all the way to Indonesia – I was so excited I even asked for a road-map of that country at a service station. I'd track down Sophia Munting, embrace the twins. I'd never got round to making the trip before, fearful as I was of getting sentimental, afraid of hearing my father's stick in the swish of the palm leaves, of weeping real tears over the spicy food. It occurred to me that my mother might die in the operating theatre, in which case there was the consolation of her money for my airfare.

She didn't die. Waldens live to be a hundred. The lump turned out to be benign, and after a month she was right as rain. As things returned to normal, my emotions subsided, too, and I let the matter of the twins rest. There was plenty of time to visit Indonesia, and of late I had been thinking it wasn't so much to do with me as with my father, anyway. Family? A new brother and sister? Only half-brother and half-sister, whichever way you looked at it. And the less I looked, the better I felt.

Not a word about the envelope, of course. Our lips were sealed. A family trait. So was distance, and reserve.

However, I did consult a lawyer to find out what the legal status of the document was. Nil. Notary Groeneweg had offered his name and letterhead for a good cause, he had added his rubber stamp and a gob of sealing wax to save my father's face. The papers struck me as being intended primarily for my mother, consolation in black on white that his legal spouse Sophia Munting had let him down on all fronts. There was no way he could get a divorce. Unfortunately he was unable to prevent his first wife from inheriting part of his estate.

It wasn't only the shame of not being married that made my mother shrink from putting a death notice in the paper, it was also not to draw attention to herself, in case Sophia Munting was out there somewhere, ready to claim her rightful share. Not that there was much to share. And all of it paid out of my mother's purse, too: a camera, a watch, thirty jackets and trousers, a sheaf of ties and twenty pairs of shoes (my father liked to show off his good taste, and she indulged him, the cast-offs of her anthroposophical friends being good enough for her). The jackets went to the Walden relatives. I soon grew out of his shoes, but there was enough fabric in the hems of his trousers to let them down several times, and I wore formal trousers throughout my secondary schooldays.

The first weeks after his death I hardly dared leave the house, so frightened was I of the wicked witch who was after my thirty pairs of trousers. Jana was too grown up for this nonsense, and she told us that Sophia Munting had children, too, she'd known about them way back in Palembang, but my mother hastened to correct her: that first wife had made off with another man. She had bathed in the *kali*, and bathing in a stream, under Mohammedan law, amounted to divorce. No one seemed to know quite what that was, just that such un-Christian customs had no validity in the eyes of the Ministry of Overseas Territories. One thing was obvious: it was *kali* water that was to blame, not my father.

After the letter from my father's half-sister I was seized with the old indignation about Roeliana and Roediono all over again. For all those years I had shrugged off their existence as a comedy act, but now it was time to put the cards on the table. Too much new evidence had surfaced. I was curious to see how my mother would talk her way out of this. I decided I'd give her a bell, perhaps we could tell the truth for once, if we didn't have to look each other in the eye.

I asked: 'By the way, about Roeliana and Roediono, am I to take it that I'm related to them?'

'Who?'

'Those children my father had by his first legal wife.'

She sputtered reproaches, I was being cynical again, and what was I talking about anyway, who did I mean? She pretended she had no idea. Envelope, hospital, notary . . . 'Yes, yes . . .' she mumbled vaguely. She didn't find it in herself to scold me for opening the envelope, not keeping promises being on a par with not telling the truth, in her mind.

'I never knew what was in that envelope,' she said. 'It came from the notary and I popped it straight into a drawer.'

'Yeah, yeah,' I responded vaguely.

★

'Go on, look me in the eye,' I said to my mother a few days later at her flat. 'You must have known. Admit it.'

'No, no, I've never heard of your Roodie and Roolie.' And she too counted the months on her fingers. Nine. 'Well now, born on the 27th, too. Seven and two is nine: Mars,' she said with a chuckle. 'Goes with our family, doesn't it? Fancy that.'

Sometimes my mother amazes me.

Family. A child is conceived out of love, lust or boredom. It fattens on its mother's flesh, has its fill, bursts out of the pouch. It tears itself free in a shower of crap, makes her bleed with pain. That's the first battle got over with.

And then the slap to make you scream. You pee. Head under the tap, a clean flannel comforter and warm breath blowing your wispy hair dry. In your mother's arms, kicking your legs for the nipple to fill your mouth. Your mother weeps. This is called happiness.

Your father's so proud, he lifts you up, the world is too light, giddily light. Your sisters come and pinch you by turns. Eek, he's real, he's ours. You aren't listening, words mean nothing to you, nor do gestures and facial expressions. But your senses are keen, you can feel the love, the fears and expectations, the hot-water bottle at your feet, rubber undersheet and safety pins in your nappies.

They weigh you, 4,200 grams, suspended in a net, and you're worth your weight in ration cards. You have value. Up you go in the air again, balancing on your father's outstretched hand, this will be your very first photo. It shows you howling, you're no oil-painting.

You reject your mother's milk, you vomit, get milk blisters round your mouth. Your mother feels guilty, she was too weak when she gave birth to you and wasn't able to give you a good start. Your father's disappointed. You keep him awake at night, you're frightened of the dark and of moving shadows. It's winter and your sisters rub snow all over you. Make a man of you.

A big bad world streams through the fontanelle into your brain. You see your father's glowering eyes compelling you to stand up, sit down. Your first bruise is treated by pressing a cold coin on it. Well done, you can do it – one hand on the playpen railing, the other up in the air: Mussolini greeting his compatriots. That'll be your second picture. Mother soothes your crying: there, there, never mind.

You grow too fast, your shoulders drop. Your father stretches your muscles, gives you your first clip on the ear, introduces you to his cane. Your mother cuts up a military jacket to make you a pair of prickly shorts. They plant his cap on your head and you march round the table, while he beats time with his ruler. Your sisters clap to the rhythm, your mother looks on fondly. You're almost a man, almost like him.

Families – they fuck you up.

3

The Darkened Eye

Canada beckoned. Saskia had been hearing voices again: Jana's end was nigh. Sheila the astronaut had transmitted another nine, could be in October, or in November. My mother was banking on October. Jana's grandchild might be several weeks in coming, but she for her part was packed and ready. The prospect of the grieving twice over weighed on her, and she felt, now she was already in funeral mood, she'd better proceed directly to the next bereavement, instead of having to gear herself up all over again if she waited too long.

I declined to go, telling myself that neither dying nor giving birth required my presence for them to be accomplished. True, my eldest sister had been like a second mother to me in my early years, changing me and giving me baths, but she had become a stranger to me since. Her imminent death did not affect me very deeply, although I realised how tragic it was for my mother. I was nine years old when Jana got married all of a sudden and took off to Canada. Since then I had only seen her twice – when my father died and during my mother's illness – and both times she had been reluctant to come over. I never wrote to her, didn't know her children, and hadn't taken much to her husband Errol when I saw him again. What was I supposed to do in Canada? Her annual Christmas letters were humdrum and the enclosed snapshots made me wince. Overweight children and a careworn husband in an interior with Canadian redwood furniture and travel trophies on the walls.

Errol used to be in the merchant navy, and away at sea for long periods. He was from the Indies, too, a gawky toffee-coloured youth who lived at the other end of the boulevard. Our village was teeming with people who had become displaced as a result of the war, and the government had requisitioned all the vacant summer houses in the area to accommodate them. You could tell where they lived by the blankets hanging in front of the French windows. The more blankets, the more colonial the inhabitants. Where Errol lived there was a blanket at every window. 'But we're totally Dutch, you know,' his mother kept reminding everyone at birthday gatherings. However, Jana gave birth to two distinctly Chinese-looking children in Canada: yellow, with little snub noses and a mysterious fold of skin by the eyes. You never could tell with Eurasians.

Jana wasn't too keen on Holland, so the family said. She and my father pined the most for their native land: a garden with fruit trees, mango and jambu, soil in which you could drop a fruit stone and it would yield a harvest, moist earth, dead leaves and decay, the dusky aroma of the East Indian archipelago. They just couldn't get used to the slate-grey skies in Holland and the chill winters by the sea, the need for umpteen layers of clothing and the gloomy houses, not nice and white with *kapur*, as my father used to say. When we took tea in the garden in summer and the sand dunes glowed behind us, they would reminisce about balmy sunsets, about the *lingsir kulon*, that loveliest light of all in the Indies, the hour before the sun goes down in flames and rosy-red shadows spill from the bushes. No, you couldn't dance around in our kind of rain, nor did you see steam rising from the trees around the house in summer. It was too bad – *kassian*, they would say. And oh yes, the morning sky in the Indies was green.

'Ever homesick, those two,' my mother remarked, 'any old snapshot and there'll be floods of tears. Jana's a jungle child, she grew up without knowing the city and crowds of people. At the time we were always on the move from one remote outpost to the next. Never a girl for dolls, she was inseparable from her little pet pig.'

The summer Jana passed her final exams at secondary school my father treated her to a moped tour of the Netherlands. They wanted to visit all the places whose names they'd had to memorise in the Indies, they'd ride across the flat green lowlands from Roodeschool to Roosendaal and then to the Royal Military Academy in Breda, a castle with a moat and young cadets out for a stroll – yes, they'd go there, too – and to all the places incorporating the word 'berg' in their names, such as Holterberg, Galgenberg and Tankenberg, for the promise of altitude their names contained. They did so yearn for mountain air and vast panoramas. We all huddled over the map while my father traced a pirouette of red lines to mark out their new homeland, far smaller than Sumatra of course, but they'd go out and explore every corner.

What a let-down! They'd had a week of rain and gale-force winds, too much sky and too many fences, and then all those paltry bumps in the landscape – extraordinary that the Dutch should think of them in terms of elevation at all. My father pasted the trip into the family album. There was Jana in every picture, huddled against the cold. After several weeks of wet weather and Errol's near constant presence Jana had made up her mind: they'd marry and emigrate. Who didn't in those days? The milkman's boy and his sweetheart took off to America, a Jewish family opted for South Africa, classmates applied for emigration leaflets, the public information bus made the rounds of the villages with a film projector. Ten million people packed together in a tiny country – anyone young and wanting space looked overseas for opportunity. Jana received large envelopes in the post, with the richer countries sending gift calendars as well. There was one with a picture of three red mountains, which I pinned up over my bed – the Three Sisters. Jana filled in all the forms with my mother's help and practised her English in secret by listening to the neighbour's radio. Canada was the only country that would take her, they didn't care what colour she was. My father forbade further mention of the subject over supper. 'Bad for his heart,' my mother said.

The following summer Jana posed in a white frock in front of our house. Notary Groeneweg drove the newly-weds in his black saloon car. That was the only wedding picture I came across in the family album. No wedding feast, no uncles and aunts, both families preferred to keep things simple. My father was too ill for festivities; the doctor was giving him injections every week. 'He'd resigned himself,' my mother confided in me later, 'the medicines did a good job.'

A large crate was delivered to the house, in which they would pack up their belongings. Errol fashioned a lid for it in the communal corridor. My mother knitted thick jumpers, Jana ransacked the cupboards – the Walden silver and Sunday dinner service with gold rim, bed linen, Red Cross pans, all our riches vanished into the crate. Els Groeneweg came to donate a piggy bank made of Makkum pottery with a slot you could glimpse the coins through. She made Jana promise to smash it later, for the shards would bring good luck. Our grandfather gave her two old photo albums, with Jana in every picture as usual. The neighbours did their bit, too, everyone contributed. I climbed up the kitchen ladder every day to check how full her treasure chest was. My father lay on the day-bed, bitter that the apple of his eye was about to leave him. His lips were blue and tremulous. Errol was no match for Jana, a boy from a house with blankets at the windows! Such weakness, and bad form, too. We were perfectly capable of putting up with Dutch draughts, why weren't they? And what were the boy's skills, what good would a seaman's training be in Canada? He grumbled away and invented new house-rules during supper: no more hammering in the house, complete silence in the corridors. But there was no turning back, the passage had already been booked.

Errol climbed on top of the crate, wrapped the hammer in a flannel and banged down plank after plank, for which I handed him the nails while Jana stuffed in the wood shavings. The hammer reverberated in the corridor. I winced at every blow and admired Errol for his guts. Jana giggled nervously.

We didn't hear him, but suddenly he was there behind us, unshaven and unsteady on his feet, clenched fists deep in the pockets of his dressing gown. His black eyes smouldered in his head. Without a word he stepped up to Errol. 'Get down from that crate,' he ordered. Errol laid down his hammer and jumped to the floor. My father grabbed him by the collar, swung his right arm and swiped him left and right across the face with the flat of his hand, the way he always hit us. His fingers left white marks on Errol's cheekbones. I was mortified, but also relieved to find that even someone so much older than me had allowed himself to be slapped by him.

It turned into a painful goodbye. My father locked himself in his bedroom and Jana refused to have anything to do with him. We ate vegetable patties for days. Errol's parents stopped greeting us, my dad was *mataglap*, they said. That's how I learned my pidgin Malay: *meta gelap*, the eye that goes dark – a blind rage that makes you see black instead of red.

And yet he took a photograph of their departure. My mother still has it, tucked away in her album: the young couple standing beside a lorry with suitcases and crate at the ready. Errol averts his eyes, but Jana stares fixedly into the lens, uncertain but good-looking. When I picture her nowadays I realise she meant more to me than I care to admit. She was pretty, the prettiest mother in the house, anyway.

The morning my mother left for Canada with Saskia she had been woken by a strange dream. It was so early when she rang to tell me about it I was still in bed. 'There was a storm and your father went out to hitch a pair of lifeboat horses. You were in your oilskins, watching, and you had trouble climbing into the dinghy, you were that small. Your father took the oars and the horses dragged the dinghy into the surf. The waves splashed over you and when you reached calmer waters and the horses swam back, I saw that you were the man and Aram the child. You rowed away together. Strange, as if the waves had washed you into a grown man. Your hair was grey with foam.'

Not as bad as being bald, I thought.

'D'you suppose it means anything?' she asked.

'It means I'm not going to Canada, that I'm staying

here to look after Aram. I'll be like a father to him, a pillar for him to lean on.'

She boarded the plane feeling reassured.

That Sunday I took Aram to the beach. I hadn't been in touch since the funeral.

'You know what's really weird,' Aram said to me in the car, 'I don't even miss Ada one little bit.' His anorak creaked and his flashlight lay on his lap; we were going to take a look at the old bunkers.

'Well, all that may change. I didn't miss my father until I discovered I didn't know how to shave.'

'What would I miss about her?' His right hand passed lightly over his cheeks, which I noted from the corner of my eye just as I had noted the stains on his trousers, his scuffed shoes and grimy fingernails.

'Music, maybe. You used to play together, didn't you?'

'I haven't played for weeks. When I practise I keep thinking of her and I'd rather not. Is that bad?'

'How do you mean?'

'Sometimes I'm even sort of glad she's gone.' Aram nudged me, unzipped his anorak and displayed his T-shirt with a knight in armour and a bloody snake crawling out of the visor. A rubber-print, I could barely take my eyes off it and couldn't resist touching it. The snake felt sticky. 'It's Black Sabbath, bought it with my pocket money.'

'Would Ada have minded, d'you think?'

'She was afraid I'd go deaf. She loathed heavy metal, said it was vulgar. Fascist caterwauling. That was dumb.

Having an opinion but refusing to listen. She never listened to the actual words they were singing. Pieter and I smuggled the CDs upstairs, and we played them very softly. At his house it's OK to turn the volume up. And we're against violence, it's just that we want to show the world the way it is. That stuff about hell and devils is just to shock.' Aram stared out of the window. A strong wind was flattening the marram grass against the dunes, but it was a clear day and the sun glinted off the bonnet. 'It hasn't been much fun these last few years. Mum was always worried sick.'

'Did she worry about you, too?'

'About my father and me. She thought I was insolent. But my father's hopeless, and he won't let me do anything. I've got to sit there with him, do my homework and stay indoors. I make too much noise, eat too quickly, I'm not supposed to play music in the evening, the slightest thing upsets him. My father is a very old man.'

'I think he and I are more or less the same age.'

'But he's an invalid, he can't even go for a walk on the beach.'

I stopped the car by the entrance to what we called the Old Kraut Road, a gravelled path leading to the wartime bunkers beyond the sand dunes. The area was closed to the public nowadays, it belonged to the water company. Ignoring the 'No Trespassing' signs, we raised the barbed wire and crawled underneath. These dunes were mine, I knew them like the back of my hand, the quicksands by the grassy marshes, the subterranean eddies that sometimes rose to the surface after a storm. Could be dangerous, but that was part of it, too – all this emptiness was etched in my memory. If anyone stopped us I'd say I had a right.

Aram ran ahead of me, zigzagging left and right as if he were the hound and I the hunter. He was glad for a day without his father. He'd had to promise Ada on her deathbed that he would look after his father, so he took the dirty washing to the launderette every week – a big bag, because Maarten peed in his pants sometimes – and in the evenings he had to spoon-feed him. Just the final mouthfuls, when the spoon became too heavy for him to hold. We all knew things were getting out of hand, but Maarten wouldn't hear of any change. The disposable lightweight plastic cutlery I bought for them went straight into the bin. He'd rather die than use plastic. So everything went on as usual: Saskia came by to help between therapy sessions, while my mother consulted the Tarot cards with her friends and concluded that this state of affairs was, for the time being, the best option.

We tramped over the foundations of the bunkers, which had been knocked down to chunks of concrete half-submerged in the sand. What wonderful bonfires we'd made in the old days with gangs of summer orphans from the city. Put out the flames with litres of our own piss, and we'd measure our pricks. I could still smell the piss. 'I wouldn't have minded fighting in the war,' Aram said, 'bombing bunkers and that.'

'With people inside?'

'Well, maybe not, I'm not keen on blood all over the

place. But shooting is great – kerpow! and everything's in smithereens.' He ran round the concrete ruins and scooped handfuls of sand, which he threw up in the wind. Something glittered among the fallen grains. I bent down to retrieve a metal cartridge.

'From the war?' asked Aram.

'Or a poacher.'

'I think it must be a German shell. Can I keep it?'

I blew off the dust and showed him how to whistle on it by putting my lips against the ridge. An icy tone shrilled out over the dunes: I hadn't lost the knack.

'A *Wunderhorn*,'Aram said. He stuffed the cartridge into his trouser pocket. 'I bet Ada wouldn't approve. She hated war.' He threw me an earnest look. 'Sometimes I'm scared she can see what I'm doing and doesn't like it.'

'Dead is dead. The dead can't see, and the older you get the more their faces fade.' I said this as firmly as I could, standing there in those bluff-coloured dunes of mine, with the sand and the wind making my eyes water. I loved this empty wilderness, the way it always lured me with its peril and underground eddies, it was where I felt closest to my father.

We charged up the slope of a dune, Aram's sandy hand in mine. We fell down and crawled up to the crest on our hands and knees. Behind us lay the wilderness bordering the pine trees, and ahead were the waves breaking on the sand. A black kite soared and dipped over the beach, with two boys running at the end of the string. We sat down shoulder to shoulder with the windblown sand pattering on his anorak. I knew this wind from the days when I used to tie little notes to my kite, notes to heaven, to my dead father. I was short of breath and had a coughing fit – I'd been smoking again in a big way since Ada died. I was past caring, having seen what a healthy lifestyle could lead to. I almost choked for lack of air. God, how old I felt. Yet I wasn't anxious, just glad I wasn't a child any more.

After dropping Aram off at his gloomy home, I wondered for the umpteenth time whether I should take him under my wing. I'd dismissed the idea just as often as I'd entertained it. My girlfriend wasn't keen, obviously. I'd been chasing her for eight years, but she kept taking off to cities halfway across the world. She was a literary agent, always with her nose in a manuscript, there was just the odd moment between lines for a kiss. Fostering a brand-new son wouldn't be her thing at all. She wasn't one for problems, and since Ada's death I hadn't seen much of her, although she faxed me a message every day (her favourite word was 'later'). I wasn't cut out for domesticity and children, and anyway, I didn't have the space. Being a kindly uncle somewhere in the background, that was about as much as I could offer.

And yet, what a fantastic vindication it would be – to raise a kid without ever raising your hand against him! But heavy metal in the house, and graffiti? I'd want to protect him, and that would mean restricting his freedom. I didn't have the patience to let him make his own mistakes. My concern was a pose, I was conscious of the undertone of compulsion in my voice, of bottled-up swearing, of the anger that made me see black instead of red. I wasn't even capable of looking after a dog.

How shocked I had been at my own reactions when I acquired a puppy a few years ago, a little companion to roam the dunes with, a hairy child that would impose some regularity on my daily life. The hair grew in two whorls on its behind, a bit like two eyes that were fixed on me at all times, even though the dog stopped and turned at every crest or bend to check whether I was still following. I called him Janus because of his two faces.

With Janus I would make up for how my first dog, a playful mongrel, had fared. We had never got round to giving him a name. We were still living by the sea at the time, and I found the stray in the grounds of the water company, where the wind had sculpted a crust of ridges on the quicksand. No idea how he got there. In the distance I heard drawn-out, high-pitched yelping, like a call for help; I ran to where the sound was coming from and found the dog buried up to his belly, digging himself into quicksand. It was a dangerous place, one foot wrongly placed and the ground sucked at your shoe, it was only safe along the edge of the marram plantation, where the sand had compacted. That was the route taken by poachers.

The dog was up to his flanks in the sand. I grabbed hold of a tussock of marram with one hand and tried to reach him with the other. I was leaning over the ridged crust as far as I could, waving a branch in front of the snapping jaws. He tried desperately to fasten on to the stick but was sinking rapidly, and in the end my imaginary brother gave him a little push so that I was able to haul him towards me. His licks smelled of fish and he followed me gratefully.

He didn't get any further than the hall. Dogs were messy, and consequently banned from the building. But he refused to go away, just waited patiently beneath the kitchen window. We gave him food, and my mother and my sisters thought he was sweet. After two days my father filled a tub with water and soapsuds so we could give him a bath, and then he was allowed to stay. A dog! We had a dog which caught rabbits and devoured beached fish, a friend I could escape with! We used to snoop around in the secret bunker passages together.

But he wasn't properly house-trained, he chewed anything that took his fancy: pyjama pants, slippers and especially my father's expensive shoes. He was a proper beachcomber, sank his teeth into everything he came across. When he persisted in this behaviour despite threats and blows, my father handed him over to the local beach warden, who would pass him on to the fishermen in the next village. It had been discussed at length and it was understood that, being a beach-dog, he wasn't fit for an indoor life, he'd be far better off with the fishermen at the beach further north. A few days later I chanced upon him again in the dunes, solitary and smelly. He recognised me and trailed after me, wagging his tail. But this time my father was adamant: no water, not a grain of rice, not even a cardboard box to spend the night in, however hard I pleaded. The very same night he took him back to the beach warden, who drowned the dog in a sack at the back of the shed.

My new dog was allowed to chew on as many shoes as he pleased, and even got a pat on the back when he rooted around in a washed-up fish or dead bird on the beach. Janus was a doggy dog, he loved me, but he loved other dogs even more. He always wanted to play with them and when he lay in my study at home he'd prick up his ears at the faintest barking in the distance. My reclusive life-style was far too boring for him, he crouched under my desk, sighing, yawning, giving out evil-smelling farts, and fixing me with imploring eyes until I took him out to the dog-field for some sniffing and cavorting around the tracks of his pals. Janus came from a kennel, he was used to a lot of barking and jostling by the food trays. The more dogs there were around, the happier he was.

It was too quiet for him in the house, and he refused to eat. The finest dog food from a tin, the best raw steak, nothing would tempt Janus. I was getting worried and my dog could sense that. Every time I stirred towards the kitchen he made himself scarce. He got alarmingly thin.

The vet advised force-feeding, and there I was, on my knees, waving a tube of meat paste. Janus kept his jaws locked, no matter how much I stroked and cajoled. My hands were trembling, I shoved the nozzle of the tube behind his fangs, carefully at first, but soon I was applying more pressure. I pinched the sides of his jaws, making the cheeks bulge over the lips, and I slapped him. Cursing, shouting, I slapped him left and right on his head and jaws, with the flat of my hand.

The kitchen was splattered with meat paste and Janus was whimpering behind the cooker. I apologised profusely, but he stayed put. It wasn't until hours later that he emerged, cowering. Again I tried to console him and feed him, stroking and patting and wheedling, and then slapping again. I detested my hands, detested my temper. Having a go at him was hardly going to make him put on weight.

'Just give him a lot of love,' recommended the dog expert I consulted, 'and he'll start eating eventually, dogs always do.' We tried again: nice doggie, good doggie, but it didn't work. Until I discovered that Janus was quite happy to eat along with other dogs. So I took his food with me to the dog-field, and gradually he began to eat. It was several weeks before he'd eat on his own, though.

At home he never ate in my presence, and if he caught me watching him from the corner of my eye he immediately slunk behind the cooker. His trust in me had been betrayed for good. I loved him, at least so I thought, but two summers later I gave him away to a family which already had several dogs. Janus stared at me too balefully, and when I stared back he averted his head. He was afraid of the black in my eyes, and through his eyes I became frightened of myself.

Els Groeneweg's house was also near the sea, although where she lived further south the dunes had been heavily built up, every dip in the sand had been sold and developed, out of sheer greed. Now rich people lived there, all in equally hideous surroundings.

Els's house was like an old-fashioned Sunday afternoon, with the smell of *sajur* curry wafting through the corridor and a tiered cinnamon cake ready on the table. 'Just a cup of tea,' I had told her on the phone, but once there I was obliged to stay for supper. Her husband was away on business and she wanted to make a fuss of me. She knew Jana was in a bad way, and also that I felt guilty about not having gone to Canada with my mother. 'I've cooked in your sister's name, too,' she said, 'we'll be close to her in the eating.'

Els passed from the kitchen to the dining table, sat down, crossed her legs, stood up again and ran out. Her angular hips showed under her dress. 'I'm getting old,' she said. She had forgotten the spoons and the soup plates.

I sighed at the sight of her dancing blond hair, her crinkly laugh and hazel eyes. The setting sun poured in through the picture window. It was as though we were sitting in an old photograph, so lazily did the shadows pass along the white walls and the small palm tree growing in a wicker basket. Her living-room was a tropical retreat.

I weighed the spoon in my hand and quietly savoured the sensation of being in love. Next thing I was longing to be a little boy again, to sprawl naked on her lap, to blow on her breasts and feel her thighs beneath my buttocks. She walked round the table and took a framed picture from the wall.

'Have you seen this?' she asked.

'It's you, isn't it?'

'Notice anything special?'

The pencil lines were fine and scratchy, and I had to angle the picture to the light to see the contours properly. I didn't think much of the drawing, although the mouth and eyes were quite convincing: it was unmistakably her.

'Your father made it,' she said. 'His signature's hidden under the cardboard mount.' It wasn't a bad likeness, but my father hadn't captured Els's vivacity. She looked tame behind the glass.

'Yes, he was good at drawing,' she said.

'Copying, you mean.'

'Don't you have any of his pictures?'

'No, his art never made it to the walls in our house.' I felt uneasy. It was odd to hear someone praising his draughtsmanship while we used to disparage it, the way we disparaged everything he did.

'Don't frown so,' she said. 'I just thought you'd be interested.'

After the vegetable curry she led me across the room to a cabinet filled with photographs: her life in silver-framed pictures. We admired her father posing next to his black Rover, Els in her MG, her mother beside her brother Joost in his air force uniform, a stooped granny in sarong and kebaya, the family pets, dogs as well as cats: three shelves of happy moments. She held up a snapshot of herself and Jana in summer frocks with a pig on a string between them.

'Fort de Kock, just before the war,' she declared.

'I didn't realise you and Jana went back such a long way.'

'We were in the same form at school. Our mothers used to play tennis together. We were inseparable, we saw the Japs march into town in their floppy yellow uniforms, and we did everything together, like covering the window panes with blackout paper and going to school holding a wok over your head and a rubber between your teeth in case of bombs.'

Els slid open a drawer and pulled a strip of yellowed cloth from a box overflowing with snapshots and papers. She sniffed at it, then slipped it over her wrist. 'My licence plate,' she said. 'The Japs made us wear them. Mama sewed an extra bit on so I could wear it round my arm like an ID band.'

'Eliza Groeneweg' it said in print under an appliquéd red circle with a white star in the middle. The number and the Japanese characters were very faint. She slid the band further up her arm. 'I'm not as thin as I used to be,' she said, when she couldn't get it past her elbow. 'I've kept everything from the old days. Before we were interned my father gave a suitcase full of private documents and papers to one of his clerks for safekeeping. After the war he got it back. Sheer luck.' She pulled the drawer out of the cabinet and set it on the table. 'Look, Jana's smuggler notes.' She held up a handful of slips of paper.

They appeared to be scrawled notes about food, complaints about rotting vegetables, smelly meat, shortages of everything, it was never *kenjang* – never enough, Els translated for me when my index finger paused at the word.

'You're a real *totok*, you are. As Dutch as they come. So ignorant. Here's some funny ones, about the difference between body lice and bedbugs. It was her job to squash them. It says somewhere that they smelt of bitter almonds.'

'What else is there?' I asked impatiently. What I wanted to know was why Jana was so eager to escape from Holland.

'Oh, here's a very sad little note,' she said, without looking up. 'It says how much she misses me.' She rubbed the goose pimples on her arms. I had ceased to exist. 'It's all right, Jana, it's all right, I'm coming . . .'

'But weren't you in that camp together?' I ventured.

'Not until later. She went long before we did. Most of the Europeans had already been rounded up. They were crammed into a few large houses, your mother and sisters, too. It was very complicated. And my memory isn't that clear either. They took away the men, but there were also people who dug bomb shelters in the gardens for them to hide in until the Brits came, who were supposed to liberate us any moment, that was the rumour. But we just stayed in our own house.'

'So why the smuggling?'

'Our family wasn't interned at first. We had Javanese grandmothers on both sides, so we were classed as Indo-*belandas*, mixed race, not proper Dutch. The Japs weren't very strict about that kind of thing in Sumatra, but my father actually had the means to supply proof of it all. Documents, seals, rubber stamps, the Japs loved all that official stuff. Before the war people always pretended their native grandmas didn't exist, but once the Japs came they couldn't wait to trump them all up.

'They let me bring your mother some food twice a week. Look, this is Jana thanking me for the *ubi* with grated coconut,' she said, waving a slip of paper in the air before laying it on the pile in front of her.

'Wasn't it dangerous?'

'It wasn't allowed, of course, but I had less trouble than my mother – she looked too Dutch and was always being stopped. I just slipped through. Most of the Japanese soldiers were all right, as long as I bowed to them nicely and wore my identification band. I was the corn-haired *rambut djagung* of the family, and the Japs had a soft spot for blond kids.

'I used to take saucepans of food to a Chinese shopkeeper, who was the official supplier of the house where your mother and sisters were detained in the first few weeks. The Chinaman gave me bits of news to pass on to my father, because our wireless had been disabled, and I wrote notes to Jana telling her what he'd said about Germany being bombed by the Allies, and also things I'd seen with my own eyes, like when the Japs made a bonfire of our school textbooks.

'But that didn't last long, because I was caught and it took my father hours of wheedling to get me out again. My brothers weren't stopped as often, they were darker-skinned. The Japs ransacked our house, we didn't have any money left and became more and more isolated. Jana had been gone quite a while by then. The native vendors at the bazaar didn't dare serve us – yes, they were scared. My father once saw a group of Hollanders leaving a transit camp in the back of a lorry, and when they recognised him they hurled abuse at him, accusing him of being a traitor. He was terribly hurt by that. The young Indonesians in particular were hostile, everyone left us in the lurch, and my parents felt guilty towards all the people they knew who were being forcibly interned. We didn't know where we belonged.

'One day a friend of ours was stopped in the street by a group of Japanese soldiers. He hadn't bowed deeply enough, and to teach him a lesson they smashed his teeth out with the butts of their guns. That very evening my father went to register us all with the authorities. By then we actually wanted to be interned, and in the end I fetched up in Bankinang together with my mother. We were so relieved – safe at last. Jana and I were thrilled to see each other again.

'My brothers were sent to the men's camp along with my father, but they were given a hard time because Papa was regarded as a traitor. Latecomers like him were very badly treated by the Hollanders at first. That's why, after the war, he was so supportive of your mother. My father knew better than anyone how quick people are to judge.' She lifted up the drawer and slid it back into the cabinet. 'There, that's enough for now.'

'What about the letters from Canada?'

'Not much fun. Jana was right to leave, my brothers couldn't stick it here either, they emigrated directly after military service.' She sliced a triangle of cinnamon cake and took a nibble. 'A bit too sweet,' she remarked. 'I wish I'd known when your mother was leaving, I could have made a cinnamon cake for her to take to Canada. Poor Jana, so ill and not writing a word to tell me about it.'

'Had you lost touch?'

'Sort of. The last couple of years there's been just a letter at Christmas. Oh well, you know how it goes. We reminded each other too much of things we preferred to forget.'

'The camp.'

'Holland, Holland most of all, I think. It was very difficult for her here, after the war. Don't forget, Jana and I were older than our years when we left the Indies, we had worked, taken care of small children and nursed the sick. We were grown up, in a way. My mother treated me as her equal in the camp, she was my friend, she confided in me.

'Once we were in Holland we had to do a lot of adjusting. All the things we had learned didn't count for anything at school, they treated us like thickies, we were way behind in everything. I was the oldest girl in class, but also the shortest, in two and a half years of camp I hadn't grown at all.

'And how insolent the Dutch schoolchildren were! Us colonial kids were used to looking up to a teacher. But what sort of a time had my classmates had? There was talk about how bad the Krauts had been during the occupation, but in the camp I had seen how cruel people can be to each other, and how selfish. There was lying, stealing and betrayal even among the inmates, and when the war was over, in Palembang, I saw people who'd been stoned to death . . . rows of bodies by the river. Not a word about any of that in class, of course, you wouldn't dream of raising the subject. Some of the teachers were very left-wing, which meant that they had it in for children from Indonesia. They kept trying to get at us with stories about lazy planters and the extortionist, oppressive practices of colonialism. And you could tell a mile off that we came from the tropics, what with our sallow skin and hollow eyes. In the playground they used to taunt us saying we used up two lots of ration cards each. I could have died.'

Els stood up and crossed to the radiator by the window. 'Cold,' she said, and quickly left the room. She returned wearing a green cardigan.

'Was that why Jana wanted to get away?' I asked when she flopped down on the sofa beside me.

'We had gone through the same kind of experiences, she was also the oldest girl in her class, and we were both quite forward, I think. We used to write to each other about that, too. Within a year of the liberation we'd seen it all, pretty much. We had strings of admirers. My brother Joost was crazy about Jana and she was crazy about him, but your father was dead set against it. When we came to your house the two of them weren't even allowed to go to the beach together. He opened her letters, he was incredibly strict with her.'

'I thought she was his favourite?'

'Yes . . . literally so.' She jumped up and strode out of the room, agitated and irritable. 'Sorry, sorry, let's talk about something else.' She slammed the door behind her and rattled the pans in the kitchen.

Pans . . . our kitchen, my father wearing an apron and Jana on the kitchen steps clutching a rice-crust from the bottom of the pan – she was always keen on scrapings. Jana, the special one, the only one with new clothes, with the most pictures in the family album: Jana on her bike tour with him, Jana at the Keukenhof tulip show, at Schiphol airport, posing by the drawbridge of the Royal Military Academy.

'So what happened?' I asked, stepping into her white kitchen after a timid knock on the door.

'As I said,' she snapped. 'Well, they were quite close in age, you know. Jana was looking for a father figure. Maybe she brought it on herself. In any case she wanted to leave home as soon as possible, so she went and married that dim Errol. I don't think she even loved him, really, but he wanted to get away as well, and a boyfriend in the village didn't arouse suspicion. They got everything organised for their escape behind your father's back.' Els shifted the pan to one side on the white range, revealing a round, glowing hot-plate. 'Your father was authoritarian,' she said. 'Attractive, too, and we were used to flirting with danger.'

'Like with the Japs.'

'No, with the Japs we made ourselves as small and invisible as we could. During roll call we always stood all the way at the back.'

'They were nice to kids.'

'Sort of,' she said gruffly, 'but they were very disciplined, any soldier caught breaking the rules was severely punished. They treated us with respect, never came to ogle when we were washing ourselves, they were very decent. The Australians and Brits were a lot worse, right after the war.'

'But Ada's experience was different.'

'Well, yes, those things did happen sometimes. There's always some nutter among them.'

'Was my father a nutter?'

'He could be very nice, very charming, except when he lost his temper, then . . .'

'. . . he couldn't keep his hands to himself . . .'

'Something like that, yes.'

'Scum, that's what he was,' I said loudly, 'just a scum-bag with tantrums.' Els waved her arms helplessly, then spun round to rummage in a drawer. I planted myself in front of her. 'No-good scum. Go on, say it, look me straight in the eye, I won't feel insulted.' I was tempted to bang my fist hard on her white range and smash the glowing centre of the Japanese flag into a thousand pieces. But at the same time shame was welling up inside me.

And I'm no different, I thought, his character is part of my character. I look like him and my eyes have the same darkness about them. I felt too gross and sordid to remain in her presence. Suddenly I was desperate to get away, away from that whitewashed house, no more *sajur*, no more kisses, just a polite handshake and cheery-bye. I couldn't allow my secret love to be shocked by my lust.

4

In the Ranks

I'm walking to the station with my father. We've taken the way through the wood, a winding lane flanked by tall trees. The sun is up but the shadows are still struggling against the light; the pine trees put their heads together while the sea whispers in their needles, the steam tram hisses in the distance. My father consults his watch. It's a weekday, his 2,448th day away from the Indies. He always keeps track of facts and figures, his head is full of numbers. My sisters have gone to school on their bikes, seven kilometres there and back. They don't take the steam tram because they're tougher than the other children fresh from the Indies, but they do wear long stockings and thick woolly hats, as their ears are too tender – clickety-click, my mother's been knitting by the window for weeks, she's even knitted a lining for the mittens attached to their handlebars, for the girls may be tough but there's a limit to the cold they can take. I'm a man: zero degrees and still wearing short pants. He's promised me a Mekka bar if I keep it up till the new year.

We arrive at the clearing where the life-boat horses graze in summer. The grass is swathed in a haze, the bushes have been dusted white by the freezing wind. My father does his exercises and I join in: stretch, bend, breathe in, breathe out, both of us blowing white plumes into the cold air. This gives his heart more space. Lying on the day-bed by the window makes him stiff: he ought to be more active, finds the winters hard going. We run round the field, my father clicks his tongue. Giddy-up, I'm a life-saving gee-gee.

As we approach the track the cinders crunch under our shoes. There's a smell of steam and burnt coals. The tram has just left and the place is deserted. My father looks round for something to lean on, his lips quivering from pain and exhaustion. The local meter-reader comes cycling down the path along the embankment, the barrel of a rifle poking out from his pannier. We wave at him, he dismounts and asks if anything's wrong. My father tells him what we saw on the way: a buzzard as plump as a goose, and a sick rabbit dragging its paralysed hind legs through the sand. The meter-reader smiles. He's the local poacher, whose pannier smells of blood and whose gunshots we often hear around the house after supper.

'Yes, there's a lot of myxomatosis about,' he says. 'And that buzzard, where exactly did you spot it?'

My father points to the wood: 'Back there on the edge

of the clearing.' The pain fades from his face. He likes talking to the locals, even if they're not very sociable, accustomed as they have been to quiet winters without people around. They wouldn't even greet us at first and they still think we're an odd bunch. They don't take to strangers, anyway, even the summer visitors are kept at a distance, even though they all make money off them. 'I also saw a couple of Krauts in a DKW. They were looking for the bunkers,' my father says.

'They always come back, like murderers returning to the scene of the crime,' the meter-reader remarks. He gets on his bike again, swinging his right leg over the rifle. We walk on.

'I sent them in the wrong direction,' my father shouts after him.

'Good for you!' the meter-reader calls over his shoulder, winking broadly, which makes me feel proud.

We take the same route home, and when we reach the clearing I ask him, carefully, where he saw that buzzard. 'Over there,' he says, waving his finger at some point in the distance. There's nothing to be seen: no lame rabbit and no Krauts in a car either.

'When did you see the Krauts?'

'Yesterday.'

'But we didn't see anyone yesterday.'

'Then it must have been some other day.'

My father says I must never tell a lie, but he lies every day.

★

Memories gnawed at me in my sleep. I found myself jerking awake in the middle of the night, rigid with hatred at times and utterly limp at others, consumed with rage. And every morning I was dismayed by my face in the mirror.

During the day I tried to lead a quiet, orderly life. No alcohol, even one glass of wine at dinner was enough to set me on edge. I stopped smoking, too, for the hundredth time. I was up to two packs a day, perhaps that was why I was sleeping so badly. I did my work, faxed my girlfriend and did my family duties, such as sorting out Ada's papers, making regular calls to Canada and sending cheques for Jana's medical bills.

The exchanges I had with my mother on the phone didn't make me feel any better. She was incapable of holding a normal conversation, all she did was flounder and stammer things like: 'How much is this costing? I keep hearing these strange clicks' – she belonged to the generation of parents-of-emigrants who never got used to phoning halfway across the world unless there was an emergency. She was unafraid of contact with the spiritual world, but the telephone company scared the daylights out of her. I was very irritable in those days, fuming against the news on TV, flinging newspapers into the corner. War, injustice, disease, I couldn't stand it any more, I'd had it up to here with weakness, and to harden my heart I set about rubbing some salt into the family wounds, sprinkling scorn and vitriol on my father's grave – but for what purpose? It didn't help me control my anger. On the contrary, I was incensed by the humiliations that had been inflicted on my parents, and yet I wanted to punish them, and if not them, myself. I was bewildered by my own rage.

When in the depths of despair, I'd get into my car and motor down to the sea, ignoring speed limits, going at 140 kilometres an hour if I got the chance, eager for a heavy fine. To clean my lungs I walked against the wind along the tide-line, not bothering to sidestep approaching waves. I ruined my shoes and let the sand chafe blisters on my heels. Pain gave clarity, and soggy feet soothed my agitated mind.

What was the point of all this delving into the past? I was trading one addiction for another, looking forward to new thrills, such as going skinny-dipping in October. Another of those vibrant memories: the nip of the cold sea and the blissful tingling afterwards.

One windy day I took my clothes off and stepped into the water. My body fat tightened into a carapace, my scrotum shrank in the cold and became young and firm again. The waves lifted me up, my feet danced over the seabed, I swam. The skin on my fingers wrinkled, my arms and legs went numb but I kept on swimming and diving in the waves. I didn't care about cramps or underwater currents sucking me down.

My father swam ahead of me, naked. There was no one around, we'd left our clothes on the beach under a towel, with which we'd rub each other dry later on. The alternation of warm and cold was good for his heart. I felt his arms brush against my leg, his body hairs swayed in the current. The waves pushed us apart and brought us together. My father became gentle in the sea, he could hardly lash out at me surrounded by all that water.

I swam into the past and the old images slotted into my mind's eye.

It was winter and there was a gale blowing. My father and I walked up to the big bunker. It used to occupy the top of a sand dune, like a great square-nosed concrete lorry with an observation slot facing the sea, but a winter storm had blown away the sand underneath and since then it had lain, broken in two, on the beach. At high tide the nose became an island in the waves.

The tide was rising. My father took his shoes off and rolled up his trousers. All I needed to do was remove my shoes, because it wasn't New Year yet and I was hoping to develop soldier's legs. We waded to the front of the bunker; the water turned my knees purple, but my father's skin remained tropical yellow. We clambered on to the roof and waited for the top-most fringe of seaweed to get wet. It looked like human hair. Suddenly my father jumped down into the water and started wading back to the beach. His trousers got splashed up to his thighs. He motioned me to follow him, but I didn't dare. He laughed. If I didn't jump now I'd have to wait another six hours for the next opportunity. 'What are you? Milksop or fighter?' he shouted. I opted for fighter, and slithered down. The waves came up to my belt, my willy shrank in the cold and I waded to the shore, shivering. My father shook my hand and gave my curls a vigorous pull. I was a fighter. Then we set off home, the wind pushing at our backs while the sopping legs of my shorts rubbing together sounded like a marching song.

Regression. No matter how stiffly I got out of bed or emerged from the sea, my mind leaped nimbly across time. After my dip I dragged my clothes on over my wet body, I was blue with cold and cursed out loud to make myself warm again. I had to get active, run around, let the wind blow under my damp clothes. I tied my shoelaces together, hung my shoes around my neck and headed northwards, towards the remains of the big bunker. Taking the piss out of Kraut holidaymakers, sending shards of concrete skittering over the waves, drowning my father in the swell – we'd see what else the shambles of the past would reveal to me.

My father was keener on other people's wars than his own. He read books about the German occupation of Holland, pored over eye-witness accounts of survivors of the Nazi concentration camps, could reel off the names of the D-day beaches as readily as the order of the stations on the railway, and in every German he saw a camp executioner. 'Look, there's another one,' he'd say when we were exercising on the quiet beach in the early morning, and he'd point to some paunchy holidaymaker digging his private sun-bathing hollow, or to a man with wooden crutches and an empty trouser-leg flapping in the breeze. One day he mixed some cement and covered up the German word *Kinderheim*, which was carved into the doorstep of our building. He asked the neighbours to refrain from taking German lodgers, no Krauts in the communal corridor please. And when I went round selling charity stamps he made sure I knew which doorbells not to ring – collaborators were on no account to be visited.

His hatred of Germans stemmed from shame and unacknowledged pain. There was no sympathy for what he and others like him had experienced in his war, so he adopted the indignation of the Dutch about theirs. He wanted to be a patriotic Dutchman like everyone else. The first ships with returnees from the colonies had been welcomed with streamers and speeches, but by the time he arrived they'd stopped lining up guards of honour on the quay-side. The Dutch were too absorbed in reconstructing the country to care about distant heroes, and they cared even less about the unrest that was growing in the old colony. They'd had enough, too many Dutch lads had been sacrificed already. Anyone who fought over there had lost, and the less said about that the better.

In his second year in Holland he took my three sisters to a funfair. We weren't very well off, and my father was still wearing his military jacket with orange lions on the lapels and a Royal Colonial Army badge. It was the first time my sisters had been to a Dutch fair, and they wore orange bows in their hair. Some teenage boys cried: 'Here come the blueskins,' but they just laughed, so proud were they of their hair ribbons proclaiming their allegiance to the House of Orange, and anyway they thought the blue referred to blue blood. But they stopped laughing when the boys jeered that my father was a *pelopor*-killer, for all four of them knew what that meant: a *pelopor* was a native rebel against Dutch colonial rule.

It pained my father that he lacked status, a job, a proud past, all he had was a bastard son and a wife with three dark-skinned daughters, hidden away in a former holiday home by the sea at the behest of the Government Repatriation Service.

My father had foolishly declined to be invalided out of the army. Soon after leaving the camp he resigned from the military of his own volition. He knew that the fatherland needed troops to suppress the nationalist rebellion, but he also knew that he wasn't fit for armed combat. As a token of gratitude for fourteen years of loyal service in the Royal Colonial Army, they docked his wages for the cost of army clothing lost in the war: 1 beret, 1 short overcoat, 2 shirts, 1 pair of trousers, 1 jacket, 1 pair of shoes, 2 pairs of socks, suspenders, pullover, kit-bag, 3 handkerchiefs.

It was the bloody limit, he said, and my mother got so irate that she foamed at the mouth. But my father didn't dwell on the subject because he couldn't help feeling twinges of guilt. He did keep the invoice, though, and sometimes, when we had visitors for supper, he'd read out the whole list for laughs: a bill for a sergeant-major possessing nothing but the rags he stood up in, a soldier who, after three and a half years in a prison camp, didn't have the strength to go out and kill *pelopors*. That was painful, too. The charmer who could twist anyone around his finger with his banter, the conversationalist who could drive a hard bargain, had paid with his health and got practically nothing in return – just a jacket for the voyage to Holland, a silver medallion, a few brass medals and a miserable pension.

That was the injustice, so if he couldn't share in the honour of overseas service, then at least he was entitled to share in the hatred of an adopted enemy.

The shame went deeper than that. I didn't realise this until much later, after reading about survivors of death camps and other major disasters. Why them and not me? That was their question. My father had the same trouble – he was embarrassed at having the good fortune to be alive.

Trudging along the beach on my way to the bunker with my shoes dangling on my chest and my hair white with powdery sand, I thought back to the performances I used to give after the Sunday *rijsttafel* – I might have guessed how he felt then. I'd make up skits, often not much more than jokes I'd heard or read. I had no shame doing my little acts, it was fun pretending to be someone else and it was a sure way of getting attention from adults. Some dabs of cold cream gave me clown-cheeks, talc in my curls turned me into an old woman, eyebrow pencil provided moustache and beard. Best of all was smearing my face with coffee grounds to make it brown, putting on my father's military jacket, taking the medals from the sewing basket – 'insignia must be worn with campaign medals at all times' it said on the accompanying charters – and I'd be a fighter in one of those yellowed snapshots: a brave soldier of the Royal Colonial Army.

I goose-stepped over the sleepers of an imaginary rail track, bored holes with a drilling jig and hammered bolts into the wood, for that was how the POWs laboured on the Japanese railway. My audience would sit on the chairs I had lined up: they were the train and I was laying down the rails. Then I took the jacket off, stuck my legs into the sleeves, tucked the flaps into my waistband and swaggered down the carriage like a crazy Jap commander. I sold everyone a ticket for 25 cents, sat myself down on the foremost, empty chair, whistled like a locomotive and eventually fell over, chair and all. Derailed, that was the joke, and no refunding of fares. My version of his war.

The first time my father found it entertaining, because that was the way he'd told the story himself during supper. What a lot of laughs they'd had, deep in the wilds of Sumatra. Labour on the railway continued in the rainy season, eighteen hundred metres daily, thousands of men swarming in the mud, and the first time it was put to use the engine slithered off the embankment – foundations were no good, that's how dumb the Japs were. Nincompoops. Ha ha. Time for a hearty nose-blow after all that hot spicy food, for a loud belch and pats on the stomach, all out of sheer amusement. But with each repeat performance my father grew less enthusiastic. He said my act was getting stale, everyone had seen it, including the neighbours. Besides, I'd spoil his jacket. 'A lot of soldiers did great deeds in uniform, you must never forget that.' He wasn't having it any more, uniforms ought to be treated with respect, I didn't even square my shoulders properly, the way I slouched was a disgrace to the military. And the medals? They were locked away after that, never to be worn again, not even on Remembrance Day. The charters accompanying the decorations vanished, too. He hadn't really deserved them, he said, because he'd survived while his friends – the true heroes, those great guys who were his mates – were all dead. Not long afterwards my mother cut up his military jacket to make a pair of shorts.

It was a gloomy October afternoon and I couldn't locate the bunker, not the foundations, nothing, not a trace. And yet I was sure I was in the right place, because I recognised the protective wood pilings; the coast was weak here and the sea occasionally breached the ramp. I doubled back to the dunes, keeping an eye open for gravel and chunks of concrete, and soon spotted our old home in the distance. Near here was the short-cut to the village, sheltered from the wind, which took you right across the gulls' breeding grounds where the birds swooped to peck at your hair in spring. The windows were lit under the dark, massive roof, like a beacon.

I crossed the front yard of the former holiday home, still

surrounded by a wilderness of sand, thistles and marram, and couldn't resist going round to the back to check whether the never-used letterbox was still there, the oval brass mouth in the back door that howled in the wind until my mother nailed a pocket flap from my father's military jacket over it. The letterbox had gone.

I heard voices in the kitchen and as I passed the window I saw a boy laying the table for supper. I don't know how long I stood there, watching.

Laying the table. Forks to the left, tines up, spoons upturned to the right – no, we don't need knives as we always have rice. We do use glasses, though, crystal ones from the Walden inheritance, for we must always have water to cool the hot spices. Glasses go on the right also, like the napkins, while the fruit knife goes crosswise at the top, all in the strictest formation. I can smell burnt rice, and I'm allowed to have a bit of the crust with sugar. My stomach rumbles. Supper-time.

Like a Kraut veteran seeking out his wartime bunker, so I sought out the old familiar aromas that evening in town. An Indonesian restaurant, in the imaginary company of my father. I longed for some hot spices to set me ablaze and sweating, to sear my palate and my gut. Sweet coconut juice to put out the fire. A cuisine of extremes. We ordered the biggest *rijsttafel* on the menu, a lavish spread of twenty-two dishes and an extra helping of 'mother's pepper sauce' as the waiter called it. The sand that had blown into my hair drizzled on to the tablecloth.

Just like the old days. I suggested we talk about the war, his favourite and yet most glossed-over dinner topic. Here, Dad, have a clove cigarette, a glass of beer – yes, I know you wouldn't have had beer then, but it's not a luxury any more, everyone drinks it. I've given up smoking and drinking, but let's be naughty for once. I've never had much self-discipline, anyway. When I was a kid I couldn't bottle up my pain or rage for more than sixty seconds . . . counting, you remember? You were always one for keeping count. Eight days on the wagon, how many seconds is that? You were always hard on yourself, although . . .

No, you shut up, I'm the one keeping count tonight. And I'm doing the talking for you, too.

Right, the war. Drama. Theatre.

Here are the props: the knife stands for Java, the fork for Sumatra – there, I've put them at a slight angle – and these little sand heaps are the Mentawai Islands. The *sajur* dish is the Indian Ocean. Where exactly was your ship torpedoed? In the *sajur*, off the west coast of Sumatra, or down south by the Sunda Straits? Ah well, we won't argue about longitudes. Let's recapitulate the whole exciting adventure.

In your eyes war was a grand gesture, not something to niggle about, war was a paean of comradeship and bravery. Suffering didn't come into it. Physical abuse, humiliation, oh no . . . everything the Japs did was a joke, even in prison you had fun, remember all those sing-songs? You didn't mention that dozens of people died every day. Hungry? Besides your meagre ration of starch, rice and *ketela* root, you managed to prepare delicacies such as fried bat, roasted rat, python and bread made with rubber-nut flour. *Aduh* – you were full to bursting! Remember how you stepped into a flooded fire-pit after a heavy downpour and were up to your chin in mud? Your mates fell about laughing. When it rained unrelentingly for days the latrines flooded and you had to wade through waist-high effluent. And then there was that bloke who fainted from the stench and nearly drowned among the turds.

War was crap, and that was a subject that could easily come up during supper. In the Indies everyone talked about poo, even after you came here you still scooped water over your arse with your left hand, no matter how soft the bog paper was – the oriental way was more hygienic, you claimed. Was that why you never used your left hand to hit me? You were good at it, the way you twisted the palm of your hand like a butterfly before my eyes. I can't even imitate the gesture. Your wrists were so flexible, and after the blow had been delivered you cracked your knuckles one by one, like peeling off a crackly leather glove.

You told one story after another, putting on funny accents, doing impersonations, and you laughed uproariously. I was too young to understand how bitter your jokes were. Not that I was allowed to ask questions. You were the sergeant at table, you were the boss.

Here with your plate, shall I give you a helping to start

off with? Here, some nice *lontong*, a bit of *rendang*, good hearty food for a dead man, and look, a piece of chicken, a leg maybe? Pity they've removed the claw, and you can't stick the head on your finger either. But even if you were to put that awful show on here – hiding a raw chicken's head in the folds of the tablecloth, whipping it out, cock-a-doodle-doo! and waving it under my nose – you wouldn't frighten me.

No, shut up you, don't talk with your mouth full, and wipe your mouth before putting it to your glass. Don't wave your fork around, it's not a flag. What? . . . Impertinent am I? That's not how you raised me? You wait till the end, you'll be amazed at my manners.

I'll tell you a story the way you always did. I'm sitting the way you used to sit, on the edge of the chair, legs wide, buttons undone, sticking out my chin and pulling your face, lighting up my eyes and trying to locate the timbre of your voice like tuning in to a station on an old wireless. An accent a fraction more pronounced than the Indonesian waiter's, that would be good, and careful articulation of every word, no slurring, right?

Gotcha, that's your tongue I'm using! Listen here, it's you talking through me, you choosing my words, your voice reverberating in the sound box of my memory.

'Did you know swimming can make you seasick? Yes, mate, when the waves are high. (Always 'mate', I was already your mate in my cradle.) Waves as tall as houses, not like those ripples they have here. We soared and sank with only a board to hold on to, our heads kept going under. The waves were wild horses determined to shake us off their backs.

'And the thirst! Water as far as the eye could see and then this terrible thirst, I wanted to drink but the water was red, clouds of red water all around us, and I saw shark fins circling and thrashing around the drowning men. Fountains of blood. And I looked again and saw the water fade from red to blue-green, to a glassy white. I drank and vomited at once. It was a mirage. *Ajò*, the water was unbearably salty.

'There were three of us clinging on to that single board, a Scot, a Hollander and me. It was less than a metre long, three hands across maybe, and not thicker than your fist . . . a whole night long . . . The rough wood tore at our skin, it was impossible to get a firm hold, the sea was warm enough but the night wind can be cold in the tropics. We got cramp in our arms, so we hung on by jamming the wood into our armpits and treading water like mad.

'We had to watch out that no one else joined us, one more hanger-on and we'd have drowned, every man jack of us. We had to fight against sleep, however exhausted we were, if you fell asleep that was it. I hadn't slept for three nights because the ship was so overcrowded and stuffy, no room to lie down, we were all stuck together, driven mad by the pounding ship's engines and the wails of the Javanese *romusjas*.

'When the wind dropped it was even harder to stay awake. We sang songs, swore, prayed out loud, and yet we kept nodding off, the only thing that helped was pinching each other, or slapping. A good hard slap, yes, that's what kept you awake. We couldn't see properly, the sun glinting off the water all day long blinded us, and the salt stung in our eyes.

'The second night we were still hoping to be rescued, scanning the horizon and trying to attract the attention of the escort vessels. They fished all the Japs out of the water, rafts and dinghies full of Japs, they saw us all right but couldn't be bothered to turn back, so they ignored us and carried on, no matter how much we shouted and waved.

'The third day, or the second, I don't recall which, there was a storm. No puffs of smoke, no ships on the horizon. We grabbed hold of a beam that was floating past, which we wanted to tie to our plank to increase the buoyancy, but our fingers were too stiff to handle the straps we salvaged from abandoned kit-bags. It started to rain, the water was sweet and we opened our mouths wide to catch the drops. I licked my face like a cat. The wind made us numb, the rain was ice-cold, and yet only a few hours before we'd been parched in the scorching sun. Scottie was threatening to lose his grip, we hauled him up, and I bit hard in his ear and shouted to wake him up, and so we drifted, until a gunboat headed towards us.

'I remember a pole with an iron hook being clawed into our plank, then a hand, a Jap's hand and an evil grin. I was swung up on deck, got caught on a nail or a sharp corner. Something tore in my back, I can remember that. I felt a warm trickle down my haunches. Then they kicked me, and I gave up. I was finished, my last ounce of strength drained away, my legs slid back into the water and I just let it happen. Until someone hauled me up by the shoulders. I looked up and saw a white apparition, sparkling in the sunlight. This must be an angel, I thought, I must be dead.

'D'you know what it was? A British officer in white dress uniform with shiny brass buttons and blancoed shoes. You know what he said? "Worse things happen at sea." Like, it's not the end of the world. As if he were Neptune himself, stiff upper lip and all that. And he was the one who saved me. He had a little suitcase, which he kept by his side at all times no matter how people complained that his *barang* took up too much space. He didn't let it out of his sight, for the case contained his pride. Camp in, camp out, from Flores and Ambon to Java, for two whole years he'd rather have starved than give it up. Other prisoners had tried to steal it because they thought he had a stash of money or jewels, but all he had was a white jacket, white trousers and white shoes. His spare uniform. He had been saving it to present himself correctly attired on the day the liberators came, but when he found himself half-naked in the midst of all those Japs he decided to put it on for us, for the chaps who'd pulled through.

'And that man became my friend, my guardian angel who lent me his legs. He carried me down the gangway because I couldn't walk, then slung me over his back and dragged me up to the prison. Then the Japs picked him out of the line, that was the last I ever saw of him, a white streak in the dusk.'

That was the story, wasn't it, Dad? That's the way you told it, sitting at our long dinner table. Of course you peppered it with more Malay words — sorry about that, but I seem to have forgotten most of them. You at the head, half hidden behind steaming dishes, ladling out the food. Visitors always got the best bits. Now that you're dead it doesn't scare me to look in your eyes, they're not as dark and forbidding as they used to be, they've faded over time, bleached by the sun just like your framed portrait. Our sun is stronger than you thought.

Let me give you another helping, let me dye the rice red with hot pepper sauce, like blood, and I'll wallow in my spice-induced sniffles.

You used to alter your stories a lot, sometimes it wasn't a plank you clung on to but a raft lashed together with straps from kit-bags; sometimes you went under for ages, at other times the weather changed. A full moon and a mysteriously calm ocean, so that the wailing of the Javanese *romusjas* carried far across the water. But your stories were always exciting, and you wanted us to laugh, too, although mostly we shuddered with horror.

That Javanese boy, remember? It's just come back to me. He was hoisted up hanging from one leg, the other had been bitten off by a shark. A medic wanted to tie a rope round the stump to stop the bleeding, but the Japs wouldn't let him — a man lying down took up as much space as three people standing, so he was dumped overboard. Not that you allowed our appetite to be spoiled. If there was any sniffling or nervous fidgeting with napkins, you'd turn into that funny boilerman from Rotterdam who leaped into the sea right in front of the Japs' noses. 'I'd rather swim,' he shouted, but he didn't get very far, did he? The Japs fished him out of the water, beat him up and threw him into the hold. Did that poor boilerman ever make it to Rotterdam?

You weren't up to pulling my sledge in winter, nor could you make it to the top of a dune to let up a kite, but at the dinner table you were the toughest father in the village.

Let's have another beer. Go on, man, drink, forget all that anthroposophic drivel about clean living, even vegetables ferment into alcohol in your gut – did you know that? And there's no doctor here to say you can't have any. Tonight as I write you're in good health, my pen and I are in command here.

Yes, I'm a writer now. You used your ruler to drum the alphabet into my head, and it stuck – did I ever thank you for that? I still make spelling mistakes, but my sentences are fluent. You wanted me to be able to read and write by the age of four, and you succeeded. I had to pronounce long words without faltering – a matter of rhythm, that was all. You made me read aloud with you beating time: a tap of your ruler every other line. *Robin the Giant*, that was my first book, and we read it to the end. To mark the occasion you took me to the cinema, where they were showing *Gulliver's Travels*, another giant. You treated me to fizzy lemonade and a coconut macaroon with wafer-paper stuck on the bottom, which prompted you to ridicule the Catholics' communion wafers. You wanted me to skip the first year of primary school. But I'm still a fan of Gulliver's for being a giant who got people to dance in the palm of his hand. Which is what I'm doing, too – just shut your eyes . . . here's a pair of shoes (black, a gentleman never wears brown, you used to say, and I respect your taste), you shall have a new suit, too – give the clothes in your cabin trunk a good airing – and I'll set you down in the European quarter of Palembang, in the street where my future mother lives. You're holding a flower, go on, give it to her, don't break the stem, gently does it. Ask her to dance. See what a giant I am, I can make you dance, right there in the street, like common folk, who you didn't approve of, did you? No jacket, sweaty shirt stuck to your back, and don't pump your arm like that – slide and sway, mate, sway to the rhythm of my story . . .

What? Too tired? Can't keep up? Your heart giving you trouble already? I'll let you rest when I'm good and ready, but first I'll have you dancing. I'd have you dying, too, but I've done that already. So for the time being you're in the prime of life.

I went in search of your past, Dad, and a lot of it turned out different than I thought. I asked round in the family, but their stories are contradictory. My mother is keen to forget, and she's in luck, because her memory has faded just like your photograph. I had to venture further afield.

About ten years ago I wrote a story about my boyhood by the sea. I'd never heard of Pakan Baru then, and had no idea where and when your ship was torpedoed. All I knew was that you had a raft, or rather a plank, and I can't recall how many days I said you were adrift in the sea — one, two, or was it three? I don't mind telling a fib or two on your behalf.

I received a letter from a reader who recognised the story of the torpedo attack. He wrote: 'The ship your father was on was the SS *Junyo Maru*, and was heading from Tandjung Priok, the harbour of Batavia, towards Sumatra. Monday, eighteenth of September 1944, it was struck by a torpedo. Of the 2,300 POWs embarked in Priok, 680 were present at the final roll-call, of the 4,200 press-ganged *romusjas* 200 survived. In all 5,620 people died, 880 were rescued, but a further 30 died of exhaustion the week after. The Pakan Baru Death Railway, where the survivors ended up with thousands of POWs, also took its toll: mortality among military prisoners was 36.9 per cent, among *romusjas* it was 83.3 per cent.'

What a stickler for detail, he had you dying and surviving down to the decimal point, with due account of racial differences, too. And to think that I had devoted less than a paragraph to your being torpedoed. You never mentioned the name of the vessel, nor that there were so many casualties. Mother said she couldn't remember, but the name *Junyo Maru* did ring a bell.

A year passed before I wrote back to say I'd like to meet this man. I never did, though. Laziness, fear of the truth? No idea. I have never been to Indonesia, either, although there were plenty of opportunities. The family lies did me fine, I thought. After Ada died I continued delving. I read books about Pakan Baru, came across your name on lists of *Junyo Maru* survivors, and wrote to witnesses; there were a few who remembered you, and I paid each of them a visit. Little old gents they were, stiff-jointed and dignified, and they were prepared to dive into the Indian Ocean over afternoon tea for my benefit. But it was all too long ago, they got names and dates mixed up and kept returning to their own tall stories. (As I sat there in their living-rooms watching them scan their memories with their eyes closed, it would be you sitting there, as an old man. And I'd felt ashamed at having shirked military service, and that I hadn't turned into your kind of man. How did you do it?) Their hands were old and sinewy, with sunspots from long years in the tropics. I didn't dare ask if they used to hit their children. They all struck me as gentle fathers.

In the end I tracked down someone in Limburg who claimed to have had the bunk next to yours in the infantry in Batavia. His memory was pretty moth-eaten, and he didn't have much to tell me except that he found you 'a decent sort'. He said he'd been struck down by malaria after being approved for transport. 'I could barely walk, was in very bad shape. Your father drew a portrait of a Japanese sentry in exchange for some quinine. He made the Japs look braver than they were, he was very good at that, his drawings were snapped up by the guards. He was able to use his talent to get things done, I think.' That was good of you. When he saw me out he said I resembled you: 'Only your father was much shorter, as I recall.' A meagre harvest, hardly worth driving halfway across the country for.

But in the end I was able, little by little, to piece together the story of how you got to Sumatra.

Fall in! You're standing in line on the parade ground of the former Tenth Infantry Battalion in Batavia.

Hundreds of half-starved POWs from different camps are waiting to be selected for transport to an unknown destination. Roll-call. Counting, recounting, for hours on end . . . *ichi, ni, san, shi, go*. Bedlam, without an abacus it's hopeless. The noise is deafening. Civilians and soldiers all milling together, Hollanders, British, Americans, the occasional Australian, as well as a group of native soldiers from the Royal Colonial Army who, despite promises from the Japanese, now see their loyalty to the Dutch rewarded with imprisonment.

You've already spent two and a half years in a camp. Somewhere in Java, most likely, since you attended the military academy there and probably hung around afterwards; I've been unable to establish the exact facts. Odd that you should still have been in Java, though, since most of the young men had already been rounded up. How old were you, anyway? Twenty-nine? Perhaps they overlooked you.

It's before sunrise, and you're marching down the unlit streets of Batavia, a wordless procession trudging in the direction of the station. The clatter of hundreds of wooden sandals reverberates against the houses (you've long since lost your army boots), the straps made from tyres cut into your instep. You inhale the aromas of the bazaar, oil lamps flicker in the stalls, the market folk watch in silence.

What was it like to have to march like that in your home town? Your Papa ran a funeral service–cum–stables there, didn't he? Motor cars and carriages aplenty, so you didn't wear out your shoes when you were a boy. And if there weren't any dead to bury your father switched the curtains on his vehicles and drove wedding parties. Your father's business ought to be booming, what with more people dying than ever, but it's no longer up to him. You have to bow to the Japanese – humiliating, you say? And yet, to them it's a normal greeting. Think how often you made a native sink to his haunches before you when you were a kid.

You know all the streets from your privileged boyhood, when you rode your father's horses with the stable boys running alongside. On Sunday four horses would be harnessed to the carriage – giddy-up, past the kampongs, how high and mighty you felt, giddy-up, to the plantations in the hills, sun, vistas and the scent of a hundred flowers in your nostrils.

No point in dwelling on sentimental memories – it's Shanks's pony from now on. You've been vetted for transport. A few days ago you were filing past the Jap inspectors holding a turd in the palm of your hand. Dysentery parade: faeces on a slip of cellophane to demonstrate your fitness for the job. You cheated, everyone did. Mushy dog turds or ground peanut could work wonders. The men with dysentery sold their faeces, because crap with blood in it could get you off, and if you couldn't get hold of any you went to a mate with the sniffles and borrowed a gob of phlegm, to which you added a little blood. But when it was your turn the damn slit-eye looked the other way, and so you came a cropper. Into the truck with you.

The locomotive is facing north, a sure sign of transport overseas, say the prisoners who have come from the other islands. They tell stories of bombardments and torpedoed ships, but hardly anyone believes them. You have all been issued with mosquito nets, which you take to mean you're being taken somewhere hot. At the end of a journey in a shuttered goods train you catch the scent of the sea despite the vomit and shit of the men with dysentery. They march you off to the sheltered harbour, where you're kept waiting, waiting.

There come the *romusjas*, the emaciated, ragged coolies, some covered in suppurating sores. They've sold themselves for five guilders, most of them having been singled out by the headman of their kampongs for the labour camps. Old men, children, makes no difference, there's even a seven-year-old lad among them.

(These details were not supplied by your old colonial mates, I garnered them from archives and history books. But one of them said: 'Over the years you find you've blotted out a lot of things, you have more pressing problems, and pity doesn't get you anywhere.' Did you see those Javanese kids? Or didn't you bother to look?)

It is light, but you have no idea where you are. To you the dockyards are coolie territory. The *Junyo Maru*, rusty and dilapidated, is rocking alongside the quay. In a moment the Japanese and Korean guards will start beating the lot of you into the holds. The ship casts off and rides at anchor for hours in the blazing sun, anyone left on deck suffers burns from the scorching sheet iron. Open sea at last. Sun and rain by turns, a chill wind at night and suffocating heat during the day. The ship is overcrowded, not every prisoner can find a pallet to sleep on. A scaffold collapses, leaving dozens injured. The latrines are overflowing and hard to reach, so the weaker men urinate in the holds. The dysentery patients hang on to ropes to lean overboard, often too late, so the deck is ankle-deep in brown slurry.

Is that where you get your poo-jokes from? Or did you hide behind the sacks of cement, all grey like an old man? Or in the coal hold, in mourning with your friends, or did you find some nook on the upper deck?

The food isn't bad: soup, rice, vegetables and salt pork, better than anything you've had in the camp for months. But the queues by the kitchen are long, the holds are cramped and scuffles break out over water and rice.

Although there's enough to go round, those too weak to stand are ignored; the sick start dying and their bodies are dumped overboard. You can tell how many have gone by the number of wristwatches worn by the Korean guards. One of them has nine.

The *Junyo Maru* zigzags in a north-westerly direction, the coast of Sumatra looms into view and with any luck you'll see the Bukit Mountains. At 18.10 hours Tokyo time the first torpedo strikes the bow, sending men and timbers flying through the air. A few seconds later the stern is hit. As the vessel doesn't list no one on deck realises how fast she's sinking. Sure, take your time! Go on arguing about whether it was a British, Dutch or American submarine that hit you, go on blaming each other. If only the Japs had stuck to the Geneva Convention: ships carrying POWs are supposed to sail under the flag of the Red Cross.

Panic breaks out in the holds, the men kick each other down the ladders, the wounded and the sick are trampled underfoot. The stern starts sinking and panic spreads to the upper deck. You fight your way to the railing. There aren't any lifejackets. The Japs claim the lifeboats, flailing their sabres to stop the *romusjas* and POWs from climbing on board. One group of prisoners manage to occupy a lifeboat, but the ropes are paid out too quickly and the boat shatters on impact with the waves. Pallets and rafts are thrown overboard, people jump into the water from all sides, some of them hit their heads on the flotsam and go right under. The bodies of the drowned are swept together by the current: a feast for sharks.

A final explosion and the *Junyo Maru* sinks under the surface amid columns of bubbles. The sea turns red. Not from blood, though, as you were perfectly aware: it was red-lead oxide leaking from a burst vat in the cargo hold.

So you're adrift for days on end, it doesn't matter exactly how many, and at last you're spotted by a convoy vessel and hauled on deck. It must have been then that you caught your back on a piece of iron, hence the odd-looking scars between your shoulder blades – a vertical slash on the left, another on the right. They used to swell up in cold water, as if you were sprouting little pink wings. Touched by an angel of the ocean. Worse things happen at sea . . .

After several hellish days you end up in the prison of Padang like all the other survivors. No bunks, no bedding, just dry rice and a soggy leaf, unboiled water, crap all over the place and maggot-infested open sewers. You huddle together for warmth, but the men who were beaten off the boats and rafts lie cold and lifeless in your midst next morning. No time to recuperate, for in a day or two the first group is dispatched by train. Chugging up mountain-sides with the cold creeping into the shuttered carriages, careening down into valleys leading to goodness knows where. At the end of the railway there are open army trucks to convey you across dense forest, past waterfalls and ravines. Just after the highest peak you cross the Equator. Did you see the monument, the stone globe with the thick red line round the middle?

The trucks wind their way down to the low-lying

plains, the heat from the marshes inflames the wounds on your back. Your first camp: the bridge camp. I lose sight of you here. Ahead of you stretch 220 kilometres of mud, ravines and jungle. Rails and sleepers are piled high in readiness. There is work to be done.

Only now do I realise that you had lost everything. You couldn't barter because you had nothing left to barter with, nor could you curry favour with your drawings because your pencil was floating around in the ocean. No mess kit, either – the *Junyo Maru* survivors had to receive their rations in their cupped hands. No mosquito net, no clothes, no shoes, just a rag for a loincloth. It was a while before you could bring yourself to wear dead men's shirts and trousers.

I'm not saying it was because you were so bereft in the camp that you set such store by material possessions in later life. Things like cutlery became an obsession to you, you have to admit. The way we had to hold it, as though dining with royalty, just the thought of it brings cramp to my fingers. You used to say the way people held their knives and forks revealed their class – you who'd stuffed food into your mouth with a piece of wood. Once your loincloth days were over how fussy you were about your clothes, forever pressing trousers and brushing up jackets.

And where did your mania for numbers come from? The Japs? In the morning on the way to the latrine you held your own roll-call of the dead, counting the bare feet sticking out of the mortuary shed: ten, twelve, thirteen pairs . . . How many dead, how many hammer blows reverberated in your skull after eleven months on the railway? Was that what you were adding and subtracting when you lay on the day-bed recovering from one of your fits of rage?

Thirty times thirteen is three hundred and ninety, times eleven is four thousand two hundred and ninety. Four thousand two hundred and ninety plus five thousand six hundred and twenty is . . . you'd lie there for hours doing mental arithmetic out loud. Those were the stocking-feet hours. Shush, no parking of bikes in the hall, no rattling in the kitchen, no flushing the loo. Do stop playing the recorder, Ada. Shush . . . Saskia, your crayons. Mother takes the foot scraper inside. A cloth muffles the doorbell, curtains are drawn. *Ajò*, no giggling in the bedrooms, no sighing while you read. Quiet, quiet, on tiptoe. Hush, Daddy's counting.

Come along, Dad, my plate's empty. I'll ask for the bill and we won't bother to check it.

Shortly after my wintry dip in the sea one of the *Junyo Maru* survivors I had got in touch with sent me a copy of a report that shed new light on my father's obsession with figures. It was the statement of one Mr de J., formerly employed by a drilling company in the East Indies. After the war this Mr de J. had tried to bring charges against a fellow prisoner by the name of Mr X, 'a traitor who was responsible for the death of at least one of my comrades'. The report had seemingly been copied umpteen times, as the typescript was so faint as to be barely legible, but the margins were cluttered with notes in different hands. It took me a while but in the end I figured out that Mr X had served as interpreter at various camps along the railway. He'd spent some time in Japan in the thirties as a shipping agent, and claimed to be fluent in the language. In reality his knowledge didn't extend further than a small range of civilities, but when he got the chance he used them to ingratiate himself with the Japanese. Mr X had already caused trouble several times with his unsolicited services, and was shunned by his fellow-prisoners for that reason.

Mr de J.'s report didn't specify the phoney interpreter's guilt or eventual punishment. Not that it mattered, really. Everyone was out to save his own skin. What interested me was just the one sentence that concerned my father.

Mr de J. described how, after a day's work, he had gone into the paddy fields with a gang of six men, supposedly to track down a stack of sleepers that had washed away during a flood, but in reality to catch a buffalo that had broken its tether. Heedless of the risk they were taking, they grabbed the animal by the horns and led it back to the camp. All this took place under the watchful eye of the Korean guard and a Japanese soldier, who, in exchange for half the booty, would look the other way. Unfortunately the men didn't succeed in effecting the slaughter in silence: not only did they not keep their voices down, none of them had a proper knife with which to hack the beast to pieces. The lot of them were caught with blood on their hands. The interpreter, fearing repercussions, had reported them to the commanding officer: 'better for six to be punished than the whole company' was his motive.

The men had been tortured for two days. Their names were given in a footnote. My father had been among them. One man succumbed the following night, and four of them, including Mr de J., were locked up in solitary for a week. My father apparently made such an impression on the Japanese that he was the only one to be granted time in the sick bay to recover. During those two days of torture he had behaved 'like a fakir', and, so the report went on, 'thanks to a form of self-hypnosis he felt no pain'. Just that one brief sentence made me eager to talk to Mr de J.

Pension funds work miracles. Mr de J. was still alive and residing in respectable Wassenaar. We agreed to meet on neutral ground, a teashop on a square carpeted in brown leaves. De J. had been far too busy all his life to dwell on the past, all that travelling and drilling for oil – Brunei, South America, Nigeria, all over the world – damned interesting, but now he was old he, 'a chap from the Indies', had opted for the fatherland. And here, with everyone going on about the war, those damned memories kept coming back. 'What d'you want to know?' he said gruffly. No, not the story of his life, thank you, nor was I keen to hear about the camp all over again. It was my father I was interested in – what did he think of him?

'A man able to put himself in someone else's shoes, I'd

say. A mind traveller. He could endure pain as though it were happening to someone else. When they pulled out one of his fingernails – a live nail – he never flinched. Justin could hold a bucket filled with water over his head, elbows straight, not just for five minutes like the rest of us, but for a quarter of an hour, all of fifteen minutes, without spilling a drop.'

Mr de J. took his time, making sure I noted everything down correctly. 'Write that down – a quarter of an hour . . . that was quite extraordinary, and I remember it well because your father counted every second and every minute. That was his secret method.' And as I wrote he slurped his coffee and gazed dreamily at a dog pawing the leaves outside.

'If you let the bucket sag you were whipped, we all were, your father included, but he could take it. The Japs didn't know what to make of him. Strong chap, your father. Bad heart? I'm surprised . . . He was a great mimic, too, imitated the sound of a toad, for instance, or a roaring tiger, so convincingly you thought they were right next to you. He scared the daylights out of the guards. Justin acted as if he didn't feel pain – that's what it was. He concentrated so hard that he stepped out of his own body. But if it suited him he could be a terrible wimp – talked himself into the sick bay with all sorts of ailments. That's what saved him in the end.

'The Japs amused themselves with us for two days, dragging us into those cages every six hours, one by one, so I didn't actually see your father. But I didn't hear him, either. The rest of us groaned until we were half-dead. Soon afterwards our group was split up for good. I was sent to the coal mines for punishment.

'After the liberation I ran into your father again in the convalescent camp, and I asked him how on earth he did it. By doing complicated sums, he said, a trick he'd picked up from some fakir. Remarkable chap, very remarkable,' Mr de J. said, his eyes shifting to the dog playing on the square.

My father taught me arithmetic, too, no blows, no pain. I just picked it up as I went along.

I didn't know what to think of my father's fellow-prisoners. Mr de J. looked so blank that I didn't dare ask how he had coped with his own pain. Had he bundled it up to take it with him on his travels, had he poured it all out into one of the shafts he had drilled? His voice sounded dry: 'Never shed a tear since, except that one time . . . well, that's another story.' I left it at that. And the others?

They had suffered, that was obvious, and were proud of it, too. Three and a half years of prison camp, three and a half years of bullying. They had seen the arse of the world, yet they radiated a sense of victory. Those triumphant looks when they recalled the tricks they played on the Japs, mischievous lads, that's what they'd been. They had no time for weakness, but I confronted them with it anyway.

I said: 'He used to hit me.'

'You still bothered by that?' one of them asked.

'Yes, I am.'

'No harm in a box on the ears.'

'The war was troubling him,' I said carefully.

'Surely not. Rubbish.'

They reacted uneasily, I reminded them too much of the nastier sides of survival. Hadn't they all, on occasion, taken the rations of a man who lay dying or filched clothing from the morgue? That's war for you, they had no choice.

So the camp had got the better of my father in the end? Indeed it had, and a glazed look came into their eyes. Well, it hadn't affected them that way. There was nothing wrong with them, but when I looked into their eyes I could see that the dead man's shirts and dying men's rations hadn't done them any good. No point in looking back, the past was locked away and what's done is done.

My own response was much the same: how was I to imagine my father under torture? I saw contorted features, but no pain. A father without feeling. Could insight dispel hatred? I wasn't ready to let the new facts settle in my mind.

After meeting the old colonials I'd had enough of war and bravery, I longed to hear gentler voices recalling the lush mornings of Java when my father was young, the stamp of hooves and the creaking carriage in Batavia with wedding curtains over the windows. I decided to pay my father's half-sister Edmee a visit. There was the distasteful prospect of shaking hands with a professed member of the Aryan race, but it would be worth it if it brought me closer to my father.

My new aunt came forward unsteadily and flung her arms around my neck, almost stifling me with her face powder and rouged cheeks. In spite of her wrinkles she didn't look that old. What a tart, though. She was wearing something pink and fluttery, batting her owlish black lashes at me.

I had written to tell her when to expect me – tea time – very proper, a bunch of flowers at the ready, but I didn't even have time to ring the doorbell, for she was lying in wait for me. 'At last!' she exclaimed. 'How nice and tall you are, let me give you a big hug – wonderful to have some family around at last!' Crushing the flowers, she bustled me into her living room. She'd lit several candles and put out glasses and a dish of nibbles, although she insisted that she'd forgotten all about our appointment. She gave off a faint smell of paraffin – sherry, no doubt, judging by the labels on the empty bottles lined up by the magazine rack. Her rouge didn't conceal her liking for drink, and when she let go of me to fill the glasses I noticed that the entire room was pink: lamp shades, cushions, antimacassars all in shrieking, fairground pink. Over the door hung a repulsive Christ on the cross.

Hardly had I raised a toast to this new family bond when she made me stand next to a photo of my father, a touched-up portrait she had placed on the television for the occasion, on top of a lace doily and flanked by a burning candle. How strong the resemblance was! Justin was only nineteen in that picture, the darling. Edmee took both my hands in hers and drew me back a pace so that we might admire the portrait together, side by side. When I extricated myself from her grasp she made a quick sign of the cross and tried to throw her arms around me again. Going through the motions, and I wasn't fooled. Dropping me like a hot brick, and now refusing to let me go. The irritation I had felt at the first hug turned into nausea, like burying my face in candy-floss. Everything about her was fake, eyelashes, jewellery, the string of pearls resting on her ample bosom, and I dare say her long, unevenly varnished nails were, too. She was unable to talk without clinging on to me all the time. She probably hadn't seen a soul in weeks. How she whined! She couldn't make ends meet, her husband the British officer had traded her in for a bimbo. Some thanks! She'd followed him dutifully throughout his career, living in Aden, in Cyprus – 'he did the killing, I did the cooking.' Eventually they'd emigrated to Rhodesia, where, after thirty-four years, he'd dumped her, just like that. Their only son, Ken, her darling boy, had been killed in the Rhodesian war. Her alimony was next to nothing, what with the devaluation of the pound, her solicitor had cheated her and her ex wasn't replying to her letters. Couldn't I do something? She couldn't expect much help from the rest of the family, her last surviving half-sister had died a year ago. Who? Aunt Pop, Aunt Régine? Both of them gone, yes, *kassian*, her brother too, Pop had been the last, it was her heart (weak genes – I was seized with anxiety there and then). There were still a brother and sister living in Australia, but they weren't great letter-writers, and the nephews and nieces I'd never heard of were scattered across the globe. And then there was me, turned into a writer she'd been told, and surely family was what counted in times of need. My father was her darling brother: 'I miss Justin desperately.'

No kidding, I thought, so how come you were never around when he was alive? Tell me about my father, and about his first wife and the twins, Roeliana and Roediono. But she hadn't reached the end of her litany of miseries yet, and as she pressed on I felt as if I were leafing through back issues of a woman's magazine. Dizzy spells, hyper-ventilation, agoraphobia, lumps in her breasts, and she'd just been reading about some new disease which affected the sense of balance, now she had that too, truly, she was spared nothing. She'd had to give up her car, just look how ancient her fridge was, and those dreadful stains in the carpet . . .

As she rattled on, her pancake make-up started flaking. Excuses for making a getaway flashed across my mind, but I got bogged down, lamely offering advice and motioning to Jesus, a hanger-on if ever there was one. And I took another look at her: was there any resemblance to my father or not? Same black eyes, same long nose, flattened no doubt by too much pressing against windows, and, it could not be denied, a touch of the tar-brush.

Well, that's how these things go. You give in, you have

a second glass of sherry to rinse away the cheap chemical taste of the first, you finish the bottle together, you take her out to dinner and you know that she'll choose the most expensive thing on the menu. Feeling heady with booze she reapplies her make-up, girds up her old bosom and leaves her wine glass thickly smeared with lipstick. You give her an encouraging look and ask about the Indies. She's not listening, she dodges all your questions, she slips, lands on a little story, you help her up and mention an island, Java, then a city, Batavia, with its leafy residential quarter, and with some effort you find a path to follow her in her ramblings.

So at long last you're sitting on the veranda together. The hornbill screeches, the *chee-chak* plants its little sucker feet on the wire mesh and two native boys sell you a parakeet for one *gobang* (a two-and-a-half cent coin, you still had them then) – and the pet gecko changes colour, the whole sky is tinged deep pink by the encroaching night, the houseboy is going about his business. You can hear the cicadas in the rattle of her pearls.

'Our garden at sunset . . . all those different shades of green melting into a single blur of reddish black, and all the plants fusing together in one single fragrance – gardenia, jasmine, the pale yellow frangipani, and lemon grass, which was a smell that went right to your head. I can just see us sitting out on the veranda on Saturday evening, in the rattan chairs, a jug of lemonade to hand, my hair still wet from my bath. Justin in his new tropical whites, his chin resting on the starched collar. He's on leave, brimming with stories about the army. I'm at his feet, listening with my eyes shut so as to picture his adventures more clearly, even my half-sisters have stopped bickering. The servants hover behind the screen, and our mother is filing her nails. She does so excruciatingly slowly, as if in deliberate contrast to Justin's enthusiasm, as if she's playing the violin and wants to add her own counterpoint to the darkness outside.

'We had a beautiful mother, a mother you could admire from a distance. A mother who didn't need words, one stern look and you'd button up. The pupils of her eyes were sparkly pools and her lashes long and thick. She was bored during the day, the heat made her lazy and tired, but towards sundown her spirits rose. On Saturday nights she went out, her dresses were laid out for her and she'd let me help her choose which one to wear.'

Edmee bit on her pearls and tapped them against her teeth – false, like the rest of her, to judge by the dull sound. 'Oh dear, here we go again,' she groaned. How could she get carried away like this? It was all such a long time ago and the Indies were finished. Gone to the dogs since Sukarno. Ever been back? Good heavens, no, no point in raking over past loves. She for her part preferred the beauties of the African night. 'Those tom-toms sending messages across the fields, the dry heat and the fragrance of burning wood. You know what I mean . . .'

'Let's talk about Justin, then.'

'In spite of her indolence my mother was temperamental,

deceitful even, how else can I put it, she delighted in secret rendezvous, scheming, going out on the sly. Her evening was ruined if she hadn't garnered a sheaf of business cards from admirers. She'd always been like that, even as a girl, men noticed her. At parties there was always whispering behind her back. The Rose of Surabaya, there goes the Rose of Surabaya — that's where her family was from. Nobles, they were, fled from the French Revolution. You haven't asked, but I'll tell you anyway: it's not easy to live up to such a name. She was a star and dazzled everyone, wanted to be sphinx, a temptress in the eyes of each and every man. She pretended she wasn't a mother, and according to my half-sisters no one ever saw her pregnant, either. She liked billowing frocks anyway, and disappeared to give birth in out-of-the-way places. None of us children were allowed to call her Mummy or Mother in front of strangers, we always had to say Odile, or Madame. Sometimes she went out for several days in a row, she'd come home of course, but we didn't get to see her as she thought it would make us sad to have to keep saying goodbye.'

Edmee had some more wine and sighed deeply, then pulled a face, whether it was the wine or the memory was unclear.

'She was always busy with her wardrobe, not a day went by without her talking to her dressmaker. I've still got an evening bag of hers, with little black beads . . .'

'My father was quite a bit older than you . . .'

'Husbands, sons, it made no difference, she'd dance

with anything in trousers. She spoiled the servants, got the dressmaker to make them the smartest uniforms, they looked like dandies. Being the youngest, I'd be left with the *babu* whenever there was a party. There was something going on every Saturday night, she loved the social whirl, and we didn't celebrate birthdays because she hated calendars. Her age was a taboo subject, no one knew exactly how old she was. Oh, she was so colonial, she made a great fuss about wanting to send the laundry to be done in Paris, the way the rich planters did. Daddy got badly into debt because of her. And d'you know, having been raised by servants most of the time I had an awful lot of bad habits to get rid of. I was better at eating with my fingers than with a spoon, I preferred a banana leaf to a plate, and those dreadful diseases, tape-worms, lice and . . .'

'Did your mother make my father dance with her, too?

Edmee smiled at the concern in my voice.

'It was particularly hard for his sisters,' she said. 'You know how pretty they were, Odile was terribly jealous. She either kept her daughters out of sight and denied point blank she had any children, or she made them parade around in her own clothes. She tied their hair into chignons, gave them make-up and jewellery to wear so they'd look as grown up as possible. She'd pretend the girls were her friends when she went out for a drive.'

'In the hearse.'

'Oh no, it was later, the carriage business had been sold by then and the family were all together. What I've been telling you happened after the drama.'

She tapped against the empty wine bottle with her ring, and I ordered another one.

'You know about that, do you?'

'My mother told me.'

'What could she know about it?'

'My father told her, I expect.'

'It was too awful.'

'You weren't born yet, were you?'

'But it affected my entire life.'

The waiter made to pour the wine, but when he noticed the lipstick smears on her glass he fetched her a clean one.

'Nice of you to bring me here. Best treat I've had in years.'

'Was it her fault?' I asked.

'Fault, fault, Odile's first husband was an absolute fool, I'm sorry but you did ask so I'll tell you: it was his own fault, that man refused to see what was going on before his very eyes.'

'All I know is that none of the children were actually his.'

'They all looked like her, all six of them, so there was nothing untoward there. As far as that's concerned it need never have happened. No one knows whether she was telling the truth. Odile was a great one for smokescreens, even on her deathbed she kept mum. Not even Daddy found out who her mysterious lover was. And if he did have a name he took it with him to the grave. Daddy was much older than Odile, he was content to show her off.'

'You look like my father.'

'What are you hinting at?'

'Oh, nothing, just that you both look like your mother.'

'Thank you. Yes, I adored Justin, he was the eldest and the only one I really got on with at home. He was twelve years older, but he always confided in me, he didn't care about the age difference.'

'No, he didn't, he —'

'Look here, I got it from the horse's mouth, your father was the chief witness. One Sunday after mass all the children were summoned. Odile was out, and their father, your supposed grandfather, was waiting for them in the hall. He was in his riding habit, tapping his crop impatiently against his boot. They stood in a neat line, paying attention. That's when those poor children heard that their mother had been having an affair with a secret lover. It had gone on for years. He could barely believe it himself, for he was deaf to rumour and innuendo, but there had been a terrible scene in the night during which she had confessed everything. So he wasn't their real father at all. He was very sorry, and told them to pray for their mother. The children didn't understand, only Justin suspected something was seriously wrong. Their father started up the stairs, a broken man. Halfway up he pulled a pistol from his boot and shot himself in the head. He keeled over and fell down the stairs, landing on the wooden floor at Justin's feet. Wham.' Edmee slapped her hand on the table and gave me a doleful look.

'I don't think that was the way he told it to my mother.'

'When the gun went off the horses started whinnying in the stables. Your father never forgot that. Justin was a sensitive lad.'

'Not in my book, he wasn't.'

'My dear nephew, don't be cheeky. Our darling mother packed her children off to the orphanage even before the funeral, she had a nervous breakdown and couldn't cope. You should have heard what your Aunt Pop had to say about that: all their fine clothes were taken away, their hair was shorn because of the lice, and the food was stolen from their plates while they said grace. They weren't used to discipline, so it was that much harder on them.

'For two whole years Madame left her children there. Oh, she did visit them now and then, acting the destitute widow and pinning fresh mourning bands on their orphans' uniforms. She didn't really care for her children, but she cared all the more about them showing their grief, on their sleeves if not in their hearts. Odile squandered the inheritance in no time, took a trip to Paris – to forget – and apparently came back with suitcases full of black evening frocks. It was on the return ship that she met my father. They got married as soon as they arrived in Batavia. She wore black, the Rose of Surabaya in mourning! The priest would only give his blessing if Daddy took in all the children from his wife's first marriage. Soon after I was born he bought a big house for the family, and from then on he had six extra mouths to feed. Daddy was far too good for this world, poor man. He kept to his study and rarely went out, but loved being surrounded by women enjoying themselves.'

Edmee folded her arms dramatically over her breasts, emitting a sickly-sweet smell.

'Yes, indeed, our Odile was a great actress. I don't know how many men she took for a ride, including the priest. Don't forget, to the outside world she led a life of virtue, attending mass twice on Sunday, and often matins on weekdays. Her fondness for parties and dancing was regarded as an innocent distraction. It was different for us children, behind the scenes. We knew how heartless she could be.

'The suicide remained a secret, of course. It was never mentioned, not even by the children. I was already grown up when Justin first told me about it, which was odd, considering how close we were. He didn't dare tell me until we were in Holland. Your father was a great talker, but that was just to give the impression there was nothing to hide. It was from him that I heard about Odile donating some of her inheritance to the church so as to have her first husband buried in hallowed ground. Appearances, that's all she cared about.

' "Sorry" was a word our mother didn't know the meaning of. Talk about insensitive – she was as hard as nails.'

Edmee had hardened her heart, too, she said. Feelings? She didn't believe in them, she didn't have much faith in human nature, and with good reason.

We downed another bottle, then a glass of Armagnac,

and a second, and a third . . . the kitchen crew were marking time with a game of cards behind the bar. She started snivelling, I lent her my handkerchief and got it back smeared with red. Ah well, that was Batavia for you, different manners and different customs, no Hollander would understand.

I tried to get up from my chair, but she stopped me. She hadn't finished yet, and we were family after all. She'd been living in Holland for the past fifteen years, and still she wasn't used to it. Everything was so small it was like toy-land, so stuffy and so quiet indoors, no servants to liven things up. She practically lived on tranquillisers. What she was doing here was beyond her. The social services were good, admittedly, although she'd had to wait for ages to get a house. For some complicated reason she had retained her Dutch nationality. 'When it comes down to it you need your roots, family, you know.' That was what she was after: her uprooted family.

She turned up my left hand and started tracing the lines in my palm with the tip of her little finger. 'You'll embark on a second life,' she said, 'after a break-up everything will be all right again.' Her nail crept under my cuff and her shoe brushed against my ankles. 'You don't wear a ring,' she remarked.

I fought down the urge to kick her. She was supposed to be a dear long-lost auntie, and I was appalled. I snatched my hand away and wiped it on my napkin – just think of all the germs floating around at table, for all I knew family mania could be contagious.

I looked into her moist black eyes and asked in a conspiratorial tone how white she reckoned her mother was.

'Odile Didier?' she echoed, in a high-pitched voice. 'She was all white, lily-white I may say, her parents spoke French at home, you know.' Her Indies accent was thicker than ever.

What about Odile's lover?

She shrugged.

'Come now, could anyone keep a secret in the Indies?'

'Er . . . he was a foreigner, I think.'

'A foreigner? Everyone would be a foreigner to a Frenchwoman. Even a Javanese.'

'Don't be silly, a woman of her station wouldn't go near a native.'

After much fawning and wheedling I got her to tell me that Odile's lover had been Italian. She'd had a ten-year affair with her Neapolitan hairdresser. Some coiffeur! But that didn't necessarily mean he was the father of her children. No one knew for sure. 'Honest!' she said, adding that the hairdresser had boarded a ship bound for Europe. 'You know what Italians are like, scaredy-cats, the man was terrified, of course.' Edmee looked at me triumphantly, there, it was all out in the open now, *aduh*, all this talking had made her quite hot. 'Right then, now you know our big family secret.'

As if I hadn't heard such tales before! Italian blood indeed – half the colony had Italian blood in their veins, thanks no doubt to an entire regiment of Italian hairdressers.

'You shouldn't speak so harshly of your father,' she said crossly. 'Justin and his brothers and sisters may have been a little swarthy-looking, but they were definitely white. For goodness' sake, lots of French people have dark complexions.'

I said nothing, waited for her to talk herself into a corner.

'Don't look at me like that, Papa van Bennekom was pure-blooded, too, and that's the truth.' Anything wrong with that? Or was it better to be brown nowadays? Edmee sniffed loudly, she was proud of her European blood.

'Aryan, you mean,' I said, and to prove she understood my meaning she threw the remainder of her cognac in my face.

Well, things got out of hand after that. I said I didn't believe in Neapolitan hairdressers and we quarrelled bitterly. She didn't even want me to give her a lift home, insisted on calling a taxi – which I'd be paying for, needless to say. We never got round to the addresses of my distant cousins, but by then I had lost every inclination to see any member of my father's family again.

And yet, I hadn't quite finished with this aunt. I regretted having quarrelled, and we hadn't talked about my father very much either. Had she met Sophia Munting and Roeliana and Roediono? Who else but Edmee could tell me about his first marriage? And perhaps I ought to do something to help after all, she was on the brink of ruin, just a wee bit of money and attention and she'd be fine again. I could talk her into believing she suffered from camp trauma, she could apply to the social services, have a good cry in front of some qualified therapist and claim some nice benefits. I'd ask Saskia for the necessary forms. That was the excuse I had for getting in touch with Edmee again.

Our second encounter was more successful. We arranged to meet in the morning, Edmee without alcohol on her breath and steadier on her feet, although she still held on to me as we walked. Her sense of balance was impaired, definitely so, and I resolved to find her a good specialist.

I had to work my way through a slice of pink cake first and had some trouble dissuading her from indulging in a teeny-weeny glass of sherry, but after that she proved remarkably willing to talk. She too regretted the way our first meeting had gone; my resemblance to Justin had got her all muddled. If I was so eager to know more about my father, why didn't I start by taking a look at the letters he'd written home soon after the liberation ('addressed to my mother for the sake of form,' she said, 'but really they were for me').

She unlocked the door of a small side room where she kept her past stored away in a battered old cupboard. We promptly sank to our knees for some communal delving into the fragrant tropics. 'I haven't read his letters since then,' Edmee said. 'Most of them came straight from the camp, as I remember.'

'Where were you at the time?'

'Java.' She pulled a wicker box from the rummage and took out a sheaf of crumpled papers. 'Here, take your time, I don't know if they're in the right order.' Shutting the door behind her she left me alone in the unheated lumber-room.

First I inhaled the smell . . . the few things of my father's that were still in my possession smelled of tiger balm, the stuff he smeared on his body every day to stimulate the circulation of the blood, and it was a distinctive, long-lasting smell. But here my nose was picking up entirely different essences – those of a distant past, of before my time. The letters – notes, rather – were pencilled on torn strips of wartime paper, numbered but not dated, and sharply creased, probably because they had been posted without a covering envelope. The sender's address was on the back: Recovery Camp Pakan Baru, Sumatra.

Letter number one was also the longest, and I had difficulty reading the pencilled scrawl.

Madame,

First of all I want to tell you I have emerged from this hell in excellent health and I hope you and the rest of the family are well too. Have you heard from Sophie? I haven't heard anything, not through the Red Cross either. The news from Java is good and bad. Oh well, I've always been pretty fit and now I'm working as a cook in the recovery camp. A job in the kitchen means you can get extras. We're fine, being showered with tinned food, cigarettes, etc. In the beginning they were dropped by parachute from airplanes, but now they come overland. All the Englishmen who were ill have been relocated. There were four hundred Hollanders who didn't make it, a lot of chaps you used to know. Paul, Mrs 't Hin's son, died a week before the liberation. The last few months were especially bad, there were people dying every day. I could send you a list, but I can't remember a lot of the names. We all have trouble remembering things. They say it's vitamin deficiency. That will pass. No point complaining. My teeth seem to be improving, all of them were loose due to lack of vitamins. I take twenty-five tablets a day. Once we're together again I want to sleep for three years, and wake up like Rip van Winkle in peacetime. All of us here feel very tired.

The Australians and English are being evacuated to Singapore this week, and I hope it won't be long before they send me to Batavia. The Dutch aren't lifting a finger. What can you expect?

And how is my beloved little sister? Edmee must be eighteen now, will I recognise her among the others on the quay in Priok when I get there? I have no money left, but that doesn't matter, I don't need it here anyway. Are they having balls again in Batavia? I can hear the last call for the post. So I'll have to keep it short. See you soon, J.

P.S. If an opportunity arises to get the family to Australia, seize it. Safety first. I'll follow later. A kiss for Edmee.

How different this handwriting was from the careful script I remembered as his! Some of the words had been gone over twice while others were so faint as to be illegible, the lines were wavy, and all the full stops were heavily marked. You could tell by the unaccustomed scrawl that he hadn't written anything for years. I wondered whether I'd ever read any of my father's letters before. Signatures on school reports, captions beneath photographs, lists of house rules and directions for the use of appliances, anything to do with discipline and order, that was what his handwriting meant to me, but these scribbled lines were closer to the heart, however insignificant the content. In this letter my father stepped out of his handwriting and stood beside me, this told me more than some old snapshot or tie of his which I'd kept for sentimental reasons. His mood rippled across the paper, hopeful and despairing, harsh and fond by turns. Reading, writing and arithmetic, I had to master the three Rs before starting primary school. My father had all the time in the world to instruct me, and he had methods of his own devising. A crayon was pressed into my hand before I was even a toddler. At an age when other children are given colouring books I was already tracing the letters of the alphabet. The cheeks of my *b*'s and *d*'s fitted exactly between the indicated lines, the strokes of my *e*'s lay down like obedient dogs, and the loops of my *l*'s were shapely. I still have the letters he made me write, sitting beside me at the table. They were kept, treasured even. What a timid impression my boyish handwriting made. Not any more, I thought, but this camp letter brought back the sting of all those times he hit me. Even in this lumber-room I felt the menace of my father. His letter in my hand brought back the bitter taste of lead, and I remembered how, on my first day of school, I snapped a pencil between my teeth, out of rage at being taught to write by the teacher. I could write already, I was a big boy and my writing was fine. She gave me a new pencil, and I broke that one, too. She put down two or three shiny yellow pencils in front of me, to see if I could continue destroying them, and I was wild enough to go on until my mouth was full of lead and splinters. So much for the evocative power of handwriting!

I leafed through the other letters. Brief notes about still more cigarettes, tinned food and the family, and the occasional aside about the political situation:

Don't see much of Sukarno and his boys, things pretty quiet here . . . We listen to the news every day. Doesn't look too good for now. Sukarno etc. making trouble. Am getting a bit worried about you all. KLM flights resume as of 15th of October. You should try to get away. Book tickets now. It's riskiest of all for Edmee, she's prey for hungry soldiers. We should all try to get to Australia, and return when things are truly back to normal. I'm arranging a flight from here.

Skint, without even the fare for a fourth-class passage, and there he was, fantasising about flying. Delusions of grandeur, even then. Not a word about what it had been like in the camp, let alone any mention of his first wife Sophie, not a thought for the state of her health or that of her children. I didn't come across the names Roeliana and Roediono anywhere. But then how was he to know of their existence?

Twenty letters on and Justin had been on a plane. His handwriting is suitably jaunty:

Flew from Pakan Baru to Palembang today. Little time to write: the post leaves in 5 min. Beds, sheets, electric light. Fantastic. My first flight, and it went very well, with a DC3 machine. My address is Camp Transit, Palembang.

And still later:

We have social evenings in this place, which is nice. I've been billeted here with the same chaps as before, we get on like a house on fire. Music and dancing at the club, which is in what used to be the mayor's residence.

I've laid hands on a fine pair of black American shoes, as well as pyjamas and underwear. Proper clothes take some getting used to.

The Hollanders are back in the saddle again. Quite a lot of men on the outside have been detained for collaborating with the Japs and Germans.

'He doesn't mention getting to know my mother,' I remarked when Edmee came in with a cup of tea to warm me.

'He talks about me, though, did you notice how he adores me?' She gathered the letters together and perched on the corner of a small table. She was less made up, and looked the better for it. From the notes I figured out that she had to be sixty-six or sixty-seven now. The tropics had been kind to her.

I had got very cold, so I took the tea and the letter with me to the pink living-room. The candles were lit and she had prepared sandwiches.

Edmee took a folder from the table and held it out to me. 'For you,' she said. 'Your father was a sick man for as long as you knew him, but here he is in his heyday.' She drew a snapshot with a serrated edge from the folder: a pretty woman posing next to a pale bloated man in a creased linen suit and an adolescent with a toddler on his shoulders. 'That's Justin,' Edmee said, 'just after leaving the orphanage. Look at his hollow eyes! The baby is me, and those two are Odile and Daddy van Bennekom.'

It was the first picture of my grandmother I'd ever seen, and the young Justin looked a lot like her. Same flashing eyes and sensual lips, and I saw the similarity with mine, too. I also recognised the weakness in the boy, the same weakness that my father hated in me.

In another picture Justin was sitting under a tree, sketching. Tilting his head back slightly, he looked confident, aware of his good looks. A succession of snapshots showed him going from shorts to double-

breasted suit, from schoolboy to soldier. Edmee spread
out the pictures in front of her like a game of patience.
From left to right: in uniform, with cap and without,
pockets at his knees or stiff high collar, in puttees or
boots. Next came Justin the sports hero, in jodhpurs,
tennis clothes, and with a boxing glove aimed at the
lens, his shoulders broader each time. She slapped the
final picture down with a triumphant gesture: Justin
wearing a frock and a hat, posing wide-legged on a
flight of stone steps.

My father in drag. The man who was out to beat some
manhood into me – wearing a dress. And it suited him,
too, chin raised, looking askance at the camera, a fan
pressed languidly to his chest. I held the picture up and
laughed. 'I'll have this one framed, I've never seen him
look so sexy.'

'The dress was Odile's, for a fancy dress ball.' Edmee
snatched the picture from me and slipped it back into the
folder. 'If that's what you think you can't have it. Clothes
are just show. Here, look at all these different faces: child,
boy, man, more serious-looking every time.'

'And more severe.'

'The first months he'd be proud when he came on
leave, always brought me little presents, a wooden bird or
a pretty veined pebble. In the beginning he used to bring
drawings, too, landscapes of Surabaya for Odile, I think
that's where he did his training. But later on all that
stopped, he withdrew into his shell, was away for longer
stretches, too – that's the infantry for you – nasty jobs, and

all those patrols he had to go on. He had problems with his commanding officer, a horrible, fanatical chap, Odile wrote to me about it after the war. He was one of the lovers she had rejected, and he made trouble for Justin the whole time he was in the army. Just look at the pictures, each time there's less of a smile.'

'And less hair,' I said, pointing to one of the photographs of him in uniform, in which his unruly curls had been reduced to a few dark streaks.

'Ah, *kepala botak*, that's a sad story.'

'I know, I know,' I cried enthusiastically, '*kepala* means head and *botak* means bald, he told us umpteen times. It always cropped up when we had visitors, they'd ask questions.' In my mind I ran through my father's stories and came upon us sitting at a lavish Sunday *rijsttafel*, Aunt Pop and Aunt Régine with their jangly gold bangles on either side of him, flicking their purple nails against the crystal glasses and rolling their colonial *r*'s. My father on the edge of his chair, holding forth as usual. 'Where was it, was it Djambi?' I asked.

'No, it was Dyogyakarta,' Edmee said, sitting down quickly and helping herself to a sandwich.

'Yes, of course, Dyogyakarta, land of steep slopes, dense forests and man-high *kembang sepatu*.' I imitated his accent, which brought a pained look to Edmee's face.

'Don't be like that,' she said, 'don't make fun of him.'

But I couldn't stop myself.

'Close your eyes, Auntie, and I'll take you to the foot

of the Merbabu. Justin's first posting after the military academy. His rank there was *dardanel*, nice word, but it didn't amount to much: dogsbody to an officer, an orderly, that was all. Not much for a young infantryman to write home about.'

Edmee looked perturbed. She couldn't go on. 'What's wrong?' I asked.

'You're being unfair,' she said at last, with her mouth full. 'Justin had to leave home when he was sixteen, it was either a monastery or the army. Daddy couldn't afford to send him to Holland, he was badly in debt as it was. Besides, Odile wanted all the children to be independent as soon as possible.'

'Unfair? So what did he accomplish? Fourteen years in the army and never made it past the rank of sergeant major.'

'Justin was a reserve officer and if he'd stayed in the service after the war he'd have had a good career. It was your mother who persuaded him to leave the army.'

'Well, Dyogyakarta wasn't a good start, he said so himself, that was how he always began his story. No head-hunters, no rebels, no savages running amok, just endless hanging around and waiting for the big shots from Batavia to come and pay their respects to the Sultan of Dyogyakarta. After visiting the palace, they would climb the Merbabu under military escort.'

'The Kraton.'

'Who?'

'The Sultan's palace was called a Kraton, and it wasn't

really a palace but a walled-off section of town inhabited by thousands of people. I went there once with Daddy for a private audience with the Sultan. Most visitors didn't get any further than the open ballroom, which was the only building still in the traditional Javanese style. It was gorgeous, with golden pillars and a marble floor. At the entrance there were *pangerans*, courtiers who linked arms with each guest and led them to the Sultan, even the men. I had to stand on tiptoe to reach their elbows . . . God, what year would that have been?'

'Your beloved Justin was bored stiff. All those climbing parties, zigzagging up slippery paths, across forests and past slumbering kampongs, getting their breath back at the summit in the long grass, pointing to the landscape down below. And the Hollanders crying ooh and ah, look, the irrigation works, the terraces, the roads, all constructed by us! – while the coolies waved at them from the paddy fields.'

'Why don't you go there and see for yourself? Then you'll change your tune. You'll see what the aristocracy of Java –'

'He longed for promotion and dreamed of a stripe down his trousers and embroidery on his cuffs, a hat with a plume on his head, just like all those princes and ministers and generals he saw at the Sultan's court. He thought: so long as I hold my little finger by the seam of my trousers, never complain, and obey orders promptly, I'll be all set for the military academy in Breda. To be an officer, that's what he dreamed of. He'd have looked better in a cadet's uniform than in fatigues with pockets on the knees.

'As long as he did as he was told things were fine. His superior's wife took to him, too. How many times he'd fetched her horse from the stables, and adjusted the stirrups with her in the saddle! At the end of a ride she liked dropping her bag so that they'd both stoop at the same time and he'd feel her flowing blond hair brushing against his temple. He wasn't looking for perks like that, he was wary and avoided her if he could. Which wasn't easy, as he had to be available round the clock, spreading out the ordnance maps, marking mountain passes, planning itineraries, and acting as guide and interpreter.

'Justin's superior knew very little Malay, whereas our Justin spoke it fluently. He also knew sufficient high and low Javanese to get by. With his keen eye for class and status he always managed to use the right word in the right situation. All this was just native gibberish to the superior, whose Dutch didn't extend much further than barking orders, either. He looked down on the natives and he probably looked down on his orderly, too, for, let's be honest, wasn't Justin just a shade too dark to be a pure-blooded Hollander?'

Edmee's eyes flashed, but I wasn't going to let that stop me. Indeed, I'd lay it on even thicker, let's have some drama here! My father was off-stage, directing the show. Shshsh.

'He'd put up with anything for the sake of Breda, you know what your brother was like, always prepared to bend in order to succeed. Should the superior's wife drop her bag again in the stable, from now on he'd keep his eyes shut when he bent down.

'But the superior was a difficult man. He couldn't stand the sounds of the night, and he'd lie awake for hours, sweating under the fan. His wife was too frigid to console him, so he took to drink and sought out the company of his men. It was the same every night, drinking gin and playing cards on the veranda. There was plenty of gin, he kept sending for more bottles from Batavia. Whenever Justin wasn't around, the superior would keep the handle of his field telephone turning until he'd been tracked down.

'The stakes were usually low, as the superior played for the honour. Sometimes the loser had to tie his laces together and hop to the barracks and back, or he was dunked twice in the crocodile river. The superior would eat the feathers of his dress helmet. The men thought this was a great idea, he was a great guy, the chief, so friendly, didn't care about rank, either. Pity he never lost, he was the best rummy player in the whole of Dyogya.

'One night he came up with a new forfeit: the loser would have to pay with his hair. Every man reached for his head, horrified. Poor Justin, it was unthinkable, the best-looking bloke around, what he lacked in braid and embroidery grew abundantly on his head. And what did the inveterate winner risk losing? Just a few dull strands.

'The superior had the best hand of cards, as usual. The

boy had already been dispatched to the kampong to fetch a barber, the gin was flowing, the men jeered and Justin was losing. The superior's wife tried to communicate his opponents' cards with winks and sign language, but he hardly dared look at her. How brazen she was that evening, the way she danced around the table, hair piled high, bare shoulders swathed in an ostrich boa and long earrings sparkling in the lamplight. She kept dropping her boa so as to peek at the cards when she stooped to pick it up. But even a bit of cheating couldn't save Justin. He lost.

'In the meantime the barber arrived. They gave him some gin, which he drank even though he was a Moslem because they told him it was "Holland water". He liked the taste and soon he was drooling *kepala, kepala botak*, and he set about sharpening his razor on a grimy strop.

'"Bald,"' commanded the superior, "shave it all off." "Baldie, baldie," the men jeered. "*Botak, botak,*" the servants cried, and the bushes rustled with soldiers who had come running. The superior's wife, too tipsy to conceal her infatuation, laid her hands on the curls she was so eager to caress: "No," she said, leaning forward to kiss the top of his head. The superior stood up, flung down his cards and pushed his wife into a chair. He untied her chignon and held up a strand of long blond hair. "Cut it," he ordered the barber, "cut this lady's hair."

'The men protested and the barber hung back. Then

they seized Justin and forced the barber to shear off his hair instead. His curls bounced as they hit the ground, that's how thick they were, and the barber stamped his feet with delight. The superior's wife ran into the house and her husband was able to smile again. More gin. The men were relieved, too.'

'That's not the way he told it to me,' Edmee said.

'This is a special performance, a family matinée! I could have said it all in four sentences.' And I thought: my father's stories are swelling up in my head, and if I'm not careful I'll find myself turning all the things he didn't say into a book, too. Thinking about his stories it's as if it's him talking inside me, and when I lie it's his truth I'm stretching.

'Not only do you sound like him,' Edmee remarked, 'you have the same body language, the same smile, the same look in your eyes, and you wave your hands a lot when you talk, just like him. You're so alike it's uncanny.'

'But I still have all my curls, and I'm already about four years older than he ever was. I remember that when he got around to the bit about the barber he'd grab his fruit knife and wave it in the air, which used to make your sisters shriek.'

'*Kassian*,' Edmee said. She drew up her knees, curled up on the couch and shut her eyes. 'Go on, finish the story, give us another little imitation, get him to tell another fib.'

'The barber rinsed his razor in the gin and drew white

furrows across Justin's skull. The men picked up the fallen curls and held them under their noses to make moustaches. They roared with laugher and slapped the barber on the back. The razor slipped and a trickle of blood ran down the side of Justin's face.

'The *dardanel* was bald, the superior was satisfied. Next day my father bent over the ordnance maps with a red slash on his head. Nobody saw it, though, because he wore his cap by way of a sticking plaster, and he didn't complain. It had been a great night, and the loser a good sport. But losing his hair also cost him his name: Justin was known as *Kepala Botak* for the rest of his days as a serviceman.

'The following morning he felt feverish, the wound had turned septic on account of the dirty blade, a week later there wasn't any hair sprouting on his scalp, just mould. The doctor disinfected the wound and prescribed bed rest. The superior's wife brought him tea and changed the bandage. His head was inflamed for weeks. It took a whole year for some downy stubble to appear, but that fell out, too, leaving only a rim of thin hair on the back of his head. Measly little curls, as soft as Persian lamb.'

We ate our sandwiches and stared wordlessly at the ceiling, the only place in Edmee's house where your thoughts could roam free. I spotted my father momentarily in a corner, not as the demanding stage director, but good-natured, wistful. I had tamed him with his own stories.

'I never got used to him without his hair,' Edmee

remarked. One by one she picked up the photos from the table. 'Still, he was able to laugh at the whole thing later, he said he'd come out of it stronger. Hardship builds character, he used to say. The experience reminded him never to put too much trust in people. Hard, you had to be hard, or you'd just be disillusioned . . . as he well knew, the darling.'

'Were his brothers like that, too?'

'Well, they weren't sentimental, no.'

'Why did we never hear from you after he died?'

'Your mother wasn't keen.'

'What about me, his full-blooded son?'

She laughed grimly. 'Well, you know what it was like in those years, the whole world was on the move, we were in the middle of the Cyprus trouble.'

'Do you have any pictures of the twins?'

'So you know about them, too.'

'Did you ever meet his first wife?'

'No, I didn't. Justin married her in Surabaya, far away. You know how it goes.'

'Just one day by train from Batavia.'

'The whole family knew that his marrying Sophia wasn't a good idea, she'd already shacked up with a Mohammedan during the war. But Odile strongly disapproved of divorce, and she was dead set against Justin's affair with your mother, a Protestant, and she had those Indo daughters; there were all those rumours about her first husband – a native, mind you. She wanted to save Justin from ruin.'

'Long live maternal love.'

'As long as Daddy prevented the divorce from going through, Justin couldn't marry your mother or he'd have been a bigamist.'

I broke out in a sweat, what a dodgy bunch they were. Had I come across the name Van Bennekom in my father's affidavit of denial? The family jigsaw puzzle was getting very complicated. Had my mother known about all this scheming?

'Now we're letting our hair down,' Edmee said, 'there's one more thing you ought to know. Sophia Munting had already died.'

'No! When?'

'A few years after the liberation.'

'Impossible. Our notary corresponded with her until a few years before my father died.'

'It was Daddy who replied to the letters. As her solicitor he kept a tight rein on everything, he acted as her executor, too.' Edmee gave an apologetic shrug. 'Daddy got wound up rather easily, and goodness knows what grudge he bore Justin, perhaps he was jealous of his wife's flirting with her own sons.'

'So my father could have married my mother any time?'

'I think so. Justin was a widower, although he didn't know it.'

'Revenge.'

'Yes, I suppose so.'

'But why?'

'Look here, things were different then. I was the youngest, it was a problem for my step-family, and my mind was on other things anyway. I was in love with a British officer, I wanted to get married and leave the country as soon as possible. The struggle for independence had started, and it was extremely dangerous out there.'

'And his brothers and sisters lied along with the rest, did they?'

'It had gone too far, no one wanted to back down. All of us were against Justin's relationship with your mother to begin with, we wanted him to stay in the colonial army. He didn't have much education so what else could he do? How was he going to manage in Holland with a wife and three children?'

'My my, such concern for three little Indo kids!'

'We didn't discuss it, we were accustomed to living with secrets. The few occasions we visited your father once we were in Holland we couldn't get a word in edgeways, he talked non-stop. All we could talk about was the food.'

'What a relief it must have been when he died.'

'We were able to bury the lie.'

'That's why we never heard from you.'

'We didn't want to be reminded.'

So I needn't have gone through life as a bastard at all, it had all been for nothing, my mother's embarrassment, the juggling with surnames to keep up appearances in the village, the childish fiddling with my school reports and certificates: what was I really called? It had to be my official name, or it wasn't valid.

'Thanks a lot,' I said, pushing my plate away with such force that it chipped the rim of a saucer.

'I understand,' Edmee said contritely.

She put the photos back in the folder and slid it towards me. 'And Roeliana and Roediono?' I asked. Edmee was nervously collecting the chips of china with a moistened fingertip. 'What happened to the twins?'

'No idea.'

'My God, what a heartless lot you were. Children aren't puppies, you can't just dump them.'

Edmee looked hurt. 'I didn't know Sophia, I didn't know the twins, I never set eyes on them.'

'What about your mother, surely Grandmother Odile cared about them?'

'My mother and children! She thought babies stank, she wouldn't touch them if she could help it.' She got up and paced the room, snorting with indignation. Then she took a bottle of sherry from the cabinet and poured two glasses. A drink, what other option was there? 'Daddy must have thought of something. He was the cleverest lawyer in Java, he managed to keep us all out of the camps, too.'

Oops – she clapped her hand over her mouth. A slip of the tongue. Quick, another sip of sherry.

'Odile was exempt anyway,' she said hurriedly. 'She was French, I don't know the ins and outs of it, the Vichy government was pro-Japanese I think, and Daddy fixed things for us, too.'

'How?'

'A trick.'

'How? Murder, betrayal, bribery, I wouldn't put it past you lot.'

Edmee floundered like a child caught red-handed. My palms itched. It turned out that the Italian lover had been trumped up as the native father of all the children, including Edmee. This kind of thing was easier in Java than elsewhere. Odile gathered her family around her, young and old, plus hangers-on. She stayed in her own house all through the war. Daddy van Bennekom tried to find himself a native forbear as well, but that didn't work, so in the end he couldn't escape going behind barbed wire, the fool. The price of being pure-blooded.

My father was unaware of these family intrigues. He was the son destined to serve a fatherland he had never seen, and as the eldest he was the first to be sacrificed, in keeping with good Catholic tradition.

'Freedom is worth a lie or two,' said Edmee, looking peevish all of a sudden. So much for her qualifying as a camp victim, then – forget about those extra benefits. How many lies? Was there any point in dissecting this family tree any further? How had they wangled the papers for the native lover? I didn't want to speculate about how honourably or otherwise the family had got through the Japanese occupation. Edmee was after purity and consoled herself with a lily-white escutcheon. I for my part was looking for evidence of native blood because I have such pink skin, and if I didn't watch out I'd find myself going round in the same absurd circles.

That crazy longing for purity, my father, too, was infected by it, ever preoccupied with rank and class, respectability and vulgarity, right and wrong, more and less, higher and lower, left and right, strong and weak, bitter and sweet – even in the kitchen. Was that why he embraced anthroposophy? It stood for the brotherhood of all men, regardless of race, religion, sex, caste or colour, the search for truth being the ultimate goal: fancy theories to cover up the lies of his youth. No doubt that was also why he held with anthroposophic notions of education: the harmonious development of emotion and will. Learning *per se* was not paramount, what was important was creativity, music, singing, eurhythmics. Beauty would breed understanding.

It was all a bit hazy with him, though. Emotion signified pain, will the denial of pain, rhythm amounted to tapping his ruler, beauty and creativity resided in neatly drawn margins and meticulous penmanship. We had to strive after a higher self, after purity of spirit. The conscious mind was to master the subconscious. My father had a way with words, he clung on to them, so scared was he of the dark side of his own nature and of the hell in his heart. In anthroposophy he found something soft to camouflage his hardness.

'Don't you want me to be your auntie any more?' Edmee asked when I put on my coat to leave.

'Yes, I do, but not too often.'

She gave me a woozy kiss, bitter and sweet, and pressed a photograph into my hand.

My father in a frock.

5

Quicksand

We were rocking in the nave of the church. The pulpit was a light machine and thunder crashed overhead. I felt myself in a tank full of seaweed, arms writhing over and under me. Standing still was impossible, we were carried upwards in a pulsating, seething mass. The ground fell away under our feet, white smoke coiled around our ankles. I was dancing on the waves.

My eyes searched for something to latch on to, something solid and stable, but a bolt of lightning struck the columns and the roof flashed on and off and up and down in stroboscopic pandemonium.

Aram wasn't dancing, he was teetering on tiptoe, pulling himself up by my shoulder to catch a glimpse of the band. Five bare-chested youths with rings in their nipples, noses and ears, heads shaven or with flowing, shoulder-length hair. The singer wore cut-off jogging pants. The drummer was a leather Christmas tree, the studs at his crotch glittering in the light. The guitarists fucked their instruments, looked mean and spat down on us. A raw voice into the mike: 'When there's no peace, there's no sanity.' The world was a shit-hole, God and money a rip-off, fuck the universe – something like that, I couldn't catch all the words. Nor could Aram, but that wasn't what it was all about, he said, it was the feeling that counted.

Four more musicians got up on stage, kids from the Bronx. They pulled their pants down to moon us with their tattooed buttocks and amid screams from the audience. Big and brutish they were, hurling insults: motherfuckers! dumb headbangers! On their last tour they'd been made out to be fascists. That was all wrong, screamed the singer, they weren't into politics, theirs was a positive message: 'Fuck fascism, fuck ignorance. You know who's to blame, the motherfucking media's to blame.' They invoked Satan and the gamut of toyshop monsters: dragons, vampires, piranhas and black widows.

'Gothic,' Aram yelled in my ear, 'this is Gothic.' I nodded vaguely, trying not to look out of place. The music gained speed, boys and girls clambered up on stage, did a frenzied jig among cable coils and amplifiers and plunged back into the sea of waving arms.

Right in front of us a girl fainted, a boy had blood pouring from his nose. Someone's elbow jabbed into my bottom lip. I ducked, grabbed Aram by his waist and forced our way backwards through the crowd. Plastic cups crackled under our feet until we bumped against something hard. It was the drinks counter. Beer cans whizzed around our ears.

It had been my idea to take Aram to a headbanging night. I'd seen kids his age handing out flyers in town – 'Church Metal' – and I'd seized this opportunity for an initiation into his world. I rang him up and after a surreal exchange with his father ('What concert? He hasn't practised for weeks') asked him to come for the weekend. Aram didn't look back when he got into my car. His father was by the window, waving his son's French horn. No, I shook my head at him, he won't be needing that, after which he dropped the curtain.

We'd go to my house first and listen to some CDs and read the lyrics on the covers, and later on we'd go pogoing and moshing – which meant dancing, leaping up and down in clumpy boots.

'Must we?' I asked.

'Yeah, it doesn't sound right in these,' he said, pointing disdainfully to his crêpe-soled shoes. So that afternoon we bought boots at an army surplus store, and jeans with rips at the knees. And because I wanted to look tough – shades of Robin the Giant there – I picked out a pair of combat boots for myself. Aram's snake-and-visor T-shirt fitted the bill that evening, but the sight of him in that converted church made me wonder whether I was doing the right thing. He struck me as too young, and the rawness of the whole scene made him look even more vulnerable than he was. But Aram was miles away already: it was cool, far-out, fab. Yes, I was a popular uncle. The naked torsos, the smell of leather and sweat and marijuana, I took it all in and gawped at the tattoos. One youth had dedicated his back to Jesus: the saviour on the cross forming a bow in the devil's fist and an arrow hovering over the crown of thorns. Others had had the name of their favourite bands shaved into the hair on the back of their heads, and one girl had a pair of snakes writhing down her shoulders to her boobs. I gazed enviously at all those young bodies, the washboard stomachs and trellises of muscles across their backs. Once I'd bought the tickets for the headbangers' night I couldn't stop thinking about my figure. Would they laugh at me, was my hair too grey, was my arse too big to wear jeans? I'd spent an hour in front of the mirror checking my appearance and adjusting details – shirt tucked in or hanging out, collar up, top buttons undone, stomach sucked in, boots over the trouser legs or not? All this posturing had made me look older and older. James Dean with a pudding belly.

The bar in the side–aisle struck me as a safer place, and we'd have a reasonable view of the stage. Hundreds of boots stomped on the wooden floor, arms writhed in the light like electric eels. One of the Bronx boys smashed his guitar to pieces.

'Was that an expensive guitar?' I asked Aram.

'Bog,' he replied.

'What?'

'Bog.' I held my ear to his mouth. 'Bog-standard guitar,' he bellowed.

I was beginning to feel I'd had enough, but Aram had

more moshing to do. He drew a deep breath and bounced up and down flailing his arms above his head. The girl behind the bar was dancing, too, no time for punters. I leaned against the counter. The thudding intensified, the bottles rattled behind my back, but I also felt something soft, another rhythm, a hand along my shoulders and down my side.

Veering round I found myself staring at a silver nose-ring worn by a tall pale-looking girl. She sparkled in the light. White clothes, white lips, rocking to the music, totally blank expression, lanky hair swinging stiffly like glass, frozen white. She said something I couldn't hear and she didn't bother to say it again. She tugged at my sleeve and nodded towards the dancers.

'I'd rather watch,' I shouted, looking straight ahead. Aram bounced up and lunged towards the edge of the dancing crowd, beaming. His hair was far from outrageous compared with the others, and yet, with him jumping in the strobe lights, it looked like the wings of an eagle flapping in slow motion, up and down, up and down. He beckoned to me, the pale girl beside me waved back, grabbed me by both wrists and pulled me into the moshing throng. The music sucked us into the centre of the dance floor and we jumped as high as we could: the eagle, the pudding and the nose-ring. My lower lip throbbed, my boots pinched my toes.

The pulpit spewed out fireworks. Bengal lights flared overhead, smoke billowed in the spotlights. The Bronx boys sang about death and body snatchers: 'it's a shame you found out too late, reality's when you die.' The girl danced with her eyes shut. She took a sniff from a boy-scout whistle hanging on a leather thong round her neck, which brought a flush to her sallow cheek-bones. She snorted a few more times, then held the whistle under my nose. I caught the smell of sweaty feet. It was an inhaler. The blood rushed to my cheeks and I tingled and soared in the soap-bubble light. The pain vanished and so did the stiffness and embarrassment.

Suddenly the music died, the lights went out, there was a dull crash and for a moment we went on dancing in the vacuum left by the noise, a final spasm before coming to a stop.

'Blown fuse,' shouted someone from the pulpit. After a chorus of 'fucks' and 'shits', he set off a string of Chinese crackers. Blinded by all the smoke and numbed by the rapid explosions we hadn't a clue where the exit was. Aram took me by the hand and we moved with the surging flow until an arm barred my way. It was the pale girl. She led us to the bar, asked for a candle, and waved Aram to a bar stool.

'Hiccup in the fuse box, that's all,' she said, 'fixed in no time.'

'Creepy,' Aram said. 'I thought it was a raid or something.'

She held the burning candle up to his face and said: 'Your first concert, right?'

'No,' said Aram, 'I play music myself.'

She didn't introduce herself, accepted a drink without thanks and asked which instrument.

'French horn,' Aram said.

'What?'

'Horn,'

'What's that?'

To rescue him I said he was in a school band.

'Metal?' she asked.

'No, brass,' Aram shouted over the final bursts of cracker-fire. He cupped his hands and trumpeted into her ear. She smiled and returned the gesture, then put her arms around him. The kid didn't need me at all.

The three of us decided to go outside and have a pizza across the street. In the neon lighting I noted that the girl had bad skin and that the insides of her arms were bruised. She kept looking round restlessly. Her voice faltered now there was no need to shout – no she didn't really feel like a pi . . . pizza after all. She'd rather have an ice-cream or a coke. She kept sniffing loudly, made herself a ragged roll-up and asked the waiter the time twice over.

'In a hurry?' I asked.

'Nah,' she said, 'there's a gig across town, no money for a taxi though.'

'But it's nearly midnight,' Aram said.

'I'm not tired.'

'I have to go to bed at nine-fifteen.'

'I sleep during the day.'

'Every day?'

'E–every day.' Yes, she was aware that it aged you and was bad for your health, but she did so like music and dancing. She sniffed several times. Aram gazed at her admiringly. She let him touch her nose-ring and her white-sprayed hair.

'Like angel's hair,' he said.

'You're sweet,' she said when he offered her a wedge of his pizza. Aram blushed and asked how often she went to concerts. Then she lied about the bands she'd followed around and the foreign cities she'd been to and he bragged about the number of CDs he owned. He wanted to be a light man for a band later on, he said, or, even better, a roadie.

'Is that OK with your dad?' she asked, giving me a mocking look.

'He'll be dead by then,' Aram said.

'You're gross, you know that?'

Aram shrugged self-importantly. 'Reality is when you die.'

The girl and I chuckled indulgently. 'You're OK,' Aram said, and she patted him on the hand. 'You're not that old at all.'

'Thanks,' she said softly. She stubbed out her fag in the remains of her pizza and brushed the tobacco from her lap.

'I could've had a kid like you,' she said when she kissed him goodbye on the forehead. She poked me in the stomach: 'Hey, Dad, how about lending me the fare for my taxi?' Aram was convulsed with laughter. I gave her some money and he held up his hand, too.

'You can't take it with you, anyway,' she said.

'I'm not his father, I'm his uncle.'

'Oh, sorry.'

Out in the street she tapped on the window in passing. Aram looked at me questioningly, still holding up his hand.

'You've had plenty,' I said.

'It's not that. Just hold my hand,' he said. I laid my hand in his. 'Sort of nice, wasn't it, just now? Like happy families.'

I was shocked. He did need me.

But there was still Aram's father. Two days without his son and the urine was crusted around his flies. His food was still in the oven because he hadn't been able to get the door open and he couldn't understand what was going on – surely Aram was only going to be away for one night? He wanted to pat Aram on the head but his son was too tall and he let his hand drop back midway.

'It *was* only one night,' I said.

Aram opened the curtains. Maarten had spent the entire weekend in the dark.

I heated his meal, brewed some coffee and made a note of the district nurse's phone number. Something had to be done, things couldn't go on like this. Aram clumped up to his room in his boots, put on some heavy metal and stomped to the beat of the bass. Maarten sat wide-legged on the sofa, smiling at the racket overhead. 'Better this than silence,' he said. 'I've missed him.'

His father needed him, too.

★

What was I to do? I rang the social services: the district nurse would visit daily from now on. I made an appointment with the principal of Aram's school. There was some cause for concern. The boy's marks were poor: three fives and two fours, although he'd made up for the four for Greek with an eight later. We'd have to wait and see, he said, and if the worst came to the worst did I intend to look after Aram? I didn't give a straight answer. Was there a hint of mockery in his voice, or did I imagine it? From then on the idea of having my nephew move in with me became a constant preoccupation. I had to behave like a sensible adult, be a man. Either I decided I wasn't up to it, or I'd have to change my lifestyle and accept the responsibilities of being a parent to a fourteen-year-old boy. And if I was too scared or too selfish to take it on I should have the courage to admit it.

I went for a drive in my dunes again, without asking myself whether this was wise. I couldn't concentrate on my work anyway and wanted to think things over in a quiet place. My girlfriend, as usual these days, had no time to come along, and yet I needed to involve her in my decision. Aram would complicate our relationship. She had never wanted children and now I was foisting one on her. Choosing for Aram might well mean she'd leave me. A lot of things would become clear, but the consequences were anything but clear.

The village looked bleak and deserted. I took a room in the little hotel with sea views. The field opposite our old home was scraggier than ever, the rosehip-dotted bushes were shedding their leaves and the yard by the old stable was littered with deckchairs and dismantled beach tents. I let my eyes wander along the footpaths: the pine trees were making a comeback, and I saw myself as a little boy gazing up at the big Zeeland horses in the meadow. But a few hours later I was already regretting having come. What I needed to do was put the past behind me, not dwell on it. It was time to prove I could make up my own mind. Forget about the sea rolling in and out with desperate fatalism, there had to be some way of breaking free from fate, of taking one's life into one's own hands and making decisions that go against the grain of expectation. A breakwater was what I wanted to be.

I did my best not to look at the countryside through the eyes of my boyhood. After all, nothing looked the same, even the old sand dunes had shifted. Storms had blown away the horizon I used to know. Just look at how the moss had invaded the dips in the dunes, you could easily walk there in ordinary shoes nowadays. And how narrow the beach had become, and how insubstantial the new dyke along the boulevard looked. The sea breeze was permanently tainted by the smell of rancid fat from the chippie, and all over the village there were signs in German offering bed and breakfast. Fens and marshes had fallen dry, the groundwater level had dropped. Bushes lay uprooted in the dunes, the water company was laying concrete pipes. No more quicksands and treacherous plains. Arrows and signs gave directions, and every few kilometres there were coloured maps behind glass indicating local species of plants and animals. I bought a walking map and followed its directions. Before me stretched virgin territory and everything I saw was new.

But the crows were still there, wheeling around the highest dune. This was where, nearly two hundred years ago, ten thousand English and Russian troops had been butchered in a vain attempt by the Prince of Orange to win his country back from the Republicans. No doubt that was why the dunes were tipped bright orange by the low sun. Hundreds of crows alighted to peck at the ground – blood and iron kept them black. There was a paved footpath across the valley now, which was also indicated on my little map. I stamped my feet to frighten the birds feeding on death like vultures.

That night I felt a hand brush against mine. It stroked my arms, making the hairs stand on end, and for a moment I was lifted up as if I had left my own body. I was weightless, painless, fell into a deep daze from which I woke with tear-stained cheeks. I spent the rest of the night wide awake, anxious about memories slipping out of control. I listened to the sand blowing against the window of my room – the wind scraping its hind legs on the beach – and set off reluctantly across the seasons of my boyhood.

My village in the autumn. A huddle of horses forlorn in the mist. Our home was on the outskirts, across from the wood and the stable with the life-boat horses. The roof was like a beacon in the dunes, red and broad. The belfry on top had lost its bell – melted down to make German bullets. If you climbed up to the top you could see the sea and the water-tank for the steam tram.

The last of the summer visitors had left, the holiday homes stood empty and the sea lit up for the last time. My sisters went to secondary school in town and no longer came out to play. The other children in the building were too old, too. My father and mother sat and shivered by the stove.

In the autumn the dunes were mine again, when gale-force winds swept up the sand – sand that nipped at your cheeks and brought tears to your eyes so you had double vision: two lighthouses, two beach pavilions, two stables, two footprints for each step. A double landscape, to be shared with no one else.

Not long after the great flood of 1953 the local council installed a telephone in our communal hallway. The dune next to the big bunker had been seriously weakened, the water had come all the way to the back of the house twice already. We were to alert the beach warden if anything happened. There were three telephones in the village, and even though we weren't supposed to use ours except in an emergency we were very proud of the black, antler-like contraption in the hall. Now and then the lighthouse keeper further north would ring the village down the coast to tell them to get the horses and the life-boat ready. My father had offered to keep an eye on the stable nights and Sundays. He spent most of his time resting by the window anyway, and the beach warden lived too far away. Besides, he knew all about horses. How many hours hadn't he spent in his father's stables as a boy, he could handle any horse, even the wildest Arabs (with a dimple in the forehead and lips so delicate they could take water from a coconut shell) – indeed he was the best man in the village to take charge of half a dozen Zeeland nags.

In times of emergency the life-boat volunteers assembled in our hallway, which was where the chest containing flares, oilskins and waders was kept because it was too damp in the stable. The key hung on a red hook in the kitchen, and when the gale reached force nine my mother would prepare a Thermos of hot coffee.

So my father was in charge of the rescue horses. At least, I liked to think so. Whenever strangers approached the stable I'd warn them off: those are our horses and my father saves lives and helps vessels in distress. We've got a telephone that talks to lighthouses, a chest filled with fireworks and lamps with nickel-plated reflectors, not to mention a drum of paraffin and medals from the Queen.

But no ship was ever stranded on our beach, there were no cliffs or sandbanks, our horses gorged themselves on fresh hay and the oil lamps gathered dust in the cupboards. Autumn was a clammy time of year, nothing but veils of sea mist and flotsam offshore. Driftwood that the older lads used to build huts with. When the temperature dropped below freezing the sea cast ice-floes ashore, shards from faraway places. They piled up all over the beach. I was an Eskimo and sank to my knees in the crumbly ice.

In spring life returned, when the marram turned green again and traced arcs in the sand. Deckchairs were taken out of storage and the *plok* of carpet-beaters echoed between the houses. House-painters climbed up ladders and a bulldozer cleared the sand off the boulevard.

And in summer the orphans arrived. Coaches rumbled on the roads: the High House was being invaded. Blankets and mattresses hung out of the windows and the flag was raised over the steps leading to the entrance. The boys wore blue overalls and the girls blue skirts and jerkins with a zipper. They were pale and poor, the seaside was supposed to put some colour into their cheeks.

They spent their first day lurking behind the fences, spitting through the wire netting when anyone came too near. I used to go there every year to spy on their unfamiliar faces from a safe distance. They were from the city, they had city accents and wore shiny black gumboots. Their arrival meant it was summer, even if the sun didn't shine and the sand was pocked by showers.

Now began the season of forbidden things: skirts hoisted up, black underpants, boobs butting against jerkins. The girls clung together, humming and taking dance steps. They put on lipstick and smiled at me with stained teeth. The boys toyed with their combs and used spit to sculpt their hair into quiffs dancing on their foreheads and duck-tails at the back. I wanted my hair to be like that, too, straight and slick. I hated my curls, the sand got into them and they turned ropy when it rained. No amount of spit would restrain them.

When my father spent days on end lying on the divan in the darkened room and had me read to him – with my back turned so the light from the standard lamp didn't hurt his eyes – he'd plait my hair into tight little braids the way he plaited the horses' manes (tap, tap, went the ruler as it edged up my neck to measure the length of a drawn-out curl.) I had to be a man in every respect – except for my hair. My father loved my curls.

The orphanage boys wrestled and boxed for fun, flexing their muscles and swearing loudly. When the retired major went out wearing his medals to take his dog for a walk they threw pine-cones at him, and when they spotted the man from the high dune going down to the beach in his bathrobe they chanted, '*Wir fahren gegen Eng-e-land . . . plonk, plonk.*' But that was all right, because he'd been a collaborator in the war. They said all sorts of things I didn't dare say ever, without lowering their eyes. Not one of them had a forbidding father.

By the end of their first week the orphans knew the secrets of the duneland. They sauntered through my marshes and broke the crust on the dangerous sand. They knew where the quicksands were and where the key to the stable was kept. They picked my blackberries and pinched my shells.

On Saturday afternoons the orphans had to take a bath to scour away the week's dirt. Their windows steamed up and their singing could be heard from the road. Songs for the beach. I knew the tunes, but each winter I'd forget the words. They sang about the city and about losing their hearts to some tower or other. When they emerged, their hair still wet and some of the tough boys hiding fags in their cupped hands, they smelled of coal tar. That was another summer smell.

After their bath they trooped to the beach to watch the sun slide into the sea. Single file, chins up and at a smart pace. In the glowing twilight their blue uniforms turned black. They sang: 'Glory, glory hallelujah, the lasses in Batavia are black, pitch black.' But when they reached our house they'd stop singing, they'd nudge each other, talk in low voices and march on, their gumboots slapping against the back of their legs with every step.

I stood on the front doorstep, straight-backed like a general inspecting his troops. My sisters shut the curtains. I inhaled the smell of coal tar and tried to look as grim as I could.

My father loathed the orphans. Each summer he'd ask the supervisors to pick a different song. They could see his point and said they'd see what they could do. They had banned the song in the past, but somehow each new group took it up all over again, singing it in the dunes beyond our house, in the wood opposite, but never – and surely that proved their good intentions – never actually in front of our house. When they got there they swallowed the words and just stamped their feet. The orphans must have sensed that this was even more of an aggravation for my father. They passed it on over the years, and every fresh contingent knew what to do from day one: Glory glory hallelujah, the lasses in Batavia are

. . . shshsh . . . not in front of that house. The orphans knew our secret.

My father kept his temper, but he'd clench his fists at the sound of their boots. They were nothing, trash from the city. It would pass, they'd be gone by the time the autumn winds blew. The Japs hadn't got the better of him, and neither would a bunch of orphans. One fine day he'd teach them a lesson. I thought it was beastly of them, too, but to me the smell of tar signified a kind of freedom, even though they were fenced in and had to wear uniforms. Orphans made their own rules, it seemed to me. I dreamt of being an orphan myself, a Little Lord Fauntleroy. After a lot of wheedling I was given a pair of blue overalls to wear. Not rubber boots, though. In the morning I washed myself with Lifebuoy soap, which also had a tarry smell. A whiff of coal tar gave courage.

One morning I sheared off my curls. Everything that stuck out had to go, I brushed my hair down over my forehead and cut it straight across. Julius Caesar – if I couldn't have a quiff then I'd settle for an imperial hairstyle. I'd seen boys wearing their hair like that on the beach, and also a singer on a chewing-gum card. I plastered down my three crowns with Vaseline from the stable. Swaggering in my overalls, collar up, I slipped into my new role. I twirled in front of the mirror just like my sisters. This was who I wanted to be, I felt close to this cool customer, I was no longer alone. I spat on the mirror and swore: those weren't tears dribbling down, it was spunk. You could be a rebel by changing your hair – what was there to be scared of? I washed my face with Lifebuoy soap and stepped into the living-room.

My father was hidden behind his newspaper. I went across the room, tried to draw his attention by spinning round a few times. The draught riffled his paper. He lowered it and his eyes flashed, not a word, there was just the fury of his shaking fists. He shook out his newspaper and continued reading. His knuckles were white. My mother left the room.

'Did you know,' my father said during supper after an afternoon of excruciating silence, 'did you know that in the Middle Ages thieves used to comb their hair over their foreheads? To hide the brands. You look like a thief.'

The next day my mother pushed my shorn curls into an airmail envelope which she pasted into the family album.

The west wind storms gathered one afternoon in late summer, earlier than expected. My sisters were away and the blue coach had just delivered the last party of orphans. Tiles rattled on the roof, the phone rang and we knew what to expect. Lamp duty. We set to topping up the oil in the lamps, polishing the nickel reflectors, trimming wicks and testing the size of flames. All the lamps had to burn at exactly the same height. When my father wasn't looking I reached out to stroke the waders.

We huddled anxiously round the wireless, the lightning crackled through the loudspeaker. High tide, winds travelling a hundred kilometres per hour, vigilance was required from the population on the coast. I was allowed to stay up past my bedtime, and noted down the names of the ships in distress. Hard by the lighthouse was a ship named *Despina*, a steamer under the Corsican flag, which was listing heavily. The wind veered north-north-west and all the life-boat crews and coast patrols were on the alert.

The ships' piloting service was suspended. The *Mecklenburg*, a ferry boat, was listing forty degrees, the furniture in the passenger areas snapped like matchwood and dozens of people were hurt. Hundreds of campers saw their tents ripped to shreds before their eyes. The dyke-guards were poised for action, some outlying polders were already flooded. On an offshore island a boy had been blown out to sea with his kite. The newsreader spoke of 'treacherous winds'.

The phone rang again. The *Despina* had a broken rudder and was threatening to run aground on our beach. The horses neighed in the stable, my mother poured coffee for the life-boat volunteers. They were keen for the vessel to come our way, any wreck was welcome, as was the bonus they were bound to get in the end. They wound each other up with tall stories, they'd get the job done this way, that way, just leave it to them, and their oilskins creaked with fervour. My father sat by the phone, short of breath, while the wireless blared in the communal hallway. He swore under his breath because he knew he was too weak to act the hero in these weather conditions. I might as well join the crew, he said, what with my new shifty haircut I certainly looked old enough. He threw me some oilskins for a joke, and the life-boat volunteers roared with laughter. I hadn't learnt to swim yet.

The storm persisted, more bad weather was on the way. There were news bulletins every half-hour. The *Despina* had smashed a wooden breakwater but had drifted out to sea again, leaving the floating piles aimed like battering rams at the shore. The phone issued a ban on all wooden craft putting to sea. The life-boat crew returned to their homes, crestfallen. There was sand between my sheets and I thanked the good Lord from beneath my blankets.

The next morning we heard that the *Despina* had been towed away. Our village had failed to make the headlines yet again.

As for me, I would never forget that stormy night. One of the horses had been badly bitten above the knee. It was Sjors, the one with the braided mane, and he lay sprawled on the ground in the stable, foaming at the mouth. Two tendons had been severed. The beach warden said a rabid fox must have got in, because the horses had kicked down the partitions – a sure sign of panic – and were bleeding from the forelegs. This wasn't discovered until later in the day. The stable door was wide open, no one in our building had noticed anything as we had all been too agitated about the shipwreck that didn't happen. Some villain had meddled with the lock, the key wasn't on the hook. Sjors would have to be put down because a draught horse with a limp was useless. The meter-reader came round later in the day to put a bullet through his head. We searched for tracks, as it was hard to believe in hungry foxes on the prowl before the end of summer. But the wind had swept everything clean, the paths in the dunes and through the wood were pristine.

The ex-collaborator had seen someone lurking by the stable, but since my father always ignored him he hadn't reported this to the beach warden until the following day. The suspect had been wearing overalls.

My father took me aside. 'You'd better own up,' he said, gasping for breath. He had hardly slept last night and his lips had been blue when he got up in the morning. I lowered my eyes. 'No, no, it wasn't me.' I could hear the orphans singing. He drew himself up, grabbed me by my overalls and, twisting the fabric round his fist, dragged me into the road, where the band of orphans had just begun their wordless stomping routine. My father raised his hand and eyed the rows narrowly. The stomping died down. His expression of rage could be so compelling as to stop people in their tracks. He called this 'talking through the eyes'. He put on his sergeant-major's voice and ordered the boys to disperse. The supervisors accompanying them protested, but my father's unflinching eyes made them step aside meekly.

'Who left the stable door open?' he asked. The boys said nothing, a few of the elder ones risked a chuckle. I was cowering behind my father. He barked at them one by one.

'You? You?'

No response.

'Answer me!' my father roared.

'No.'

'No, what? Speak properly when you're spoken to!'

'No, sir,' one of them said, 'no . . . sir,' someone echoed. The tough boys spat on the ground and tossed back their quiffs. They didn't avoid his gaze, but they didn't look at him either, they looked right past him at me, nudging each other. They pointed to the scrunched-up front of my overalls which still bore the imprint of my father's fist. I felt ashamed and they could sense my shame. The smell of coal tar wasn't working. My father walked past the boys with his hand raised in a frozen salute, hesitating as to which cheek to slap first. The biggest boy, with a blond quiff, squared his shoulders and stepped forward.

The girls shrieked and crowded round the supervisors. The blond boy put up his fists and pranced like a boxer. My father recoiled, flailing his arms. The boys jeered and stood in a circle. I was pushed, stumbled and fell against my father. They came closer, edging us to the curb. My father staggered, trembling all over his body. I thought he was going to faint and held him tight. But he recovered his composure, seized hold of my shoulders and shoved me against a tree.

'It was you,' he roared, 'it was you who left the stable door open.'

His voice was like gunfire from a way off, harsh and with the Indies intonation. All the accents were in the wrong places. The orphans burst out laughing. They imitated him – 'peanut, peanut'. He was a peanut-man from the Indies. I tried to hold my head up straight. Everything turned blue through my tears.

'No,' I said, 'no, it wasn't me.'

'What's that?'

'No, Dad,' I whispered. And I felt the fire in his hand. He went on and on, fingers fluttering before my eyes. I didn't duck, I fell over only to be yanked upright by my hair. He held me with one hand while he slapped me with the other. Left and right across my face. My nose began to bleed. The orphans hooted, the supervisors tried to restrain him but he fought them off. I was his flesh and blood, he thundered, he had every right to beat his own shifty-faced son. I was his punch-bag and again he dragged me up by my hair.

I was ready to admit anything, but couldn't find the strength to lie. I fell against the tree and collapsed in a heap. I don't know how long I lay there, but I remember his hand on my neck pushing me into the house. His hand was limp, all the rage had been slapped away.

And my mother combed my hair. She combed it forwards like Caesar's, and stroked my head softly, softly, watching the tufts fall on her lap with tears in her eyes. I wasn't crying any more, I was just afraid of going bald.

My father locked himself in the bedroom and started counting out loud in a steady, clockwork rhythm. 'He's counting his mates,' she said, 'the mates he had during the war.'

There was no way I could ever become a mate like them.

After the storms the sky turned a dazzling blue. A warm, lazy east wind brought a sense of lethargy to our house. I was so exhausted I couldn't manage to wheel my bike outside, my eyes kept shutting and I tripped over my feet. I was sent back to bed, and my mother gave me a cracker spread with wild strawberries. But I was beyond consoling with kind words or tasty morsels: a heavy hand was clamped over me, pressing me down. The next morning I couldn't move my arms, and couldn't get out of bed. I was paralysed. A few hours later I was in hospital.

Some mysterious virus, the doctor said, a relative of polio. I could only move my head. There had been several cases already in the coastal provinces, and four of the orphans were struck down, too. So it couldn't be that dangerous. What was dangerous was my faeces. They took samples of my blood, too, and wouldn't allow other children near me. I was put in quarantine, in a glass cubicle. No pain, just numbness. I was a head, nothing more.

During the first days I practised using my eyes, gazing endlessly at the whitewashed ceiling, scanning it for brushstrokes, and I slurped up all the sounds I could hear: the squelch of soles on polished floors, the crackle of starched pinafores. The nurses wore masks over their mouths, the doctors dropped their rubber gloves in the bin outside my glass door after examining me. I was dangerous and everyone loved me. My sisters delivered sweets for me at reception. My father came to the window every day, making encouraging gestures and planting a kiss on the glass when he said goodbye. I had never felt happier or more secure, I inhaled the world outside and invented stories to go with the sounds and smells. I may have been paralysed, but my head was out and about all day.

My father made me a book-support out of a piece of driftwood, which fitted snugly across my bed. And although he disapproved of comics, he gave me an Illustrated Classic each time he visited. I turned the pages with a rod which I held between my teeth, a little bamboo pointer fitted with a rubber potato-peeler thimble on the end. An idea of my father's, from a photograph in a book about basket cases.

Basket cases – I didn't even know such people existed. They were soldiers who had lost all their limbs, men who were condemned to spend the rest of their lives in a basket, far removed from the eyes of the world. The war had made them innocent for ever. And I could see myself dangling in a basket, being rocked and fed and always having my way. But it also meant never playing Eskimos again on the beach, as well as lifelong imprisonment in my father's sight.

The heroes in my Classics talked to me and my mattress became as vast as the universe. Horizons fell away and I travelled to the centre of the earth, to the moon in a rocket, twenty thousand leagues under the sea. I shared

Uncle Tom's cabin, became the man who never stopped laughing, turned into Pip with his great expectations and into Noman tricking the Cyclops. I joined the Three Musketeers on their chase across the French countryside and helped nobles find places to hide. I drove the money-changers out of the temple and shuddered at the Man in the Iron Mask. Benjamin Franklin held my kite-string for me, and I stayed awake for a thousand-and-one-nights. Black tulips blossomed on my ceiling.

After a week a tingling sensation returned in my arms and legs. I was allowed to be kissed again, and my mother shed a tear when she hugged me. Full recovery required physiotherapy, which I did in the morning with a nurse and in the afternoons with the doctor as well as my father, so that there would be someone to show me how to carry on once I got home.

I was instructed to tap the little finger of my right hand ten times. The doctor counted out loud, my father joined in. One, two, three: my finger was obeying. The doctor lifted my left arm, I felt nothing. A stranger's arm dropped to my side. Right leg. The doctor pressed my ankle, told me to make an effort. I clenched my teeth and dragged my leg up from what felt like a bed of thick treacle. He raised my left leg, pricked in my thigh with a safety pin and let it go. A strange leg thumped on to the mattress. My right side was responding, my left was not. Next came my back. My father turned me on my side, the doctor curved my spine and started counting the vertebrae. My father counted aloud with him. They stopped at six. The doctor rummaged in his bag, I could hear metal being screwed into metal, the rustle of cellophane, a fingernail flicking against glass. They were draining fluid from my back, but I didn't feel a thing. The doctor and my father laid me on my back again, pulled the sheet up under my arms and tucked it in tightly. With a large pillow under my head, the book-support across my stomach and the bamboo rod stuck in my mouth I was all ready for some more reading.

I memorised hundreds of pictures, ten times the same adventure, and because I found it easy to concentrate I learned more and more every day. I knew how to survive on a desert island, for instance, and how to get bees to leave their hives. The Swiss Family Robinson showed me how to build a tree house, and how to improvise clothing in the wilderness. I knew the names of exotic plants: cassava, sisal, sago, copra. A new side to the Indies.

I, too, would travel one day, and write down what I'd seen. My father gave me a Swiss army knife to be going on with. It had a magnifying glass and a little saw as attachments. Once I was better we'd do exercises together and build huts, burn off the grass, cut bamboo stakes and weave baskets. With each visit he repeated his old army slogan: 'Keep on going and you'll win through.'

After three weeks in hospital I could use both arms and both legs. My nerves and muscles emerged from paralysis undamaged. I was given two crutches, learned to walk with them and after a few days didn't need them any

more. Only my feet and my back were still a bit
unreliable.

I was well enough to be discharged. My father came
with me in the ambulance which took me home through
the rain. He had never been so kind and gentle. He
stroked my tingling arms and we listened to the squeaky
hum of thick rubber tyres on wet asphalt.

Over the fields and far away
Where the cows crap every day
Where the tram chuffs by the river
We go faster and faster
Against the driving rain
I'll win through

Past the lake where eels are caught
Where the child molester stalks
Kids playing in the paddling pool
We go faster and faster
Ahead of all the others
I'll win through

Hello avenue with trees so grand
Where the rich kids' houses stand
After the bend the weather changes
We go faster and faster
Leaving the rain behind
I'll win through

My father took charge of my exercising schedule. Several hours daily. The doctor in the hospital had given him a book about physiotherapy.

The rod was a multi-purpose instrument. It could be used for rolling up the plastic tablecloth, but also for stretching a crooked spine, for trotting like a horse, for wedging my torso at table, for balancing and for hitting me with when I slacked. It was a fine, straight stick, sanded down to an even gloss, with oval knots in the wood and rounded knobs on either end.

Rolling: me lying flat on my stomach, my father on his knees rolling the rod from neck to buttocks over my spine. There and back, there and back, like a baker rolling out dough.

Stretching: my father sitting on a chair, me kneeling on the floor with the rod passed through the crooks of my arms behind my back. With each upward thrust the ribs expanded. Hold the breath, push out the chest, hands flat on the nipples. Between the pair of us we were weaving a tough mantle of muscles, later I'd be able to lift railway sleepers.

Trotting: first a mug of Sanatogen, a calcium drink to strengthen the bones (my mother had been too weak when I was born). Next the rod was passed through my elbows and I was off: a horse with a shaft on my back. I was growing fast and my muscles weren't keeping up, there was a risk of a hump developing between my shoulder blades.

Wedging: sitting at table, stomach pressed against the

edge. Rod wedged down the back of the trousers and
secured with a belt round the chest. Sit up straight! Pull in
that stomach and square those shoulders! Hold your spoon
high, no spilling now. My table manners would be those
of a nobleman.

Balancing: a cup of herbal tea before the afternoon nap,
to loosen the muscles because the cramps pulled me out of
shape. Lying down with the rod across my chest, keeping
it in balance while breathing in and out. Not twisting or
turning. If the rod fell I'd had it. The backbone had to be
in equilibrium, that's what it said in the book. Nerves and
muscles were to be given their fair due. Lying down
crookedly was fatal.

There were further refinements: jumping to avoid the
rod swinging low over the ground, ducking when he
whizzed it round at eye-level. While this was going on we
reeled off the names of our lost islands: Sumatra, Bangka,
Billiton, Borneo, Celebes, Java, Bali, Lombok, Soemba,
Soembawa, Flores, and of course Timor, which was half
Portuguese. It was my sisters' skipping song. For the pain
I was given an hour-glass with sixty grains in it. The pain
was not to last longer than sixty seconds.

Everything was carefully counted out.

Until my muscles recovered properly I was to stay home
from school. I knew how to read and write already.
Lessons in living, that's what I needed, for the newspapers
were full of foreboding. There were dangerous times
ahead: the Russians were advancing on the West and this

time they weren't coming as liberators. The crows cawed joyfully behind the dunes. I had to be strong and fit and able to walk long distances in case we suddenly had to flee, but my feet were misshapen and weak. Something had to be done about that.

A marble in the arch of my instep. My father tied them in place with the same yellow bandages that were used to wrap round the horses' legs when the beach warden wanted to show them off. The bandages served as socks, otherwise I wouldn't fit in my shoes. I had to circle round the dinner-table twenty times with my father beating time. Tap, tap, tap.

He'd speed up the rhythm with every 'ouch' I uttered, his ruler slicing through the air. Scrunching my toes lessened the pain from the marble but if he caught me doing it he'd take a swipe at me. Walking on the outside of my soles was forbidden, too, it was the arches that needed massaging. I concealed the pain in my legs, my face would not give me away. I won.

After that came the foot-baths. A ten-minute session daily. Submersion in cold water was good for the muscles. Meanwhile my father rubbed the marbles until they were hot, held them over my head to make my hair stand up on end. My curls were growing back. This was how I learned about electricity. My father favoured exercising body and brain in conjunction.

(They say pain doesn't last in the memory. And yet I could feel the marbles under the arches of my feet as I strolled through my old village. Not as a recollection, but as pure physical sensation. Hysterical imagination. It went on for hours, never mind the hour-glass.

I was imprisoned in the mind of a child. To know what had happened in the last few years I'd have had to check in old diaries, but the most banal recollections from my childhood were in razor-sharp focus. I was perturbed by my ability to summon up the minutest details: the little ochre-yellow drawers in the attic of our communal home, the convex brass screw-heads in the stairs to the kitchen, the waist-high geraniums outside the window (champion geraniums they were, with fist-size blooms, grown from cuttings taken at full moon and pampered with violin music), the grouting between the floor-tiles in the hallway and in particular the little lump sticking out in one place, the pits in the lino, the metal *Kinderheim* bedpans, the knots in the wooden wardrobes and the faces I read into them. All that old stuff was clogging up my brain. It was a disease, a tumour occupying more space by the day.

I must have absorbed it all when I was a boy, and had retained it the way a cactus holds water. It's my imagination, I used to think, a web of dreams and inventions. Memory as a magic lantern. Yet I went back to our old house where that boy had been laying the table and I actually rang the bell. Nothing had changed. The new occupants weren't very well off either, they just rented the place so they'd done nothing except general maintenance and painting. I could find the lump in the grouting blindfold, the screws, the notches in the kitchen doorpost – marks made by my father with the aid of a Swiss army knife and a ruler to show how much I'd grown each year. It was exactly the same, all of it, although I was surprised at how small I had been.)

The threat of war was mounting. The local authority installed a siren by the station and the civil defence force practised stretcher-bearing in the dunes. There were Communists everywhere, including in the free West, infiltrating factories and firing up the workers. Soldiers' leave was cancelled and in Siberia people froze to death in prison camps, which I knew about because Biggles had flown his plane over there. The Russians were at the ready behind the Iron Curtain.

No ifs and buts, I was to follow the instructions in the book faithfully. Training and more training, get strong legs. There was no time to be lost.

The GP's visits became more frequent, my father's nerves were playing up and his heart was getting worse. His eyes sank even deeper into their sockets and his lips were permanently tinged blue. My sisters whispered about an operation, there was a chance he'd be given a new valve for his heart. A notice came in the post saying the chief surgeon had placed him at the top of the waiting-list.

My mother ceased to exist for me in those weeks, although she often offered encouragement: 'Don't give up, do it for his sake.' She drew my horoscope, broke bread with the sick and cycled to the health-food store in town twice a week. Her organic pills and powders didn't help, but neither did the doctor's injections. The day-bed became the nerve-centre of the household. We were constantly issued orders, which had to be carried out at the double or he'd hurl abuse at us. My mother paid visits to all her relatives and managed to borrow some money from the Waldens. She couldn't cope with the strain so we got home help, and there was a lady who came to cook an anthroposophical meal for us once a week. My father was too tired for elaborate *rijsttafels*, so we had raw chicory with oat flakes for supper. My mother wrote two long letters to the hospital begging the chief surgeon to bring forward the date of the operation.

We had to be on our best behaviour for my father's sake. And provided I kept up my exercises I'd soon be strong enough to pull my weight along with the others. There was so much to be done before the Russians invaded! First the cellar had to be cleared out. I lugged stacks of old newspapers upstairs and swept up the coal-dust, which would give me miner's arms. Blowing my nose left black smuts on my handkerchief. We borrowed a pair of oil lamps from the life-saver chest and stored them in the cellar. My father screwed twenty bicycle lamps on to a plank just in case – he already had the batteries. We would not be without light. My mother sewed bags from old sheets, which I filled with sand and carried downstairs. Sand kept out atomic radiation. And we'd have food till kingdom come: twenty kilos of string beans in preserving jars. I wore a red band round my

upper arm and strutted about like a martinet. Red was a
dangerous colour. Pears had to be preserved, too, and
onions. The greengrocer delivered two crates of tinned
beans. How we'd fart! But the fug would go unnoticed.
My father covered the hatch with a piece of carpet so no
one would know we lived in the cellar.

And in the evenings we read the paper together. He
showed me the photos and I spelled out the headlines
without faltering. Words became more exciting than
pictures. Uprising in Hungary. Attack on Budapest. The
people smeared soap all over the bridges and the streets so
the Russian tanks swivelled round in circles. Barbed wire
was put up everywhere and tens of thousands of
Hungarians fled to the West. There was a popular song
about Budapest. War was imminent. My father wept by
the wireless.

It was stocking-feet time again. Hush. No ball games in
the corridor, don't bump against the bikes. No bright
lights. Turn the wireless off. Disconnect the record-
player. Don't ring the doorbell. Put straw on the doorstep.
No visitors. Stop flushing the lav. Turn that tap off. Don't
let the butter hiss in the pan. The clock's too noisy. My
father counted the days, hours, minutes out loud.

His overnight bag was ready in the hall. A summons
from the hospital might come any day.

The cellar wasn't deep enough, I'd better hunt for a safer
refuge. Besides, our red roof would attract attention from

bomber aircraft. I thought a hiding place at the back of the house would be better, so I went out into the dunes to find an area of drift sand where enemy tanks couldn't go. Besides, the instruction book recommended digging holes in sand. Not with a spade but with bare hands, so the fingers would grow strong. I'd dig a hole deep enough for me to stand up in. The sand clotted under my fingernails, the deeper I dug the colder and wetter it was. I counted my sixty seconds. My nails were bleeding, but I didn't mind: clean sand acts as a disinfectant.

After an hour I gave up, I was simply too weak to go on. But I went back the next day, although my father maintained that no hiding place would ever be safe from the Russians, not even if I cut a lot of marram grass to thatch a chameleon-roof for us. One day we'd have to flee together, the day when all men would be enslaved and nobody could think what they liked any more. Which was why I had to exercise, I had to be swifter than the evil threatening us. Indeed, my father would teach me foreign languages, we'd buy a globe and plot an escape route. Then we'd go on a vast journey, leaving everything behind, my sisters, even my mother maybe. That's what happened in wars, you had to be tough, cut your losses.

After digging it was time to rest; the afternoon nap remained compulsory for a long time. Herbal tea and a session of rod-balancing. My father rested in the mornings and in the afternoons, and if he wasn't lying on the day-bed he'd be shuffling around the house. He was weak, but not too tired to supervise my physical training. We didn't trot any more when I had the rod across my back, we just ambled.

To soothe my muscles between periods of effort he rubbed me with tiger balm. From now on we smelled the same. And if he had any strength left he'd give me a massage, rolling my muscles firmly between his fingers, loosening and plucking from thigh to heel, testing their resilience until the tears came. I let out a shriek, the tiger was snapping at my legs. 'Concentrate on something else,' he whispered and continued kneading. 'Tears are allowed, but you must never cry out, pain must be borne in silence. Think of your hour-glass.' And when it was over and I lay sobbing quietly he'd console me with a story, a classic of his own invention which he'd embroider into a thousand-and-second fable like Sheherazade.

My father on the edge of my bed. The stories go on unfolding in my memory, with different words each time, although the tone of his voice is constant.

'Seeing you cry like that, my old mate, reminds me of something. Did you know that according to ancient oriental wisdom it's possible to raise the dead with tears?'

He passed me his handkerchief and I blew my tears away.

'Funny thing, that. An old ship's peddler told me about it in Port Said. You were still in your mother's belly, we were sailing to Holland. It had actually happened to him, believe it or not.

'It was hot, unexpectedly hot for the time of year. Yes,

indeed: Port Said on the edge of the desert, even camels scorching their feet on the sand. The peddler was in his craft, in the lee of a jetty, weary but content. He'd sold out and had a bundle of money next to his chest. He needed more merchandise, but where could he find it? He didn't know the city very well, he was from the South and had sailed with his wares from Suez across the Bitter Lakes to the entrance to the canal.

'There was more money to be made in Port Said than in Suez, since it was a refuelling base set up specially for the construction of the canal. Our ship was moored there for two whole days to take on water and oil supplies and to scrub the desert sand off the decks. The water around us was rarely still, for the ship was surrounded by money-divers calling and begging for coins all day long. In the evenings a mass of hawkers and street artists jostled by the railing.

'After a voyage of shuffleboard, deck-quoits and amateur theatricals it was time to bid the tropics goodbye. We set off again, and in the Mediterranean strained yellow by the silt of the Nile we all tried on our new warm clothes and paraded around on deck. We were also issued life-jackets with a little red lamp attached; the sea was full of mines. But in Port Said we were still carefree, there was dancing all over town, music everywhere. Yes, mate, before you were born you danced under a canopy of stars.

'It was forty-five degrees in the shade and the peddler needed a cloth to wipe the sweat from his brow.'

My father pulled his handkerchief from his trouser

pocket and flapped it about to dry it of my tears ('Look! Geese flying from the delta to Europe'), then mopped his bald head. He was ill, but he couldn't tell a story without due accompaniment of sound-effects and gestures.

'The peddler reached into the pockets of his burnous and guess what he found. A damp hand trying to steal his Swiss army knife. The hand was attached to a young money-diver treading water alongside. Naked except for a loincloth, his body glistened with silt and his nose was shaped like a Bedouin tent. The peddler hoisted him on board. The money-diver bowed and introduced himself as Mousapha.

'They soon reached a compromise: the peddler wouldn't report him to the police in exchange for Mousapha's help in finding his way around the Arab quarter to replenish his stock. Mousapha didn't need much time to think about it, as thieves got their hands chopped off in Port Said. They moored the boat and clambered up on to the quay. They were halfway there when the peddler remembered something – his oar! He used it as a pole to manoeuvre his boat among the merchant vessels. Mousapha was to carry the oar so no one would steal the boat, because without the oar it was useless.

'The boy couldn't read, but he knew the names of all the ships by heart, as well as their arrival and departure dates – a glance at the smokestacks was sufficient. He was a clever lad, good at wheedling coins out of foreigners. And if he didn't get his way he'd dance a little jig with the oar, much to the peddler's amusement.

'The sun dried Mousapha's loincloth and gave his hair an auburn glow. He smelled of silt and his fingernails were dyed red with henna. Yes, henna, an Arabian plant, good for diarrhoea, too. The peddler was taken aback by the vendors with day-old chicks in their inside pockets, whipping out dirty pictures for sale. That was not the kind of stock he was after.

'Mousapha was a skilled guide. He took the quickest route across the European quarter and shooed stray donkeys away. Shoo . . . shoo . . . They paused briefly to gape at the displays in the windows of the Simon Artz department store' – I knew the name because I'd seen it on packets of flat Egyptian cigarettes with a picture of a man in a fez – 'Such fine fabrics! Hand-sewn shirts, hats with silk headbands . . . alas, such items were far beyond the peddler's means. So they headed to the souk, passing sun-drenched, sleepy De Lesseps Square and avoiding the dens where planters gambled their entire fortunes away in a single night.

'By the time they reached the pigeon-sellers' street, the shrill Arab street-noise was already deafening. Thousands of plucked birds hung from strings suspended across the street ahead, leaking blood. That wasn't what the peddler was after, either. Mousapha chased off beggar children and guided him past a group of rowdies with a sled. They were deep in a maze of shaded alleys, with shops in every doorway and the sun filtering through the cloths stretched overhead. Mousapha led the way to the tanners, the tailors and the coppersmiths, but the peddler was looking for handier trade, trinkets, jewellery, items he could display in a crate which could be hauled up with a rope. To find such merchandise they had to penetrate to the very heart of the souk, a covered area with hidden mosques and bath-houses. Steam-baths, yes, to counter heat with heat.

'Mousapha halted by a battered wooden door. "This is where all the gold in the city ends up," he said, turning into a tight maze of passages and steps. The oar was too long for the sharp corners, but by holding it upright they were able to press on until they reached a wooden attic. Rrrr . . . the spiders fled as they approached.'

My father left the room to wash the tiger balm off his hands. It didn't matter which story he was telling, he always kept up the suspense. There I lay, balancing the oar on my chest, my cheeks flushed with excitement. Forty-five degrees in the shade!

'There were ten brass beds in a row,' my father said when he returned, 'with rugs over the mattresses upon which boys and men sat polishing silver pitchers, picking gems out of brooches, counting coins. Some were snoring. Not one of them looked up. The peddler was too exhausted to ask what kind of a place this was. He slid his oar under one of the beds and fell into a deep sleep.

'A few hours later he woke up with his head on Mousapha's chest. Night had fallen and there was a spider crawling up his temple. Mousapha told him the spider had spun a thread between their shoulders, and that he hadn't dared move for fear of disturbing him as well as the spider.

'"You've got excellent eyesight," the peddler remarked.

'"Stands to reason or I wouldn't be a money-diver, would I?" Mousapha said.

'They laughed and broke the spider's thread. It was long since the peddler had taken time off for friendship. He had spent his life chasing after money, and sometimes he feared that his heart was as thickly calloused as his hands. But the sensation of Mousapha's heart beating against his cheek made him realise how he missed having a son. He wanted to be a father to the boy, teach him to read and write and equip him for an honest life.

'Mousapha grinned broadly, for he had slipped out in the meantime to steal a flat bread as well as some onions and juicy olives. The peddler protested, but the smell was so mouth-watering that he gobbled it all up to the last crumb. He wiped a tear from the corner of his eye, not knowing whether it was the onions or the emotion that was making him cry – why would a money-diver want to show kindness to a rich man? Mousapha soothed him saying that tears were the blood of friendship, and then he told him the ancient wisdom about bringing the dead to life with tears.

'The attic was deserted, all the boys and men had vanished.

'"Where have they gone?" the peddler asked.

'"To work," Mousapha replied.

'"At night?"

'The young money-diver chuckled at such ignorance. This was his home, couldn't he see? His father and mother were dead, so this was where he was living in the company of his friends, the craftiest thieves of Port Said, money-changers, story-tellers, money-divers – the top gang in the harbour.

'The next morning the peddler discovered how true this was. All the beds were occupied again, young and old fast asleep with their spoils at their feet: coins of every description, rings, wallets and silver-knobbed walking-sticks.

'The peddler himself had fallen victim to their diligence, too, for he missed the money he wore under his shirt. Even his oar had gone, all he had left was his Swiss army knife. He was outraged, and accused Mousapha and his gang of having robbed him.

'Reluctantly the money-diver went through the goods stolen by his friends. He was sure the thief had come from outside, for there was no stealing among the attic dwellers. The peddler's rage lasted longer than sixty seconds . . .

'So after that night the pair of them shared not only poverty but also the same bed, the same bowl and everything else that was theirs, like the slits in the roof and the tears in the sheet and a sea of time. Mousapha offered to teach the peddler the art of stealing in exchange for lessons in how to read and write. Neither of them was particularly pleased with their newfound skills, and when the fleas had gorged themselves on the peddler's blood he longed to return to his boat. But where would he find a new oar? The city was still too young for tall trees and the desert was too dry. Wood was a precious commodity.

'Now in the Arab quarter there was just one tree, which grew by an ancient oasis where caravans used to halt in former times. The city fathers had used the trunk as a pillar to support the roof of the bath-house. It was a gigantic plane tree, and it was only from the sky that you could see its leafy boughs towering above the dome. If you looked carefully you could see a chink of light in a gap between trunk and roof, not wider than two hands, just big enough for a child to wriggle through. Mousapha decided to climb the tree to check whether there was a suitable branch to make an oar. Sticking the Swiss army knife between his teeth, he clawed his way up the flaky trunk and wormed himself through the gap. The peddler didn't dare look up for fear of getting sawdust in his eyes. There was no sound of sawing, and yet a stick as thick as a man's wrist tumbled down a moment later. His oar! He could tell it was his by the places where the wood was worn down. When he finally raised his eyes it was suddenly raining banknotes. All his earnings – and more, for he didn't recognise all the dog-eared bills.

'Mousapha had discovered a thieves' hoard in the treetop, and he had honestly stolen everything back. The peddler was rich again, he could stock up on merchandise and ply his trade as before. He was so grateful that he offered Mousapha half the money and begged him to be his ship-mate.

'It was hard for Mousapha to leave his attic friends from one day to the next. Besides, he had to catch the outside thief first, no one wanted cheats around, and the honour of the guild was at stake. After the muezzin's call for the fifth prayer he made for the plane tree despite the peddler's fears for his life. Mousapha reassured him, saying: "If you notice someone getting into bed on the right-hand side tonight, it'll be me. If it's the left-hand side it won't be me." The peddler gave up and went to sleep. Outside, the tunes played by the ships' band drifted over the city until the early hours. Red sails in the sunset, don't you know.' I could see the memory creeping across my father's skin.

'*Ajò*, gooseflesh!'

'The peddler didn't hear the music, but he felt a cool draught on his neck before dawn.

'The bed creaked on the left side and a strange body slipped under the sheet. Something was amiss. Whoever it was didn't have Mousapha's familiar silty smell, this person smelled of blood. The peddler leaped out of bed, lit a candle and shone it right in the stranger's face. You know what he saw? A head with a white turban and a scarf covering the nose and mouth, which he barely noticed because of the murderous eyes glowering above the scarf, burning even brighter than his candle.

'"Where's Mousapha?" cried the peddler.

'The scarf-man didn't reply but held up his hand, which was dripping with blood. His fingers relaxed one by one, like a sea anemone in a current. A sickly smell wafted over the sheet. The hand was holding a beating heart. The peddler reached for the calabash which served as their chamber pot and caught the heart in it.

'In the Arab quarter the muezzins climbed their minarets to call the faithful to the first prayer, the sun flooded the

horizon and Allah's bounty was praised. *Al-lahou akbarou.*
The murderer stuck his fingers in his ears and fled.

'The peddler was inconsolable. He remembered the old
saying that it was possible to bring a dead friend back to
life with tears, and tried with all his might to cry. He
huffed and puffed and screwed up his eyes, but no tears
came. When the thieves returned to the attic after a hard
night's work he hadn't even wept enough to fill a thimble
– and the few drops he had managed to squeeze out were
from regret for his very inability to cry. The thieves
understood what was going on and knew what to do. One
by one they burst into tears. By the end of the day, soon
after the last prayer, the calabash was full. To them
shedding tears was like shedding blood. *Al-lahou akbarou.*
There wasn't a thief with a tear left inside him, and they
all fell asleep right away. There was no stealing in Port
Said that night, nor story-telling.'

'What about Mousapha?' I asked.

My father laughed mysteriously. 'Good stories always
have an ending you can dream up for yourself.'

And I dreamt I heard my bed creaking on the right-hand
side. A back nestled against mine, a back I knew better
than my own – tropical yellow, muscular. Between the
shoulder blades there was a jagged scar to the left and one
to the right, like wings of puckered flesh.

I found myself staring into my father's tear-stained face.
He had come to say goodbye. The letter from the hospital
had arrived a few days ago – no, he hadn't said a word, he

didn't want to worry me unduly, 'Pain must be borne in silence, matey, you know that' – but now the time had come. Notary Groeneweg had offered to drive him there and was already waiting outside.

The Rover belched white plumes. There was snow in the air. The notary held the door open and my mother helped my father to the car. Kisses, a final wave, and they were off.

We were watching from the window, Ada, Saskia and me I. I didn't cry. My father wasn't going to die, the surgeon had promised him a new heart. My mother returned to the house, her head bowed.

The world shrank, the daily papers went unread into the magazine rack. There was only one concern: my father's heart. Would the valve work? Hadn't the surgeon's hands been shaking rather a lot when they last spoke to him? My mother was gone half the day travelling to the hospital in town and back, her fingernails rimmed with black from the grimy buses and trains. I had to write my father a letter every day, using his ruler to keep my lines straight. Saskia sent him drawings.

It was strangely quiet in the house, as if it was stocking-feet day every day; no stories during supper, no wireless, either. Only Ada seemed oblivious to the atmosphere of gloom. She played her recorder in the living-room, endlessly practising a *valse russe*.

The frost had covered the windows with ice-flowers and our preserved pears were freezing in their jars, so we had them for supper. The Russians remained behind the

Curtain. My father wouldn't be returning home just yet, it was too cold by the sea. First he would convalesce at the Waldens'.

My shorts vanished into the wardrobe and I forgot the meaning of pain and bruises just as I forgot to do my exercises, and I went to school by bus instead of by bike. My muscles were flabby and my limp got worse.

The beach warden came by every day on his bike to carry messages until the council gave permission for us to use the phone in the hallway for private calls. Whenever my mother made a call I had to watch the alarm clock and signal her to hang up after one minute. It was then that I first heard my father's voice on the phone: 'Hello, matey, I'm not dead yet, my ticker's still going strong.'

He'd be able to do everything again when he got back, cook, dance, ride the moped, yes indeed, he even promised my mother he'd look for a job, his first in civilian life, and then they'd have plenty of money. My mother varnished her nails pearly pink and went to stay with him for a week at the Waldens'. All of us took a deep breath. New heart, new father.

The postman delivered a large parcel, which contained a globe lit from the inside. It was a present from my grandfather with a note from my father saying: 'Dear son. When I'm better we'll start preparing for a long journey. You can dubbin the straps of your rucksack for a start.'

It was nearly spring when my father came back. My mother picked a bunch of early winter-aconites in the garden and gave the wok a scour. The Rover drew up and there he was, thin and shrunken. His hat looked too big for him and the creases of his trousers weren't straight. I was standing by the window, afraid he'd notice my limp if I went out to welcome him. I tried to attract his attention, but he kissed my mother and my sisters and not once did he look up at the window – look at me, please look at me I implored under my breath, but he went off into the garden to inspect the straw around the rose bushes. I tapped on the window but he didn't react, he squatted down and poked his finger into the soil. I prayed for an angel to give his chin a little nudge . . . look up, go on, look up at the window . . . but he didn't. So I went downstairs and, holding on to the front door, said: 'Daddy, Daddy.' He turned and said: 'Ah there you are, you truant, about time, too.' He smiled and I ran into his outstretched arms. When I kissed his cheek he tweaked my ear.

'Let me see you walk,' he said. I stepped forward as steadily as I could. 'You're dragging your leg. Back to your exercises tonight.'

Inside we admired the scar from the operation and I held my ear to his heart . . . thud . . . thud, it sounded brand new. My father was strong and healthy, he could give orders again without panting: Stop waving your spoon! On your toes and round the dinner-table twenty times! He called for the tiger balm from the medicine cabinet. The massage session roused his anger – my left leg was clearly thinner than my right. His ruler was given a place of honour beside his plate, the thwacking resumed. The kitchen windows steamed up from the rice on the boil and Ada practised her recorder in the bathroom. Everything was the same as before.

But the rod was reserved for rolling up the oilcloth from now on, as my father had been reading a book on anthroposophical healing methods. Rhythmic dancing, that was the cure, body and soul had to grow together. Eurhythmics with letters: feeling the space and walking an N, the N of no, *nyet, nein* and *non*. An elusive letter. Jump up off the lino, arms and legs wide, flex the muscles, try keeping off the floor. The ruler swung merrily through the air. I was to make my body the vehicle of my will. And we danced an A, a T, an H, an A, an N. Oops, that last N was a bit clumsy. Do it again. My father traced my name in the air, and poems besides: Goethe, Morgenstern, Nietzsche; and also shapes: five-pointed stars, circles and the figure 8; these things were to be expressed by means of dance, which I did until I dropped. And if I couldn't express them I'd be made to feel them: slap, slap, a flick from the ruler on each cheek.

My father had regained his strength and I had lost mine. The required harmony between brain and body wasn't happening. I was a weakling. 'Look at you – all flabby like a woman.' He put me in front of the mirror and pulled up my shirt, sure enough, I was even sprouting plump little breasts. He squeezed them and made them jiggle. Climbing trees might be a good idea. TREE – what did the eurhythmics book have to say about that? The T was a plosive and symbolised growth, roots spreading in earth, and the R was a soft rumble, a sort of mounting energy, and the E stood for Eureka and for Embrace. We crossed the road and looked for a tree my father could put his arms around. We picked the thickest in the wood. 'Go on, climb up,' he said. The trunk was thick and the first branch high. I couldn't make it up there, I wasn't Mousapha. So he took the lead, without panting, although his face was contorted with pain. His ribs were still too stiff, the chief surgeon had had to force them apart to reach the heart. He hauled me up to the first branch and pushed me up to the next one. 'Higher,' he ordered, 'pull yourself up now.'

I couldn't find the strength in my arms and my knees were scraping against the bark. I didn't dare go up and I didn't dare come down, either. My father slithered down the tree and glared up at me with smouldering eyes: 'Prove you're a man.' He turned on his heel and walked away.

I sat astride the branch and waited. Squirrels bounded from tree to tree, crept up close to me, scratched themselves and bounded off again. After an hour (or was it longer? I was too terrified to count the seconds) he came back.

'Are you a man?'

'I don't know.'

He grabbed me by my ankles and pulled himself up. My balls were squashed against the branch and I was close to vomiting from the pain. He swung my straddled legs front and back, making my groin rub against the bark.

'Still don't know?'

I howled.

'These are your balls, man, a man has balls. Now do you know?'

And I knew that when my mother rubbed ointment into my groin later on it would be because I'd had a nasty fall.

I loved my father, especially then, I wanted to earn his respect, ignore my pain like a mate from the war. But whatever I did he only found fault with me. What could I do to make him love me? I could see that he wanted to make a knight-in-shining-armour of me and that I'd have to perform many tasks before he'd accept me as his equal, but I wished he'd praise me just once in a while. The operation seemed to have made him meaner. Could they have given him a worse heart instead of a better one?

At night in bed, curled up from the ache between my legs, I gave my globe a little push and watched the illuminated snow on the Himalayas and the greenish-yellow continents go by. I'd travel the world, I thought, get away. How dare he say I'm like a woman when I'm doing all those exercises to become a proper man, how dare he say I look like a thief with my Caesar haircut, while he glorifies thieves in his stories! That evening was the first time I felt a profound loathing, a rage that rose up from my bruised balls. It was the bloody limit, my own personal bloody limit. It wasn't that I hated my father, nor indeed my mother, who dismissed welts as mere scratches and bruises as my own stupid fault. Nor did I hate my sisters for ignoring me – I was too feeble for that, too much of a wimp, not enough of a man with balls. It was myself I hated. I wished to die and vanish from the face of the earth. My eyes stung from the light in the globe, my hopes had been torpedoed in some blue ocean. I'd never return to my parents rich and successful so they'd be proud of their manly son. I was a failure. Even the heroes in my Classics looked down on me.

I pulled the sheet up over my head, bit my pillow and counted . . . I heard barking in the distance, long-drawn-out howls that went on for seconds at a time, and I thought of the quicksands, of the dog I'd rescued there, and imagined sinking down into the quagmire myself, being swallowed up by the ground. I got out of bed, crossed to the window: blackness and silence except for the muffled sound of the sea. I slunk down to the kitchen in my pyjamas and took the key of the life-saver chest from the red hook. It was dark in the hallway, my parents were listening to the wireless in the living-room. I didn't dare turn the light on and had to find the padlock on the chest by touch. The oil lamps sounded empty, the waders felt damp. I filled one of the lamps and spilled some fuel on my bare feet. There was a box of matches at the bottom of the chest which I had some trouble finding, and in the low flame I picked out a set of oilskins and waders. I slipped outside and got dressed behind the house. The waders were far too big and flapped around my thighs, I had to tie a knot in the braces. I turned up the wick and set off on the path to the water company grounds. My shadow lengthened in the night, and with my larger self by my side I was unafraid. I was a giant.

The howling was still audible but the intervals between howls were getting longer. It was hard to guess where the sound was coming from. Were those voices I heard? Or was there some echo in the dunes? The drift sand was to the north, that was the direction I should head in, past the green marshes. No one could stop me now. Everything seemed much bigger in the dark, bushes became trees and the slightest bend in the footpath put me off my sense of direction. I lowered the flame, the barking was coming from different directions now, and when I turned I saw a swaying pinpoint of light. Had they sounded the alarm, had they noticed I'd gone? Diversionary tactics, zigzag across the sand and streak up the gravelled Old Kraut Road where I wouldn't leave footprints. The light was coming nearer and I could definitely hear voices now, booming voices. This wasn't my imagination – they were after me. The dog fell silent.

The waders prevented me from running, they kept slipping down and the tops flapped so hard I had trouble keeping my balance. The lamp bumping against my stomach flickered and threatened to go out. I'd have to turn up the wick, which was risky but I needed the light because the moon and the stars were hidden behind clouds.

Following the sound of the surf I headed towards the

beach. That way I couldn't miss the Old Kraut Road to the bunkers, where I'd hole up for the time being. The stink of urine would cover my tracks. The ground underfoot was too soft for me to speed up, my left leg was hurting and my waders made such a racket that I couldn't hear the sea properly. When I stopped I still couldn't hear because of the pounding of my heart. I felt very hot, the oilskin scratched my neck . . . my heart! even my heart was weaker than my father's. My coat was scorched, I'd held the oil lamp too close. I blew it out and had only the paleness of the dunes to guide me.

The voices came closer, the barking resumed. I was Eliza fleeing from her master, the stretches of white sand were my ice-floes. A dog snarled. The ground under my waders fell away: grass, wet grass, puddles and ridges of sand, I was entering the water company duneland. I'd come the right way after all. A shot rang out, then another, 'Stop!' they shouted. The dog barked again. 'Stop right there!'

Not on your life, I thought, one more ice-floe, one more jump and I'll reach the drift sand. I jumped . . . tripped over my waders and fell in a pool of light. A dog with a beam of torchlight trained on it came towards me, panting and barking and rearing at the end of a leash. I raised my eyes and found myself staring into the meter man's face. Rifle under his arm, shoulder bag with a furry tail sticking out. He was going to shoot me, I was sure. The beach warden stood behind him. They'd got the fox at last, completely rabid it was, one of its legs caught in the trap – how it had yelped, terrible that was, but it was time they caught it after six months of trying. Those shots had been merciful, each of them had delivered a bullet. But they'd noticed something odd in the dunes, a flicker of light heading towards the drift sand, and see what they'd found – the lad from the colonials' home. Half-drowned in the marsh and disguised as a lifeboatman. What was he up to at this time of night? Spot of thieving? Now they knew who'd left the door of the stable open that night. I was to go home at once. The beach warden pulled off my boots and lifted me up on his shoulders. The waning moon peeped brightly through the clouds. I looked back and saw the drift sand dwindling in the distance like a white ice-floe. Ahead of us stood our house, light shining in all the windows. Home, in spite of everything. They had missed me.

And so I walked through the seasons of my childhood. Past the stable, the vacant orphanage, over the dunes and across the water company estate where the rain dimpled the sand and where you could hear foxes barking. For my mother I stopped in the garden to pick a sea thistle, a survivor like her, grey green with a straw heart. All that walking had flushed the anger out of my system, scattered my anguish to the wind. Now I could stroll at ease with my father, no longer in the ranks, no longer a child but a man unafraid of resembling his father.

That was how I felt, and in my newfound confidence I decided to ask Aram if he'd like to come and live with me. He had to get away from the misery of his sick father, he deserved better than that. I could handle it. It was what I wanted to do, and I would overcome my weaknesses.

I drove to his school and waited for him at the gate. He shot out of the building with two girls in his wake. Our eyes met, but he pretended not to see me and crossed to the bicycle shed. He hung around, joking and hiding a cigarette in his cupped hand, and only came towards me when everyone had gone. He was embarrassed at being collected by me after school.

'Hi, are we going moshing again?' he asked. His boots clattered on the pavement. He wore them every day now, he hadn't forgotten our metal night. Had I seen that girl with the nose-ring by any chance? No? 'You know, she fancied you,' he said.

'I've already got a girlfriend.'

'You're always alone, though. She wasn't even at the funeral.'

'What's wrong with being on your own?'

'You're too old for that.'

'So why don't you come and live with me?'

'Because I'm living with my father.'

I blushed and swallowed a few times to summon courage. 'A different environment would do you good, and we'll go on holiday together in the summer.'

Aram looked at me in surprise. 'Will Dad come along, too?'

'No, just me, we'll find a home for Maarten where they'll take good care of him.'

'Never,' Aram said fiercely, 'I want to take care of him myself. Dad has promised to keep going until after my final exams.'

'Can you count on that?'

'Of course. I'll repeat the whole year if I have to.'

I was ashamed at my own tactlessness. We stopped for tea and lots of cakes. Aram asked for an extra slice which he wrapped in a paper napkin to take home to his father.

'But he can barely swallow as it is. You already have to feed him.'

'I'll mash it up. I'm better for him than a nurse, you know.'

'Well, it's up to you. If that's what you want . . .'

'It is,' he said coolly. 'It's not really any of your business, either, is it? You're not my father.'

I apologised and said that if the need arose there was always a bed for him at my place. Perhaps I ought to have another go with a dog.

6

Repeat Performance

We were to go through the whole sorry business again. A funeral – without a coffin this time, but with music and speeches. Saskia lit a candle and placed a photo of Ada on the table. My mother laid a cushion on her chair and glanced round, relieved to see her whole family gathered together. Just as well I'd come in the end, I told myself, just as well I'd listened to my inner voice. After all, I did love my family. I read out my eulogy, after which violin music seeped from the CD player. Jana was to be part of it all whether she liked it or not. The video tape got stuck, the system in Canada was not compatible. 'Such a shame,' my mother said, 'we all look so nice on it.'

So everything had to be described, from the coffin to the rose garden, the death notice, the flowers, what we wore, the weather. Jana wasn't spared a single detail. 'Remember those rainbows?' Saskia said. 'When the cortège arrived at the cemetery there were two rainbows over the auditorium, and they disappeared just as we were coming outside.'

Wasn't that extraordinary? I didn't recall a rainbow, but then I didn't have Saskia's sensitivity to heavenly portents. My mother couldn't help glancing outside: grey polar sky . . . well, she hadn't actually noticed any rainbows on the day itself, but hearing about them now she thought they must have meant something. Anyway, it had been a sad but beautiful gathering, such a shame Jana hadn't been able to be there with them. I too looked out of the window, to conceal my irritation. Did I really have to spend an entire fortnight in the company of these loonies?

After the cake – surprise surprise, made with real Dutch butter, thanks to good old Saskia – it was time to inspect the condolence album, the cards, and the ribbons salvaged from the wreaths. Whose idea had it been to bring these tasteless mementos? Saskia raised a finger: it was all about evocation, about sharing things as a family and about closure. Jana leafed through the condolence register, surprised by the number of names. Was it easy to get time off to attend funerals in Holland? What a rich country it had become! Most of the names meant nothing to her. There was Aunt Nikki, and Els – she really ought to write her a letter, but what would she say? She'd be complaining before she knew it and she didn't want that.

A few photos slipped out. Ada lying in her coffin dressed in her pyjamas. The flash had left a halo on the glass lid. 'How thin she looks,' Jana said, 'poor thing, I wish I could have helped.' No, she wouldn't look like that when she died. Jana was swelling up. She helped herself to the two last slices of cake and wolfed them down. Her nylon wig moved as she chewed. Eating was one of the few things she still enjoyed, she never left the house nowadays unless to go to the hospital, and even that wasn't necessary any more. They'd given up, no more chemotherapy, either. She spent her days on a pile of cushions, diapers creaking.

Any liquids she ingested were retained, despite the diuretic herbs my mother had brought her. Jana's legs were swollen with water and the tumour in her groin pulsed like a toad. The cancer was erupting all over. Every morning she was propped up on a chair by a table, and every evening her husband hauled her upstairs in the stair-lift. She was unable to walk as both hips had collapsed, but she didn't want to lie down, she wanted to see the birds, the clouds, the bushes and trees in the red autumn blaze and the hills in the distance. Errol had built a glass conservatory at the back of the house for her, which was where we were gathered – the sick woman with her mother, her sister and her brother.

Tedium, small talk. 'Look, a seagull, aren't we much too far from the sea for gulls?'

'The lakes here are like seas.'

'But they're freshwater lakes, aren't they?'

'Yes, they are.'

When we had run out of things to say about the landscape and the weather, the reminiscing began. About the old holiday home in the dunes, about the early years in Holland, and eventually, somewhat reluctantly, about the Indies, too. The Indonesian archipelago, the army outposts, the green shimmer of the jungle, the flying squirrels and wild cats and elephants on the rampage. Saskia plied Jana with questions, for her sister had had a proper childhood in the Indies about which she knew so little – exactly how often had they moved, for instance? What was Bali like in those days, and what about the wild men of the Kabu tribe, had she ever actually seen any? Jana scratched her wig. Thinking made her tired. But with her mother's help she was still able to dredge up quite a lot – ooh, remember this, remember that? It wasn't that I knew the names of all the regions and volcanoes or the taste of the exotic fruits and cool drinks, but I'd heard it all before.

Saskia said she'd like to take a look at the old family albums. 'Where on earth have I put them?' Jana wondered aloud. A thorough search was conducted in cupboards and drawers, after which Saskia deposited the albums on the table with a pained expression. How could her sister treat them so carelessly? They were heirlooms, photographs that had been sent to Holland before the war to show the Walden family they were safe and well in the exotic colonies. Jana had taken the albums with her to Canada (pinched them, according to Saskia). She did look at them in the early years, 'but it used to make me sad, too. We were making a fresh start, you know. No point in looking back.'

Jana flipped through the opening pages brusquely,

making small tears in the tissue paper separating the sheets. She didn't seem pleased: how cramped and primitive their accommodation at the army outposts had been, how silly she looked in the pictures, it was all so much better and bigger in her memory. Then she paused for a long moment, absorbed in the black–and–white panoramas before her. Well yes, a childhood in the tropics did get under your skin, it did mark you for life, it was just that it was all so pointless now. All these photographs wouldn't mean a thing once she'd gone. People in Canada had never heard of the Dutch East Indies. She suddenly realised that the stories that went with the pictures would die with her. It was all the same to Errol. This was as good a time as any for making bequests, she decided, this was her legacy. She reached for the scissors lying on a pile of newspapers beside her and gave the air a few snips. 'For you, Saskia: your father paying a visit to the resident, and a tiger hanging from a pole, shot by him in person. And this one, my raccoon dog which used to nibble my clothes, why don't you give it to Aram, he can show it to his friends.' Laughing hoarsely, she gave her dreams short shrift, cutting swiftly around the rectangles and ovals. Page after page.

'Stop, Jana, stop!' my mother cried in English, for she still had the habit of blending in whenever she could. But Jana wouldn't hear of it: 'I don't want those pictures to end up in the garbage.' Saskia took them from her eagerly.

'What about the children?' my mother asked.

'My children? They're too young, they don't care, it's just history, boring old stuff to them.'

Ah yes, the children. There were framed pictures of them on the dresser, plain and stodgy-looking, the pair of them. Underachievers, unsuccessful at school and in their jobs: her son was in the army folding parachutes at some base, her daughter had a job at the local supermarket. College drop-outs, no diplomas, not children to write home about. We hardly saw them, Jana kept them in the background. 'They want to be Canadian you know, same as everyone else, they're a bit embarrassed about our background and so on.'

But the times her daughter visited after work, swollen with her eight-month pregnancy, she was eager to know all about us. She clung to my mother . . . Granny this and Granny that, she'd missed her Dutch relatives so . . . and she looked enviously at the little piles of photos lying in front of us. 'Who's that black man?' she asked. 'Your grandfather,' my mother replied, and no, he wasn't black, he was brown. Menadonese. The daughter flipped through the photos, why, she'd never known . . . tigers in Indonesia? A house on stilts? Her mother as a little girl with a pig on a string. And this one, three dark-skinned soldiers beside a cannon, with a proud lieutenant Van Capellen looking on.

Saskia clapped her hands over her eyes. How could her niece be so stupid, had her sister never told her anything at all? 'This is incredible.'

Jana went on cutting out photographs. My mother quietly levered the cardboard off the back of the pictures.

'Mummy and you are exactly the same,' Saskia said.

'Always avoiding confrontation. Not facing up to the past means being burdened with it for the rest of your life.'

'That won't be very long now.'

'You'll be in pain.'

'They've got pills for that.'

'That's what I thought, too, until recently.' Saskia drew herself up and made an effort to look scornful. 'And the camp? Surely you've told them about the camp?'

'No, I haven't,' Jana said curtly, 'what good would that do?'

'But your daughter,' Saskia cried, 'what does she look like? Half Chinese, did you explain that to her? You're depriving your children of their heritage.' She fought back her tears.

'This country's a mishmash, all colours, all sorts, that's what makes us Canadian.'

Where had I heard that before?

The scissors snipped the past into little pieces. The heating was turned up and the last maple leaf fluttered to the ground. The world shrank around us. There was little else to do but have another cup of tea, another organic biscuit, and stare out of the window. And more snipping, of course. We were getting rather good at it. There was an awful lot that needed cutting out: stacks of old newspapers with coupons, special offers in garish folders. Anything you need, save it with your scissors: Garden seats two dollars discount! Two boxes of detergent for the price of one with this coupon! Jana seized upon these last-ditch bargains and my mother approved.

The candle was kept alight, Ada's portrait was given a place of honour and Saskia expressed her grief by playing one violin CD after another. The tissues flew out of the box.

Every morning around eleven the nurse arrived: a wash, tablets, fresh bandages and off she went. Jana's legs were gangrenous, her toes were black already. How long did she still have? No one knew, even Saskia hadn't received any messages from outer space lately. To hide her impatience she threw herself into her old nursing role again. She wrapped her sister in softer diapers, peeled away the rotting flesh and bought lavender water (with a coupon) to mask the smell.

But diapers and devotion were not enough now that her sister was fading fast – there were the wounds of her soul that needed cleansing, too. The camp. Saskia insisted on discussing it. She felt so guilty, she said – Jana's collapsed hips, for instance, surely the cause was to be found in the camp? Jana had always had to carry her. She'd worked herself to the bone, cooking, fetching water, looking after the little ones, nursing her mother. Jana had been the strongest then, and now she was paying the price.

'Remember that forced march to the train?' Saskia asked. 'We were only allowed to take what we could carry. I was carrying the jug, but it was terribly heavy.

You helped me, you took the handle and I held the bottom so we carried it between us. "Mummy, I have to pee," I said. Just do it in your knickers, she told me. We couldn't stop, and the wet fabric rubbed painfully between my thighs. You lifted me up and carried me on your hip, and you were weighed down as it was. After the train, we had to get into the backs of lorries. I lost sight of you and the others and went to the front of the line. Mummy panicked, but you found me, playing under the wheels, and saved me from being run over.' How could she ever thank Jana?

Talk, talk, talk, to get rid of all the festering hurt. My mother eyed her youngest daughter with dismay, for it had been she who had told her the story in the first place, and now she was being blamed for saying so little.

I put up with all this for a week and was surprised at how well I managed to conceal my murderous feelings. The first few days I'd felt somewhat awkward and out of place in the bosom of my family, but the irritation ebbed away and a desire for mildness and gentleness came over me. Just sitting there and listening quietly, perhaps that was an expression of love, too.

My mother and Saskia kept me busy. I was their driver, joined them for breakfast and had dinner with them as well. We were in a motel fifteen minutes away because Jana's house wasn't big enough for us all. Besides, none of us liked her husband very much. His years at sea hadn't softened his ways, either. Nowadays he did something in nautical equipment and was accustomed to shouting to make himself heard over the roar of ships' engines. When he left for work in the mornings we took over; after six we returned to the motel. He didn't want us around, really, it was too much as if we were waiting for Jana to die. And for lack of a better target he unleashed his anger on our language – Dutch was useless, it didn't get you anywhere in Canada. Sometimes we had trouble understanding his English.

Jana had learned to live with her husband's crudeness. They had stopped speaking Dutch to each other when their first child was born and she for her part had given up correcting his pronunciation long ago. Strange, the way her English seemed to desert her more and more often these days, sometimes she couldn't come up with the most ordinary words, yet she'd always had a good ear for languages. With the stories about the Indies her Malay came flooding back, and she took pleasure in surprising my mother with little outbursts of *petjo*, the Indo-dialect frowned on by the Hollanders, although my father used to speak it with suspicious ease ('just for fun, mind'). She loved the old sing-song intonation, and when she was tired it crept into her Dutch, too. She sounded like my father. I used to imitate his funny accent sometimes, and I'd ask myself whether I wasn't exaggerating it out of all proportion. But listening to Jana, whose accent had been preserved under a bell jar, I knew I wasn't. It was the only part of my sister untainted by disease. A voice recalling pleasant memories – ditties sung over the washing up, bedtime stories – a past that was not dismal.

For all the satisfaction my family got from having me there, my own motives were selfish. I hadn't come for closure, I was looking for an opening. I wanted to have a serious conversation with my eldest sister for the first time in my life. But how? I was never alone with her. We were all in each other's way, stuck in that damn conservatory. I caught myself cutting out coupons, too. No place like Canada for bargains.

One evening at the motel my mother knocked on my door: 'Saskia's driving me round the bend, I haven't had a single chance to be alone with Jana.' A moment later Saskia turned up with complaints, too. Rising to the occasion I boldly decreed that each of us would have the patient to ourselves for a day. Saskia was to have the first turn.

Relieved, I took my mother for a drive in New Brunswick. The plane ride had already convinced me that Canada was not the place for me. Good mountains, lakes, vast plains, an unpolluted horizon to be sure, but you still had to share it all with the locals, and they presented a pretty depressing spectacle: overweight, loud check shirts, bushy hair sticking out of ridiculous baseball caps. A worker's paradise, not a bookshop to be found, one measly literary journal and a thousand magazines about the great outdoors. That's all they cared about, driving around in mud-bespattered pick-ups, canoe on the roof, drinking beer from a can and then crumpling it with one hand, a flexing of the muscles prior to felling trees, fishing salmon or killing Indians. If you spent longer than one minute in front of a painting in a museum they thought you were gay.

After a long drive under grey skies, the aircon turned up nice and warm and a 'terrific' conversation in which nothing painful was touched upon, my mother asked me to stop at a hardware store. No, she didn't feel like visiting the Whale Museum. She again reminded me of a chameleon in her eagerness to adjust, for there were hardware stores all over New Brunswick. Perhaps she wanted to buy a present for my brother-in-law. I was to wait outside, but after a while she called me into the store.

'How do you say "magnet" and "file" in English?'

'What do you need those for?' I asked.

'I want to put them at the foot of Jana's bed. That'll draw out the fluid, help her move her legs.' She'd seen it on television at home, had tried it and I had to admit she was a sprightly walker for her age. She made her purchases and eyed me narrowly . . . No, I wasn't angry, I was smiling . . . she poked me in the ribs and we left the store chuckling together.

The sky turned into a grimy blackboard, grey-black all over. There was snow in the air and before long the flakes were clotting around the windscreen wipers. My mother felt the winter glowing in her toes, she said. Jana's view would be transformed overnight.

Back in the motel the red signal was flashing on my phone. Front desk: 'Your sister called. It's urgent.'

I rang the house and Jana answered. Shouts and screams in the background.

'What's going on?' I asked.

'Oh it's awful,' Jana sobbed, but before she could go on the receiver was snatched from her.

It was Saskia: 'Please come and fetch me right away.'

'Why, what's wrong?'

'I can't stay here another second, take me away from here, take me away!' She slammed down the receiver.

I changed into a dry pair of shoes, went to my mother's room and knocked on her door. I could hear her talking to someone and went in. She motioned me to sit on the bed opposite hers.

'Yes, I see,' she said, frowning as she listened to the voice at the other end. 'Oh my goodness. What, in this weather? Oh. I see. Yes.' She put the phone down, distraught. Jana had just told her that Saskia had rushed out into the snow without even putting her coat on. 'What did I do wrong this time?'

'Never mind.'

She wanted to cry, her shoulders shook, but there were no tears. I sat down beside her and put my arm around her. 'Don't feel guilty,' I said, 'it isn't your fault.' And I rocked her like a child, gave her little pats on the back, stroked her hair. 'Your children are old enough to sort themselves out.'

'We should never have left the two of them alone.'

'What happened, exactly?'

'Saskia spent the whole day yammering about the

camp, asking questions, making accusations. Jana didn't feel like talking and they fell out, I don't know. She tore up the photos, apparently. Errol came home early and found them both in tears. He was furious and lashed out at Saskia. She blamed everything on him, and then I think she scratched him, called him a lot of terrible names. What are we to do?' she wailed.

I tried calling Jana but got a furious Errol on the phone. He was very sorry, he said, but I and the rest of the bloody family could go to hell, all we were doing was hastening his wife's death. She was devastated. That was her, crying in the background.

I tried to explain what was the matter with Saskia. 'She's traumatised by the war.'

'Which war?' he asked, lapsing into Dutch out of sheer incredulity.

'It's the time she spent in the prison camp, under the Japs. She's in therapy.'

'Just like the Dutch, that is,' Errol said.

'Where is she now?'

'No idea, outside somewhere. Take Grand Falls Road.'

The parking lot was blanketed with snow and it took me a while to locate my rented car. It was snowing large, fluffy flakes, my wheels slipped as I turned on to the road. With both windows wound down halfway so as to keep an eye on the curb, the snow gathered on the upholstery.

No one ventured out of doors in this weather, there were no road gritters in action, even heavy-duty tyre tracks were snowed under in no time. The staff at the Burger King tried to keep their driveway open with a small tractor, and my headlights sucked in the snow from all sides. I was approaching the outskirts of town, where vacant lots, road surface and verges blended together. I had driven this stretch countless times already. If Saskia was heading back to the motel, she'd have to come this way, surely? But maybe I'd already missed her.

I got out of the car at the highest point and stood on the curb to look back at the road, which bisected a zone with large hangars and sheds. It was deathly quiet, the only sound was the crunch of my footsteps.

An icy calm came over me. They were all completely mad, but they wouldn't get me down. Big Eskimo in search of sister.

No sign of her around Jana's house, either. Perhaps she was hiding in the garden. I walked round the back, to the conservatory, and saw Jana flopped on to the table with her arms stretched out in front of her. Her wig had slipped off: she was bald. Her fat daughter rushed in and tried to prop her up on her chair again. Errol's loud voice could be heard through the glass. They were startled when I tapped on the window. Still no sign of our loony sister? The daughter pointed reproachfully at a little pile of torn-up photographs.

Inside, with my feet on a newspaper because of the snow on my shoes, I saw the state Jana was in. She could hardly breathe, her puffy cheeks were scarlet, her lungs squeaked horribly. Her daughter tried to replace the wig, but Jana kept shaking her head. 'Satisfied?' the daughter sneered at me, her check-out fingers quivering with emotion.

'Oh what a mess,' Jana whimpered when I gave her a hug to calm her down. Yes, Errol was moody and not always very likeable, but I had to remember that they lived a very isolated life. And Saskia had been so mean. 'She called Errol a bastard. I almost lost my temper.'

'Bastard – hear that?' Errol echoed. There were two red scratches on his cheek, and his shirt was torn at the collar. Saskia was a witch: 'I'll kill her if she comes anywhere near me.' Granny could still come to the house if she liked, but that was about it. 'Nutters like Saskia should be locked up.'

The daughter clasped her belly. She looked at me as if to say her waters were breaking.

I borrowed Errol's binoculars and drove past Grand Falls again. Sister, sister, where are you?

Visibility was very poor and I realised I wasn't nearly as calm as when I'd stopped to look at the road earlier. The flurry of snowflakes racing towards me was spooky, and I almost lost my balance. I shouted, honked, drove on, stopped again. Nothing. Seriously worried now, I decided to get back to the motel as soon as possible and call the police.

There was a white bundle at the foot of a billboard on the parking lot. It was Saskia, the hysterical snow-woman. Her hair was matted with snow, she was soaked through and inconsolable. I tried to brush the snow off her head but she drew back, afraid I was going to hit her.

'I got back all right, didn't I?' she whimpered, 'I never lose my way.'

I took her to my room in the motel and sat her down on the bed while I poured two miniatures of brandy into a glass, and I felt a strong urge to lie down beside her, put my arm around her and whisper in her ear that I loved her, that I'd be nice to her from now on, that she was a brave girl, my very dearest sister. But I couldn't do it and I put the glass down brusquely on the bedside table, saying: 'Here, do you good. And I'll get you home tomorrow.'

In the meantime the receptionist had taken it upon herself to call a doctor. He gave Saskia an injection and wrote a prescription. She fell asleep at once.

I hadn't told my mother yet, but when I went to her room later her suitcase was wide open on the bed.

'I think we'd better start packing,' she said when I told her what had happened. Her face was ashen. 'Running away, as usual,' she said, sighing heavily.

'Don't we all do that?'

'It was the same in the camp. She's very restless.'

'You mean just plain nuts.'

She looked at me sternly.

'She's all mixed up, Mum, seriously,' I said.

'Do you think she can travel?'

'I'll hold her hand, don't you worry.'

'Certainly not, you just make her nervous. She and I will fly back together. Same as when we came here. I thought you wanted to stop over in New York?'

'What about Jana?'

'I've said my goodbyes.' She crossed to the chest of drawers and started folding her underwear. 'I've had quite enough. I'm exhausted.'

'Don't give up.'

She wiped a tear away with a stocking. 'A tear from very long ago,' she said with a wry smile, 'from another life.' We patted each other affectionately on the back. I had never been as touchy-feely with my family as I was during that fortnight.

It was a tremendous hassle getting my mother and Saskia on an earlier flight. There were problems with the computer system and it looked as if we'd have to come up with the full fare, but after endless phone calls I found a charter flight for the next day. Insanity didn't qualify as an emergency, but the death of a close relative of my own invention worked wonders: mother and daughter could leave tomorrow afternoon.

'Did you know your father didn't tell me anything about the prison camp to begin with?' my mother remarked, fanning her steaming spaghetti. 'It wasn't until after 1950 that he started talking. He'd been to an anthroposophy meeting and someone went up to him and said he recognised him from the ship that took them from Java to Sumatra.' She took a mouthful of pasta and spilt some on her cardigan.

'But you knew he'd worked on the railway, didn't you?' I said.

'Yes, someone in Palembang told me. He didn't mention it himself. I could tell from the look in his eyes that he'd been through a lot. But that man talked about the ship being torpedoed and about the British officer who saved your father's life. That's when it all came back to him. He'd clean forgotten. Strange, no?'

Saskia was fast asleep on my bed and my mother and I were having dinner in the restaurant festooned with little Italian flags. The motel was having a Pasta Week. My vongole tasted like cod liver oil. We ordered a bottle of wine and my mother recklessly had a second glass. It was almost as if we were secretly celebrating something – our status as survivors, if nothing else. I was glad I'd taken the initiative, at last I was being the sensible, reliable son my mother could be proud of. When she died I'd be the one to take matters in hand. Normally it would have been Ada's job, because she was so thrifty and painstaking, but now she was dead the honour would go to me. 'I've got a few years to go yet, it's written in the stars,' she giggled, 'and mind you pick some nicer music. At least you've got good taste.' She was actually fawning on me, betraying her unstable daughter and laughing at her own superstitions just to get in my good books. Behavioural mimesis. She wouldn't stop adapting until she was in her coffin.

'What did Dad see in anthroposophy?' I asked.

'Education, the idea that you can teach children anything. You mustn't forget that he didn't have many advantages himself when he was young. He did so want you to do well in life.'

'Hitting can't very well have been part of the anthroposophical idea.'

'It wasn't that bad.'

'He used to hit me every day.'

'Not every day.'

'Oh come now!'

'Well. Sundays were always nice, we'd have a *rijsttafel* and he'd be in his element.'

All this was just a skirmish, for I had a much deadlier question in store for her: why did she always leave the room when he lashed out at me? For days I'd been waiting for an opportunity to ask her, but I hadn't dared. I started out childishly, listing all the times he'd hit me. When he was teaching me to write, during supper and after supper, too, whenever I was late coming home from school . . . I heard myself witter on and was ashamed of my self-pity . . . 365 days minus 52 Sundays . . . my mother was shocked at my calculations. We bickered at length until she conceded: all right then, during the week yes but not on Sundays. 'Are you out of your mind?' I grumbled. 'Do you think that makes it all right?'

She thought I was exaggerating.

And the swipes with the ruler?

'Yes, well, I suppose so,' she said. My father had set great store by table manners.

And the rod?

'That didn't go on for long.' And hadn't it been for my own good? I'd recovered splendidly from that bout of paralysis, hadn't I?

It made no difference which painful memory I dragged up, my mother found excuses for them all. She was only trying to be fair, she insisted, but she was distorting the truth. It wasn't about how many times I'd been hit at all, it was about one thing only: why hadn't she stopped him? I must have been puzzled by this when I was little, but as I had focused all my anger on my father in subsequent years the question hadn't arisen before.

I had some more wine to bolster my confidence. I'd played out my role of sensible son, and here I was, a little boy face to face with his mother, wanting to make up for past bad behaviour, wanting to excuse hers. If there was anyone I resembled, it was her.

So I changed the subject and put the blame on others. I launched into a juicy account of how that shady lawyer Van Bennekom had concealed the fact that my father's first wife had died. She barely reacted to this bombshell, it was as if she had known all along.

But my obsession didn't go away. Why hadn't she come to my rescue? She owed me an answer, my patience was running out and I didn't have the time. Tired from our outing and the emotions over dinner – we'd already asked for the bill – I recast my question into a statement: 'I think you were scared of him.'

'Whatever gave you that idea?' she protested. 'I had a short temper myself. When he made a scene I'd say: "If you don't like it there's the door," just like that.' She gripped the handle of her fork and pulled a face to illustrate how brazen she had been.

Emboldened by her vehemence I blurted: 'But it was *you* who walked out on *me*.'

My mother cringed, screwed up her eyes and shook her head from side to side. I reached for her hand and tried to comfort her. The hoped-for sense of liberation had turned into pangs of remorse. 'No, no, no,' she said, pulling her hand away. 'If I left the room it was to pray that his troubled spirit would calm itself so he'd be all right again.'

'Like the Pope praying for the Jews in the gas chambers.'

'That's a dreadful thing to say.' She drew herself up and in her agitation knocked over her water glass. 'You take yourself too seriously,' she said loudly. 'Wallowing in self-pity. You think you had a hard time, but what about your sisters? How dare you, you selfish prat.'

I hid my shame in a large brandy. My mother fished the ice-cubes out of her water glass. There was a polar snowstorm raging outside, but the waitresses in Canada kept plonking ice-cubes into the table-water. Weird habits they had there.

'Your father was a good lover,' my mother said when the last cube had melted in the ashtray.

'Now who's being daring?'

'I think you ought to know. Your father had a very tender and loving side, too.'

'D'you think Jana felt the same about him?'

Wham. Her reply was an old-fashioned slap with the flat of the hand on my left cheek. A Jap-slap. The little flags overhead danced in the sudden breeze. There was plenty of life in her old fingers yet.

'I used to do that to your father, too, when he went too far.'

Not that I ever noticed, I thought. She reached for her handbag and I signed the check. We walked down the sparsely lit corridor in uneasy silence.

'Never forget,' she said when we reached the door of her room, 'you were a wanted baby, you know. We both longed to have a little boy.' She gave me a motherly tap on the cheek.

It had stopped snowing. The sky was clear and starry, there was a stripe of yellowish light on the horizon. I went outside and washed my face in the snow.

The receptionist handed me a long fax from my girlfriend. 'Dear matey,' it began. 'Soon I'll . . .' She said she loved me, distance evidently lent enchantment as far as she was concerned. I really had to tell her some time that I wasn't her matey and never would be.

Saskia was breathing heavily, there was a spare bed in my room and I lay down on it fully dressed. Her presence annoyed me, even asleep I couldn't stand her, although I couldn't think why. Why not like her instead of feeling sorry for her? I stretched my back muscles and relaxed again, balanced an imaginary rod across my chest and tried frantically to think fond thoughts . . . being in a room together, that last time we slept in the same wooden bed on our grandfather's farm.

'I've got a secret,' she'd said that night.

'What is it?'

'I'm not going to tell you.'
'Go on, tell me.'
'It's bad luck if I tell you.'
'I won't tell a soul.'
'Promise? Cross your heart?'
'Mum had another baby boy – before you.'
'When was that?'
'In the camp.'
'Oh,' I said, taken aback. 'So where is he now?'
'In heaven, Indonesia's heaven. He was born dead.'
'Is he in Grandpa's photograph album?'
'Mummy gave you his name.'
'Did he look like me?'
'No, he was our whole brother.'

The human memory is selective, there's plenty of input but not everything is properly filed away. I hadn't given Saskia's secret another thought, my mother had never said a word and the subject wasn't even hinted at either in the diaries or in the conversations I'd had with the old camp-aunties. Yet I missed my elder brother. Hadn't I sensed his presence when I was little? Perhaps his memory had lingered on in my mother's womb when I was on the way, perhaps that was why I used to dream of a brother. I'd asked my mother enough questions for the time being, perhaps Jana could . . .

Quebec was free of snow and the main roads had been cleared. There was nothing to prevent our departure. It was five hours' drive to the airport. We had only the morning in which to say goodbye. I would be the first to go to the house, I didn't feel like staying on by myself, couldn't see the point of waiting around for Jana to die. Her daughter hadn't gone into labour yet; it could be a while before she did, and all that time Jana might hang on. No doctor in his right mind predicts when a cancer patient will die, the nurse had told us. My mother would come to say goodbye later. Saskia was adamant, she didn't want to see her sister ever again. We put a tranquiliser in her yoghurt so she'd stay in the motel without a fuss. We could be very practical when we needed to be.

Jana was distraught. So little time! 'Mummy had looked forward to this trip so much, and so had I of course.' She'd done everything wrong. There had been too much stress, Errol and she weren't used to talking so much. 'All that's my fault, too, and I haven't even got an excuse.' It had all been so sudden and she was ashamed of the reception they'd given us. 'Our life here isn't very grand.'

We drank weak tea and I let her talk: 'Remembering Ada together like that was nice. Your eulogy was just right for Ada, she did things her way, it was her life, but she was so tired after all that caring for others. It makes me realise how cut off I've been, how alone, but it was my own choice. An easy way out, maybe, the kind of choice you make when you're young and as you get older you wonder whether you did the right thing. Maybe it was meant to be.' She chewed her lip bravely.

'Why did you go to Canada?'

'The prospects, you know, there were jobs for the asking.'

'Els Groeneweg said it was an escape.'

'Why, Els! How is she?'

'Had something happened?'

'I was a goose. Too young.'

'Did he . . .'

'You know what it was like.'

'No, I don't.'

'I was the eldest, I was a big girl. He leaned on me, too.'

'Weak heart.'

'Yes, that too. You don't realise.' She pointed outside. 'Hey, what are those? Pass me the binoculars will you?' She twisted round in her chair and trained the glasses on the line of black dots streaking across the snowbound slopes. 'Swans, wild swans. We seldom see them here, must be the last of them to fly south.'

Then there were other birds to follow in their flight. 'Well, brother dear, that's life.'

Right she was: no more skeletons in the cupboard, no more interrogations, no more reproaches, either. I went over to the window and stood there with my hands in my pockets. Had it been Jana who'd read me the story about the princess whose brothers had turned into swans and who'd saved them by weaving a cloth of nettle-fibres to throw over their wings? 'Thank you for all those stories you read me in the old days,' I said.

A car hooted. My mother's cab. I didn't know how to

say goodbye, so I licked my finger and traced a little cross on her forehead. To make it better, as our mother used to say. 'She always did that in the camp, too,' Jana said, smiling.

I went to the door to let my mother in and when she entered the conservatory on my arm Jana said to me: 'You walk exactly like your father. Feet turned out, swaying like an elephant.' Then it was my turn to bite my lip. I blushed, although I knew she didn't mean to be unkind. I couldn't help feeling ashamed. I was an elephant and my father was my keeper. I'd shaken him off, but Jana had put him right back in charge.

Saskia was waiting in the hall with the luggage. We had agreed to stop only to pick our mother up. No more farewells. But Jana couldn't bear to let her sister go without waving goodbye so she was posted at the window, leaning on her fat daughter, her face contorted with pain. Saskia looked the other way.

'Did you talk about anything in particular?' I asked my mother en route to Quebec.

'No,' she replied, 'we had talked enough already.'

'So what did you do?'

'Cut out coupons.'

On the way to New York I spent the night in Albany. The next morning, after a hearty breakfast of pancakes and maple syrup, I decided on a whim to head east instead of south. It would be a relief to drive along the Atlantic coast for a while, I'd seen quite enough ugliness for the time being. A few hours later I reached the rolling hills of the coast and passed a sign to Cape Cod. That was my signal! The name was familiar because of a famous photograph of John Kennedy as a young man in the sand dunes of Cape Cod. The dunes . . . I longed for the solace of sea air, for the wind to blast away the stench of diapers and death. The breeze tugged impatiently at the window and in the distance there was a strip of land jutting into a bay and yachts bobbing along a wooden landing stage. I took a side road and rattled over an iron bridge. I hadn't realised Cape Cod was an island.

On the map it looked like a bent arm with a clenched fist. Popeye after downing a can of spinach. The wide road traversed a landscape of woods, boulders, pools and creeks, but no dunes. It wasn't until I reached the elbow, where the landscape was flatter, that there was a promise of sand and clay on the low hills. Land like a flag striped with rust, lead and ivory, rippling in the sea breeze. The white gates of the country houses were locked, the shutters of the old seamen's homes shone with new paint. There were no beautiful people around at this time of year, just the odd senior citizen taking a stroll in pink check trousers.

A fish eagle skimmed over the marsh, then winged into the pine forest with prey in its claws. Sunshine, autumn on its best behaviour, boughs heavy with cones swaying in the soft south-westerly winds.

The island grew increasingly bare: scraggy bushes, tough

grasses, weatherbeaten sheds and wharves. Windswept and unassuming, the way things are supposed to be on a sea coast. Approaching the fist, the road narrowed and I turned into side-tracks a few times in search of dunes and a frame-house hotel with a sea view. But either the tracks didn't go anywhere or they described a loop that took you back to the main road. There didn't seem to be any dunes. Maybe I'd imagined seeing them in that photo. And where was the sea, anyway? I could hear it and smell it, but I couldn't see it. It was getting late. The sun sank behind the bushes and the lighthouses started flashing: three fingers streaking across the sky. I drove to the nearest lighthouse. Ignoring the 'No Trespassing' sign I vaulted over the fence and walked up the slope. The sound of the sea grew louder and it was only when I reached the highest point that I finally saw it crashing down below: the wild, foaming Atlantic Ocean. I had been driving in a hollow: the sides of the island were higher than the middle, and only now did I discover that the island was fringed with sprawling dunes and gullies and oddly shaped bays, dark and menacing in the dying light. The sheer scale was awesome. Here the sea reigned supreme, while storms carved the shore. This would be my beach tomorrow.

The sand was hard and untrodden, I hunched my back against the chill autumn wind tugging at my clothing. It was low tide and puffs of foam rolled on the waves lapping the shore. With each bend I found new vistas.

Suddenly a dark cloud rose from the dunes, a screeching mass heading to the ocean, where it hovered for a moment before disintegrating over the surf. Thousands of birds landed at my feet. Entire regiments of snipe flocked together on their way south for the winter, alighting here for a meal and a rest. There was order in their chaos: thousands of tiny brains had decided on this spot as a place to pass a few hours, and they weren't going to let me stop them. The vanguard, initially timid, flew up as I approached and landed behind me, but very soon the birds presented a united front. Some of them stood on one leg and eyed me dreamily. They were neither hostile nor large, but they made me nervous. A few birds tried to perch on my shoulders; to them I was a tree in motion, I turned and retraced my steps on tiptoe.

'Keep on going,' I heard my father say. 'The jungle's full of wild animals. Take no notice, just focus on a point in the distance.' It was breeding season and the gulls flew ahead of us. We were hiking in full rig, the rucksack was filled with sand. 'Back straight, muscles tense, go on, *up* with that left leg.' If it hurt I was to say: 'I'll win through, I'll win through,' ten times over. The mincing gait of a girl was to be avoided at all costs – a firm stride gave strength to the legs. My father's soles left their imprint in the sand.

That was how he'd survived on patrol, too. He had to keep going for days with a wounded soldier on his back. It was no use complaining: an injured man on his own would be easy prey for the enemy, and besides, he was not a traitor. My sand-filled rucksack was the wounded soldier. He made me wait while he added some more handfuls to my load – wet sand that leaked down my buttocks and scoured the insides of my thighs. Think blood, the blood of the soldier.

We tramped across the dunes, ankle-deep in soft sand between tufts of waving marram grass. Seagulls circled overhead, screeching. I looked up in fright. They dived down and tried to peck at us. We were in the midst of a colony of gulls, they were everywhere, squadron after squadron launched their low-flying, vicious attacks. Keeping my head down I heard their wings battering my rucksack and felt the whoosh of displaced air on my neck.

My father uprooted fistfuls of marram and shook them at the gulls, flailing his arms and shouting. But the birds didn't care, they just pecked at his hands. 'The birds are the enemy,' he shouted, to make himself heard over the pandemonium, 'this is just a diversionary tactic, we must keep going. They want to create confusion.' His lips were purple.

We pressed on, hands on our heads and eyes fixed on the horizon. I'll win through. My father was right behind me, panting as we went up to the row of dunes, away from the green wood where the nests were. I could hear his rasping breath, and looking round I saw him clutch at tussocks of grass to pull himself up the slope. He grabbed hold of me, exhausted, and lolled against my rucksack. I unbuckled the strap and flopped down on the sand. 'Keep going,' he rasped, 'don't stop. Kick the tiredness away! At the first sign of slacking they'll attack. If I'd given up back then I wouldn't be here with you now. Keep going and you'll win.'

I climbed up to the crest of the dune with my father leaning on me. The burden, heavy at first, grew lighter. The wounded soldier was an angel hovering about my shoulders.

Epilogue

The mother had buried her daughter. She'd left her in the snow, in a hole hacked out of the frozen earth. The tulips from Holland had looked waxen on the coffin. Numbed by the cold she'd stood by the grave, the icy wind taking her breath away. The love and warmth she dearly wished to give her daughter in her last resting place had congealed in her head: she couldn't think, and found nothing to say. Here she was, with chilblains on her toes, saying goodbye to her eldest daughter, delivering a child born and bred in a hot climate to a frozen grave. Jana had probably wanted it this way – being embraced by the cold so that nature would hold on to her a while longer. Jana had passed away in the conservatory, where her bed had been moved in the final weeks. She lay between two electric fires. It had been like a hothouse in there, with the snow melting beneath the windows and the birds warming their feet on the glass roof. The garden fascinated her to the end, and she was pointing to a squirrel helping itself to a peanut on a string when she died. The nurse was about to give her a wash. Errol was away at work, it was all taking too long, and he couldn't stand twiddling his thumbs while waiting for her to die.

It would be a modest funeral, not worth flying out for. The lid had already been lowered on the coffin. 'It's far too cold for you here,' Errol said on the phone. Too cold? Well, that was for her to decide! She'd wear warm clothes, goodness knows how many woollies she'd knitted in her day. Besides, there was a new baby to admire, her very first great-grandchild. No, she would not be put off. And she wanted to hold her daughter's hand one last time, surely a mother was entitled to that? There was no need for anyone to accompany her, she'd even prefer to travel alone, and if Saskia and I felt bad we could pay for her plane ticket. She had no need to share her grief. She was sorry she hadn't been able to say goodbye to Jana in a more honourable fashion. The eldest child always lost out. 'I'll hold you when you go.' That was the promise she'd made last time she flew to Canada, and the words went round and round her head. What else could you do but gently lead your child to the dark tunnel, take away the fear, which was what she'd done when Jana was born, too. Console a helpless creature, help it towards the light, towards redemption on the other side. Being born meant passing through a tunnel, too, so there wasn't that much difference between beginning and end. But Fate had intervened. Saskia was in a very bad way, and the decision had been quick: she didn't want to risk losing her youngest daughter as well. Life took priority over death.

Saskia was a bit better now, but the past weeks had been dreadful. Angry words and accusations. She blamed absolutely everything on her mother, who had not defended herself. It was easy to swallow your pride if it helped your child.

There were few mourners at the grave-side, not more than ten or so. A couple of neighbours, Errol and the children, and a fiancé she hadn't met before. Jana's son read something from the Bible and stumbled over the words. His sister clung to her grandmother. Poor Granny! But Granny would soon be relieved of this burden. She knew she was not only saying goodbye to Jana, there were her grandchildren and her son-in-law, too, but they'd become total strangers. She'd looked forward to the new baby at first, but when she held the infant in her arms, a pale blob of a boy, she felt no emotion. She didn't even inquire after the time of his birth, what good would a horoscope do him anyway?

She was back on the plane to Europe the following evening. She'd asked for a window seat so she'd get to see the white lakes. Visibility was excellent, the wind had swept the sky clean of the thick fog that had spoiled the view on her last flight. Studying the route map from the pocket in the seat in front of her, she reflected that this would be her last plane trip.

She was practised at farewells. Not that it didn't hurt

any more, it was just part of her existence. When she was only four her own mother had died while giving birth to her baby brother. The boy couldn't find favour in his father's eyes, he was raised in an atmosphere of strife and she had been stuck in the middle. She'd been mother, sister and referee all at once, there was no time for her own grief. That experience had shaped her: no matter how much you loved someone, they could slip right out of your life just like that. It was out of your hands, you were put to the test. Karma, that was it, the main outline of life was fixed beforehand. She firmly believed that, hadn't she had plenty of proof?

Take her first husband: just before war broke out he'd predicted that one day she would return to Holland alone with the girls. She thought he was alluding to divorce, that he wanted to be rid of her, but she didn't protest because she knew their marriage wasn't working. Later, in the camp, when it dawned on her that her swollen stomach was not due to oedema but to pregnancy, she knew the child she was carrying would not live, and that knowledge did a lot to ease the sense of loss.

And then there was Just Two. Convinced he'd die at forty-two, because some clairvoyant had told him so in the camp. That's why he was in such a hurry to raise his son. She'd never forget him coming home the day after his forty-second birthday with a large box of envelopes which he set on the table in front of him, he was that convinced that he was going to die. He'd had another prediction come true before. It was that Justin would be in a car crash by the time he was nine years old. So everyone took extra care, and he was never allowed to leave the house unattended. The day he turned nine the whole family heaved a sigh of relief. They dropped him off at school, saw him go through the gate, and drove off. But Justin turned round and slunk out into the street again, where he was promptly hit by a car. That was where those scars on his back came from!

Seat-belts were unbuckled and air hostesses distributed drinks. Oh dear, she'd forgotten to look at the lakes! She put her face to the window and gazed into a black hole . . . no ice-fields to be seen, just that strange yellow glow on the horizon, surely that wasn't the moon? Or was it the beginning of sunrise?

How wonderful it would be to float in space . . . just drift off towards the light, delivered from her task on earth . . . She shut her eyes and saw Ada pass by, then Jana . . . calling to her and beckoning. No, she had to be sensible, for Aram's sake. He was her favourite grandchild, clever and sensitive. The lad relied on her. She resolved to visit him every Wednesday evening, give him a hug and check his ears. An excellent plan: the bus was free for pensioners on Wednesdays.

She took a photograph out of her handbag, which Jana had saved for her in an envelope. It was one of the few pictures that had escaped Saskia's destructive frenzy, there was just one little corner missing. She'd find a frame for it and give it a nice place in her home. The whole family on the crest of a dune: her, Justin and the four children.

She wondered who could have taken the picture. She didn't recall having seen it before. Where was her magnifying glass? Let's have another look . . . the sun was sinking, you could tell by the soft shadow spreading over the dunes. Father in the middle, his small son standing between his legs, the girls sitting with their knees drawn up beside their mother. All of them swarthy-looking in the evening light, all of them equal and safe, a moment of happiness at the end of a summer's day. Her arm lay on Justin's shoulder. She thought of the hair on the back of his neck, the soft little curls she loved running her fingers through. How skinny she'd been, what on earth had he seen in her? Justin could have any woman he wanted in Palembang, everyone thought he was handsome and charming, and yet he chose her, a widow with bad teeth. She would be eternally grateful to him for giving her back her pride . . . no man had ever made her feel so womanly.

How could that boy hate his father? They adored each other, you could tell from the picture, both of them beaming! All those awful things he kept dredging up . . . the hitting, the rod. Mistakes had been made, of course, but when would he finally put that behind him? She ought to remind him that it was he who fetched the rod after supper: 'Shall we do the exercises, Daddy?' It was he who tugged at his father's sleeve to go outside, he who wanted to learn how to climb trees, even though his father wasn't really up to it. She often worried that all that tramping about in the dunes was bad for his heart. In winter, if she suggested taking the little boy for a ride on his sled he'd stamp his feet and protest that he didn't want her to pull him but his father. The child was given to tantrums, which wasn't surprising as he'd been born with red hair. Sometimes she feared that he adored his father too much, he might have a mixed-up sort of Oedipus complex, such things were possible, it seemed. He'd been very clingy, and perhaps Justin hadn't known how to deal with that, which would explain his severity.

She put her magnifying glass away and peered at the photograph. Her children playing in the dunes . . . she could hear them crying, laughing, whispering together. She comforted them, fetched and carried and made her way through a crowd of nameless faces . . . music, dancing under a starry sky, clumping around in a field in wooden clogs, tripping barefoot along the paddy fields, bowing low to the Nips, bowing before a grave . . . She riffled through her life at top speed and all the images tore apart before her eyes.

The air hostess unfolded the little table in front of her and set a tray with a defrosted roll upon it. 'Dreaming, are we?' she said as she poured coffee. 'Shall I get rid of that for you?' she offered, indicating the torn-up picture. The mother, wide-eyed, stuffed the pieces quickly into her bag.

The captain announced they were approaching the Netherlands, their descent had begun. Someone had pulled down the shutter over her window, and along the bottom edge she noticed a brilliant line of morning sun. The mother wanted to see the coast. She raised the shutter and looked down. All she saw was waves.

Z418819